Cover Art is by Bonnie Koon A third generation Floridian and self taught artist, Bonnie Koon grew up in her Grandmothers Ceramic & Beauty Salons in Tampa, she began at an early age to learn several different mediums. Today she uses an array of surfaces to express her artwork, like the very interesting horseshoe crab.

She is inspired by her Florida surroundings from The Keys to the Alafia River, where she has spent her life. Having a keen eye and steady hand, she enjoys painting miniature tropical scenes that are less than an inch square.

You can find her work at The Green World Gallery, on Duval Street in Key West, in Boynton Beach at The Fancy Flamingo near the marina, online at www.koonberries.com and on facebook.
http://www.facebook.com/pages/KoonBerries/

http://www.facebook.com/pages/Bonnies-KoonKrabs-by-KoonBerries/

Mary, without your patience, understanding and the occasional
whipping, this book may not have been possible.

And special thanks to Chris Rehm who provided several of his
pictures of the Islands.

Introduction.

The Florida Conchs are those born and raised on the rock, the islands of the Keys.

While some of the Florida Keys even today are without electricity, others contain five star resorts with private landing strips and self contained medical facilities. But you will not find that on Stock Island. Well unless you consider the Monroe County Jail a five star resort.

This is a tale of a Florida Conch turning of age and doing the unthinkable. Leaving the island, leaving the Rock. Conchs are always told to never leave the rock. But the rock, their islands are changing.

Listen to the island drums. Feel the salt air, as the light breeze comes off the ocean. Follow a Conch's journey through the streets and the music of the Keys.

Enjoy the funnier side of life through the eyes of a Florida Conch.

Chapter 1

Boner and his father (White Boots Morgan), a commercial fisherman, live aboard their houseboat in a marina on the Atlantic side of Stock Island, in the Florida Keys. His father's crab boat is tied up, in the next slip, when his father is not out working his crab traps.

According to White Boots, Boner's mother left them shortly after Boner was born and no one has heard from her since. There are rumors she ran off with a power boater from St. Louis.

The marina Boner and his father live in, originally constructed for commercial fishing and shrimp boats, is slowly becoming a marina for recreation. Boner's father knows his time is becoming more and more limited as the Island and the marina changes.

Boner's father tells him stories through the years of his family's sometimes dark heritage. White Boots tells Boner how his Great Great Great Great Great Great Grandfather is Henry Morgan, the infamous Pirate of the Caribbean. Telling him the tales handed down from father to son through the years.

White Boots tells Boner how his Great Great Great Great Great Great Grandfather is one of the greatest Pirates of the sixteen hundreds. And their family practically ran the Caribbean.

Everyone it appears has a story to tell and Boner is always more than willing to listen. As the stories carry him away from the docks and cleaning of the boat bottoms.

Boner does not have time for sports in high school. He spends his weekends, either helping his father pull their crab traps or cleaning the bottom of boat hulls. And often time at night, he sneaks out to listen to the local bands.

Even if he had time for sports, he can not take part due to the accident.

Years back while helping White Boots, Boner, trying to jump off the boat onto the dock, slipped getting his leg caught between the narrow finger pier and the boat's hull.

The accident although minor, leaves Boner with a limp and steel pins in his bone after the break heals.

Still three days a week, or so, you can find Boner in the school's weight room along side the students on the Football team. Boner really does not care about sports, but he does want to gain strength for his work on the crab boat.

Boner is much like his dad in structure. He stands six foot two and weighs in at barely two hundred pounds. Carrying the same rugged chin line as his dad, he appears older then he is. And like his dad, he keeps his haircut in the manner of the military and most police officers.

One day a member of the team, asks him to try out for Football. Pointing to his leg, he tells him about the pin in his leg. The player tells him that's a bummer, where Billy replies, "No, a boner." And laughs at himself.

From that point forward Billy Morgan carries the nickname of Boner.

As the years pass Boner gets to know the docks well. And he is always ready to lend a hand to those around the marina. Boner always has time to listen to the stories of other Boat Captains, dock hands and the strangers who come and go.

Courtesy of Chris Rehm

It is from these docks Boner learns how to size up people quickly. Dock hands come and go. Some working for a few weeks while others work only long enough to earn a few dollars for their next pint.

Although Boner takes everything in, he has no idea his world revolves around the harder side of life. A life that hides from the tourists and the snowbirds who migrate from the north during the winter.

Often cruisers come into their marina when the other marinas are full. And it is Boner, who with his slight limp, helps to handle their dock lines and cleans their boat's bottoms to earn spending money.

With occasional breaks from helping the cruisers or helping his father pull traps, he sneaks out to listen to the local bands on the island and even sometimes off Stock Island into Key West itself.

The music flows through the night air. Not just resting above the streets but carried throughout the lanes and alleyways of Old Town. The sounds mingle together in concert with the rhymes of the Island.

Afternoons and weekends provide Boner with interaction between the transient dockhands, such as the old man called Red Stripe. Red Stripe works pulling traps when White Boots needs extra help. The weekend also gives Boner time for his studies and the music that takes him away from his chores.

Living with Boner and his father is Boner's best friend, Macky. Macky very seldom talks but is a good listener and enjoys hearing Boner talk about his day. They will not allow Macky in school anymore. So Boner only gets to see him when back in the marina. Macky is the unofficial watchman for their houseboat.

Chapter 2

White Boots knows Boner is sneaking out at night. But he also knows his son needs a release. One afternoon while Boner is in school, White Boots drops off his haul from the crab traps at the fish house and sits with the other Crabbers.

The Crabbers are telling White Boots how Boner is spending a lot of time around the Hogfish, one of the local bars on Stock Island. They are telling him how Boner will just sit there listening to the likes of Barry Cuda, Howard Livingston, and Dave Aaron, some of the local Musicians who play Stock Island, Key West and points North.

White Boots decides he will do something special for Boner, for his Birthday. Once getting paid for his haul and paying Red Stripe for his help, White Boots pulls his crab boat over to one of the transient slips and ties her off.

Walking up both 2nd and 3rd Streets, he finds what he is looking for, a Pawn Shop. Being buzzed inside, White Boots tells the owner what he is looking to buy.

As the Pawn Shop owner looks at White Boots with a wary eye, he points to where he can find it.

The owner can see White Boots has no idea what he is looking at, much less how it is used.

"You buying it for yourself?", asks the owner.

"No Sir, I'm getting it for my son.", replies White Boots.

"Has your son ever used one before?", the owner asks him.

"No Sir, I'm wanting to surprise him.", White Boots tells the owner.

The Pawn Shop owner seeing this means alot to the old man, walks around the counter to help him with this life changing decision.

As White Boots starts to leave the Pawn Shop with his prize, the owner tells him, "If your son has any trouble tell him to come see me"

Walking back down the shell and gravel road to his boat, White Boots feels proud he can do this for his son.

Arriving back at the fish docks, he boards his vessel and carefully stores his prize.

Once the lumbering diesel engine comes to life, White Boots unties his boat and starts to power out of the slip, heading back to the marina. At the helm, White Boots starts to smile as he thinks of his son and how proud he is of him.

Stopping by the Pawn Shop takes away the time White Boots usually uses to re-fuel for the next day. Knowing he will have to re-fuel in the morning, he decides to give the boat a quick spray down and then hit his bunk in the Pilothouse of the crab boat, leaving a note for Boner to let him sleep.

Chapter 3

On Flagler Ave, is Key West High School, where Boner watches the clock on the classroom wall. He is exhausted, staying up all night studying for the test. And now he is only waiting for the buzzer to sound, to set him free for the rest of the day.

Still groggy from no sleep the night before, Boner boards the bus to take him home. As Boner grabs a window seat his eyes are already starting to close, with the sweet smell of the salt air drifting through the window.

Boner is able to catch a short nap during the twenty minute ride, before arriving at the bus stop for the marina.

One of his classmates starts yelling. "Hey Boner. Crab Boy. Wake up man. It's your stop."

Arriving at his bus stop, Boner gets off the bus and starts walking down the road to the marina. The road to the marina is lined with abandoned lots. Some lots are so over grown it looks more like a dense forest. On other lots, there are single-wide trailers with broken freezers and patio chairs strewn between them.

Walking down the broken shell and gravel road, he can hear the faint plucking of guitar strings. Its Red Stripe, sitting on an old broken crab trap, finger picking an old blues tune.

Boner knows Red Stripe from him helping out on his dad's crab boat and seeing him sit in with some of the local bands. Red Stripe doesn't talk much, he just picks on his guitar. No one, not even Boner knows where Red Stripe lives. Although there are rumors he is homeless and lives in the woods around the marina.

The closer he gets to Red Stripe the more pronounced are the notes he is picking, as they flow through the breeze of the sea.

Dada-dit-dit-dit-dit-dit-dit-dit.

Dada-dit-dit-dit-dit-dit-dit.

Reaching Red Stripe Boner asks him, "How's it going Red?"

"Went out with your daddy today. Made me thirty bucks."

"What's that song you're playing?"

"It's an old family song from when I lived in the Blue Ridge Mountains. My daddy said it's called Deliverance."

"I like it. Mind if I call it my families' song?"

Red Stripe laughs. "Son, you're like family to me. So I don't think my daddy will mind."

"How many pounds did you get today?"

"Didn't really look like much. Your daddy thinks someone is robbing the traps again."

"Well, keep playing, I have got to get some sleep."

As Boner starts walking into the marina, he hears Red Stripe yell at him.

"Hey Boner, I hear there might be some fancy boaters coming in this weekend. Some might need their bottoms cleaned."

"Thanks Red, see you later."

Most days, arriving home, Boner will head to the Dock Office to pickup the mail and talk to Bruce the Dockmaster.

Not today. Today Boner is exhausted from last nights studies and only wants to go to sleep for a while.

Walking down the narrow finger pier, Boner arrives at the houseboat. He tugs on the dock line to bring the houseboat closer, so he can board the vessel.

As he slides open the door he sees White Boot's note taped to the glass. "Son, it has been a long day, so Macky and I both turned in early. Please try to be quiet and let us sleep." Boner smiles and scribbles just one word. "Ditto"

Entering the houseboat he tosses his backpack on the couch and heads to his bunk. Boner, mumbles to himself "Me too dad, me too."

Closing the door, Boner heads straight to his stateroom. The only stateroom in the one bedroom houseboat.

Reaching the stateroom, still fully dressed, Boner only slides off his shoes and flops on the bed.

For hours Boner does not stir. Not even when the music starts drifting through the night air from several of the local bars. This will not be a night Boner will sneak out.

Chapter 4

At Five-thirty A.M. White Boot's alarm blares that the morning has arrived. Feeling the pain, he crawls his aching body off the Pilothouse's bunk.

"Damn it.", he thinks to himself. "I forgot to fix the coffee."

Normally White Boots sets up the coffee maker the night before so its ready when he wakes up. Not this time.

He can already hear the rumbling of some of the diesel engines idling from the other boats. It's a new start to another day. Turning on the VHF radio to catch NOAA's weather report, he starts setting up the coffee maker in the pilothouse.

White Boots knows Boner will not be getting up for another few hours, so he stays on the crab boat making the boat ready for the days work. His first stop will be the fuel dock and then the channel leading to the sea and his crab traps.

White Boots is also letting his diesel engine idle and warm up, giving him time to pour that first cup of coffee. Drinking the hot nectar of caffeine, he scans his charts reviewing the location of his traps and starts planning his daily run.

As White Boots unties the dock lines a slight smile comes over his face as he is still thinking about what he is able to do for his son.

Although White Boots barely scrapes by for him and his son, he does the best he can. As do most people living on the water in the Keys.

With his six foot four frame, the muscles he built through a lifetime of pulling crab pots and working the sea are now growing weak with age.

As the morning sun tiptoes through the forward hatch. The light brings a sheet of brightness over Boner's bunk.

Stirring, Boner can hear the marina is also waking up and coming alive. Feeling the warmth of the morning sun, he knows his dad did not wake him for the daily run of the crab pots.

And it being Saturday, he knows he can take his time. Ridding himself of the cobwebs, built inside his head during the night.

Being live aboard boaters, he and his dad continued living on the boat in the marina, as it is some of the most affordable housing on the Island.

Their slip has fresh water, coming from a Sears garden hose, and 50 amp electrical power. With water and electrical power from the dock, the houseboat is much like any other home on land. That is until a wayward cruiser happens to arrive in the middle of the night.

Some weekend cruisers have a bad habit of grabbing the nearest hose in order to rinse the salt spray from the deck and hull of their expensive power boats.

Today is one of those mornings. Boner strips off yesterdays clothes and climbs into the shower stall to rid himself of yesterday's grim.

Turning the shower knob...nothing...drip, drip drip, drip. "Crap", Boner mumbles. No hot water, no cold water...nothing, just drips of the precious liquid.

Climbing back out of the shower and grabbing his towel, Boner looks out the window and sees the problem. A forty-two foot Fountain. A go-fast boat is now in the slip on the other side of the houseboat.

Boner is upset, knowing his dad pays for their water and this power boater is stealing it. Slipping into his boxers, Boner heads for the sliding doors to get their hose and water back.

Being awake for only several minutes Boner stops at the door. As with most men when they wake from a nights sleep, Boner has one.

Covering his crotch with one hand, he pulls the door open with the other and yells at the Captain. "Hey, you took our hose. What are you doing taking our hose?"

Not hearing Boner, the man continues spraying his boat's deck while listening the music coming from his boat's speakers.

Coming from his speakers is the sound of a wall banging bass, pumping out Rap music. BOOM BOOM BOOM DA BOOM DA BOOM, BOOM BOOM. The Gansta Rap is so loud coming from the go-fast boat it is pounding the dock's pilings and vibrating the hulls of other nearby vessels.

Going back inside the houseboat, Boner makes his way to his berth. Grabbing yesterdays pants, he throws one leg in, then the other and goes back to the sliding glass door.

But before he can slide open the door, something stops his movement. Something…a feeling…Boner senses something is wrong. Something is out of place.

He turns, looking back at the salon, the living room in most land homes. And focuses his eyes onto the couch. "What the heck", he thinks to himself.

Boner, now engaged with something on the couch, he forgets about the go-fast boat stealing their water. One foot after the other, he moves slowly as if he is stalking a prey.

There, on the couch, he sees his backpack and chemistry book laying in shreds.

"Oh come on!" Boner blurts out.

As he reaches for the destroyed backpack, it hits him. He slowly turns, looking towards the starboard bulkhead.

With a disgusted voice, Boner states "Macky, you did this!"

Macky now awake, just sits there with no immediate response.

"I'll talk to you after I get back." Boner tells Macky.

Turning towards the door, Boner just shakes his head.

Sliding the door open, Boner pulls on the dock line enabling him to step onto the finger pier. As he starts to walk up the finger pier to the dock, he can barely hear himself think over the thundering bass music coming from the man's boat.

As Boner approaches, the man pays no attention and continues spraying down the go-fast boat. Undaunted, Boner walks back to the water spigot and turns off the water.

As the last of the water leaves the nozzle, the man starts yelling at Boner. "Hey, turn my water back on you moron. What do you think you are doing? Turn the water back on now!"

"It's not your water Mister. It's my water and you didn't even ask to use it."

The man, starts to jump off his boat to come after Boner. In doing so he slips, doing a back flip and falls into the water.

As Boner starts to laugh, the man starts yelling. "I can't swim!" His arms start to pound the water like a bird flapping it's wings.

"Help, I can't swim!" he continues to yell.

Boner, not thinking about how this man was ready to attack him, grabs the boat hook off the dock box and runs to the end of the dock. Stretching out the hook, the man is able to grab on, while Boner pulls him to the dock.

The man grabs hold of the slats of the finger pier. While Boner with his upper body strength is able to pull the man out of the water and onto the pier.

Out of breath, the man just lays there. Boner tries to calm him down and stop him from hyperventilating. By now several others have gathered on the dock to watch.

This is both excitement and entertainment for the other cruisers, dock hands and live aboards.

Hearing the commotion, Bruce comes down from the Dock Master's Office to see what all the yelling is about.

"Boner, what's going on?" Bruce asks him.

"He slipped and fell in the water Sir."

Coming closer, Bruce is worried. "Is he ok?"

"Hell no, I'm not alright!" The man is yelling, while still trying to catch his breath. "This kid! This kid turned off, he turned off my hose! And he made me fall in the water!"

Boner looking at the Dock Master, "No Sir, I turned off my water hose."

Just then, Martha, a lady on a nearby boat chimes in. "He tried to jumped off his boat and slipped. Boner wasn't anywhere near him Bruce."

While trying to hold back the laughter Martha tells Bruce what happened. "You should have seen him. When he tries to run off the boat, his legs go out from under him. His legs must have gone almost four feet over his head, before his butt hit the deck and he slides into the water. Funniest site you'd ever seen."

Others are standing around laughing and a few even clapping for the mornings entertainment.

The Dock Master's eyes quickly scans the pier and dock. He sees the water hose is attached to White Boot's slip. But not wanting to lose a paying customer tries to calm the man from the power boat down.

Bruce talks to the power boater. "I'm sorry. Some of these live aboards get protective of their hoses. Let me get you another one."

"Boner, why don't you take your hose back to your slip and I'll talk with you later."

Just nodding, Boner picks up the water hose and walks it back to the houseboat.

He can hear Bruce talking to the man and the man sounds like he is starting to understand. He thought the water is free and didn't know everyone has their own hose.

After Boner changes the water valve back to supplying the houseboat, he again pulls on the dock line to bring the boat closer and steps on board.

Entering the boat, Boner, seeing what used to be his backpack, remembers, shaking his head walking past Macky. All he wants is a hot shower. He will deal with the drama later.

Boner is still trying to fully wake up And now with the water spraying down his body, all Boner can do is sit on the shower seat holding his head in his hands.

He knows within hours it will be all over the marina how he pushed someone in the water. That is how it works around a marina. One person says something, then another picks it up and within hours, rumors and hearsay becomes the truth.

It is already a long morning for Boner and it is only 8 AM.

Getting out of the shower, Boner notices the Gangsta Rap is no longer pounding the dock. Now he needs to deal with Macky but he doesn't have time. The day has to get better. It just has to.

Chapter 5

Boner has two boat bottoms to clean today. A thirty-two foot Pacemaker that arrived a few day ago. And a forty-six foot Morgan to clean after he is done with the Pacemaker. Boner is always looking for a way to earn some spending money.

Drying off and putting on his swim shorts, Boner walks into the salon. As he locks everything up, he looks at Macky.

"I don't have time to talk to you right now. But when I get back, we need to talk."

Boner leaves the salon and heads to his stateroom. With the swim gear and the hookah stored on the aft deck of the houseboat, he exits through the rear sliding doors.

Boner likes using the hookah instead of dive tanks.

Looking up towards the Dock House he sees a dock cart not in use. Maybe the day is looking up. He will only have to make one trip to take his gear to the boat he is cleaning.

As Boner reaches the dock cart, Bruce comes out of the Dock House.

Bruce tells him "Boner, you can't talk like that to paying customers."

"Mr. Bruce, he didn't ask to use our hose and the new marina owner will end up charging my dad for the extra water."

The new owner of the marina looks out for the weekenders and tourists more than the locals. He is one of those people who do not understanding it is the locals keeping a business running during the off season.

"Boner, If you have a problem with one of our customers, you come to me."

Boner, does not want to get in any trouble, so he keeps it simple. "Yes Sir, I will come see you."

"May I use this cart for a little bit?"

"Just make sure you return the cart to where you found it."

As Boner is loading the dock cart with his diving gear, the marina is coming alive. Dinghies are running around. Boaters are sitting on their decks, some with their first cup of coffee. Others are readying their boats for a day a of cruising or fishing.

While Boner is setting up to clean the Pacemaker's bottom, his dad is out looking over and counting his traps. Because the current , surf and wind moves his crab traps around, he does this inspection run even on the days he does not pull the traps.

Sometimes two, three, six, or even twenty traps are moved from the day before. While he is moving the traps back in line with the others, he is also able to check the buoy line for any fraying. Losing a trap will cost White Boots money he can not afford.

Boaters try to avoid the crab trap buoys. Most boaters learn to run buoy lines, as they are usually laid out in parallel lines. However, sometimes the boaters do not notice the buoy, until it is too late and the buoy's line will end up around the boat's prop or rudder.

That is why White Boots is always counting his traps, checking his GPS, scanning the water for other boats, and listening to the VHF.

Other than Macky and the go-fast boater, it is a normal weekend for Boner and his dad. White Boots runs his trap line and Boner is dropping his dive flags into the water for a few hours work.

As Boner starts setting up to clean the bottom of the Pacemaker, he hears someone calling from the Fly bridge.

"Hey, I'm sorry. I forgot your name."

"They call me Boner."

"I guess you are getting ready to clean the bottom, now?"

"Yes Sir. It should only take me a couple of hours."

"Great Boner. I'll put a tag on the engines, so no one will try to start them. Just yell at me when you are done."

"Yes Sir. Thank you. I'll let you know."

As Boner starts putting on his wetsuit, he knows today will be a good day for him. It will take him two or three hours to clean this one and then he has one more to clean.

He puts out his two dive flags. One at each corner of the boats stern. Many times boaters are not paying attention and this way his flags are more likely to be seen.

Turning on the hookah and putting the regulator in his mouth he checks the air supply. He makes sure the wooden finger pier does not have any nails or splinters sticking out. As several times he forgot and ended up tearing his suit.

With no nails or splinters showing on the pier, he checks all his equipment and slides off the finger pier into the marina basin's water.

Boner takes his time checking the entire hull before starting the scraping of the algae, barnacles and silt.

The marina basin's depth runs between seven and fifteen feet. When the marina basin is free of current and traffic, you can see the bottom.

As Boner starts scraping the hull, White Boots is checking the last of the crab traps off the coast.

He hasn't lost any traps. But the weekend is young. And more and more people are coming down from Miami on their fancy boats. Decking out their bow with models wearing their T-backs and sipping on their sweet colored drinks. After all this is paradise.

Now that the traps are checked, it is time to relax and enjoy some of the wonderful Florida Keys sunshine. It also gives White Boots some time to start his own boat cleaning.

White Boots drops his anchor about four miles Southeast of Cow Key. As he sits there watching the boats darting about and the Planes landing at the Key West Airport, he reflects on the changes taking place in the Islands.

He remembers the times the skyline of the harbor is filled with mangroves and the houses are unseen from the shoreline.

There are more people on the White Street Pier than he has seen in long time. Even so, it is quieter and more relaxed on this side of the island. As most of the tourists flock to the other side to view the Cruise Ships at Truman.

Such a beautiful Keys day White Books thinks to himself.

"I sure wish Boner was out here with me."

White Boots enjoys the water. Especially when he gets to see small pods of Dolphins playing off his bow.

Checking his watch, he knows Boner is in the water cleaning a hull. White Boots starts the diesel up and prepares to pull anchor.

Entering the marina basin, he sees Boner's Dive Flags are in the water. Approaching the slip, he puts the boat into neutral and glides up to the finger pier. You never want to approach a dock faster than you want to hit it. A lesson he learned from his father when he was around Boner's age.

As White Boots starts tying off his dock line, Martha comes walking down the dock. "Good Morning, I just want you to hear it from me first."

Finishing tying off the boat, White Boots looks up. "Hear what Martha?"

Pointing to the forty-two foot Fountain. "A power boater came in earlier. That one over there."

"The guy took your water hose without asking and Boner took it back."

"The guy got real angry and when he goes to get off his boat, he slips, doing a back flip and goes into water."

White Boots is puzzled. "What does that have to do me?"

"Well the guy tells Bruce that Boner pushed him in the water, but he didn't! I saw it all and Boner didn't touch him."

"I just want you to know Boner didn't do anything to the guy. You know in case Bruce or somebody else tries to blame him."

"Well thank you Martha. Seems like there is a lot of that going around since this new owner took over."

Martha isn't too happy with the new owner either and lets White Boots know it. "All he cares about is the tourists and their money. Seems like we are only boat trash to him."

"Martha, you know how it is in the Keys. Everything changes and everything remains the same."

"I know. Tell Boner I said Happy Birthday." she tells White Boots, as she turns to go back to her houseboat.

"I will Martha and thank you for letting me know what happened."

Chapter 6

As White Boots cleans his crab boat from the mornings salt spray, he can not help but smile, knowing the present waiting for Boner.

While still cleaning the crab boat, Boner comes up from cleaning the hull of the Pacemaker.

Boner climbs up the ladder and walks down the rickety wooden finger pier to the dock.

"Hi Dad, how are the crab traps?"

White Boots laughs. "Hi son, looks like they're all still there. How's the water down there today?"

"Mostly clear. This one is easy. Next, I have to go clean that forty-six foot Morgan. I don't think its been cleaned in years."

"No, I don't think it has. How long do you think it will take you?"

"I'm guessing around five or six hours. Kind of kills the rest of day. But he is giving me three dollars and fifty cents a foot."

"You going to get some lunch?"

"No Sir, I want to try and get the Morgan done today."

"Ok, when you're done and cleaned up, we'll get some dinner up at the Hogfish or maybe Mangrove Mama's."

"Sounds good. I'll let you know when I'm done." Boner tells his dad, as he turns to go get the dock cart again to move his equipment from the Pacemaker to the Morgan.

White Boots already knows Boner will want to go to the Hogfish.

The Hogfish and Mangrove Mama's have been there ever since White Boots can remember. One filled with banana trees and coconut palms, the other is on the water. Both allowing you to escape from life for a little while.

As Boner goes to start cleaning the Morgan's hull, White Boots goes back to washing the salt spray from the deck, gunwales and freeboard of the crab boat.

With his dad cleaning the crab boat, Boner starts on the Morgan. He would much rather be cleaning a power boat than a sailboat. Sailboats have a keel with a draft between four feet and eight feet depending on the boat.

The Morgan only has four and half foot draft so it will not be as hard as some.

Boner starts cleaning the Morgan just below the waterline. And works his way to the keel. With all the scraping of the hull, it is making it harder to see more than a few feet.

From behind, Boner gets bumped. Something pushes him. He knows it may be a loose deck board from one of the past hurricanes.

As Boner turns in the water to push the deck board out of the way, the silt hides it from his sight. Reaching out, its not a deck board he feels.

All in one motion, Boner brings both his arm and hand into his chest, while at the same time kicking his feet and fins. Boner shoots to the surface as if he has been shot out of a torpedo tube. He is on the finger pier in all of about two seconds.

Boner hit the finger pier so fast, the water did not even have time to fill in behind him.

"What the heck?" Boner blurts out. Still shaking, he quickly moves to the dock itself. His eyes fixed on the water beside the Morgan.

After several minutes the water beside the Morgan starts to settle down, to where he can almost see to the bottom again. As his eyes scans each inch of the water below him, he looks for it. Where is it?

Boner knows the Casa Marina Resort closed its beach after a saltwater crocodile was under it's pier. And the waters off Fort Zachary Taylor State Park are closed to swimmers when saltwater crocodiles are spotted.

His body still shaking, he keeps scanning. Feeling something in the water that should not be there and not being able to see it will scare anybody.

Starting to calm down, Boner creeps back onto the finger pier. His eyes darting from side to side. "What is it?" He keeps saying under his breath "What is it?"

Slowly he reaches the end of the finger pier. Holding onto the piling he looks down. He looks from the stern of the Morgan along the waterline to the bow and back again. He scans the other side along the Beneteau.

Then, there it is. Eight or nine feet long. At the bow of the Beneteau. Nine hundred pounds, floating barely under the water, with it's snout poking through the surface. A Manatee.

Boner bursts out laughing. A Manatee.

A Manatee. "Wow, what was I thinking. Geez, ok."

Manatees come through all of the marinas during the winter months. If they are not around the warm waters of the power stations, they graze in the warm waters of the Florida Keys.

Even though it is against the law, many of the locals provide fresh water to the manatees. Fresh water from a garden hose is like a cheese burger in paradise to this gentle herbivorous Mammal.

They seek marina basins for shelter. The sound of a garden hose pouring it's water draws them even closer. Often when a Manatee is spotted in the marina, locals will grab their boat's garden hose, turn on the water and drop the hose into the basin.

The Manatee is drawn to the hose, knowing the sweet nectar it will provide. The Manatee will take the hose into it's mouth as if it is a straw and to the Manatee it is.

But today Boner doesn't have time to provide the Manatee it's cheese burger. He still has more than half of the Morgan's bottom to clean.

Putting his swim fins and gloves back on and the regulator in his mouth, he lowers himself back into the basin. Washing his mask out and placing it over his head, he slides under the water and back to the Morgan's keel.

Chapter 7

Inch by inch, Boner scrapes the barnacles from the Morgan. With one hand feeling the keel and the other scraping, Boner, now is more alert. Now he is keeping an eye on the water around him.

The Manatee must have been watching Boner enter the water, as now the Manatee is slowly guiding its massive body closer to Boner.

As Boner scrapes the keel from forward to aft, the Manatee ascends toward him. Watching, the Manatee is sensing this human is no threat and may be one of the local humans who provide the him the sweet nectar he craves.

As the Manatee rises level with Boner, it makes Boner laugh. "How could I think that thing is a crocodile?"

With Boner scraping the keel, the Manatee nudges Boner with it's snout around Boner's knee. Using his foot and flipper, Boner tries to gently push the Manatee away.

But the Manatee is thinking Boner is playing and wants more.

Slowly moving it's large frame around, the Manatee nudges Boner. This time with it's entire body against him.

Boner is thinking "Come on stop it." Using his hand, Boner again tries to push the large Mammal away. "What do you want? Go way, I have work to do."

But the Manatee appears to have other thoughts. It starts to roll over, exposing it's underside to Boner. Boner decides to take off one glove and reaches out to touch the creature.

Boner can see the creature's flippers slowly moving up and down as he strokes it. As he withdraws his hand, the Manatee using it's flat tail and flippers moves side by side with Boner. Slowly the Mammal using it's flippers, appears to want to hug Boner.

Just then, above the surface aft of the Morgan., Boner sees the hull of a boat pulling up straddling the finger pier and the Morgan.

In what is a somewhat garbled sound, Boner hears "Diver, come up! This is the FWC! Diver, come up now!"

Seeing his Dive Flag be tugged on, Boner knows something is up.

Pushing the huge Manatee away Boner kicks his flippers and heads to the surface. Raising to the side of the boat above, Boner stretches his hand through the surface grabbing the gunwale of the Florida Fish and Wildlife boat.

The officer, is just finishing tying off to the finger pier at his bow and the Morgan off his stern. He tells Boner "Get up on the dock."

Boner takes off his flippers and tosses them on the pier. The Officer steps out of his thirty-three foot Contender, onto the pier. Offering Boner a hand, he helps him up the rickety ladder.

The FWC Officer is not happy. "What did I just see you doing?"

"I'm cleaning the hull. You know, bottom cleaning."

"Son, that's not what I was seeing. Do you see how clear that water is right now?

Boner answers the Officer "It's a little murky from my scraping and the manatee. But yes Sir, I see."

"That's right, the Manatee. What are you doing with that Manatee?"

Boner is puzzled "Manatee? I don't understand." His mind racing. He knows according to law no one can touch, harass or molest a Manatee.

The Officer tells Boner to go over and sit on the dock box and he takes out his notepad. "How long were you in the water?"

"I've been cleaning this hull for about the last two and half hours Sir."

"And how long have you been masturbating the Manatee?"

Jumping to his feet, Boner exclaims "What, No Sir! No Sir, I would never I could never do something like that. What do you mean?"

"Settle down and sit back down!"

"Son, the water is clear enough anyone can see you. You do know that Manatee down there is a bull right?"

"No Sir. I didn't know you could tell the difference between a male and female Manatee."

"You were rubbing the Manatee on it's underside."

"Yes Sir, I'm sorry. I know you're not suppose to touch them."

"And when you were touching the Manatee, where were you rubbing it?"

"On it's stomach. It appears to like it Sir. Besides he came to me, I didn't like go chase it or anything."

"Do you know how to tell the difference between a Bull and a Cow?"

"No Sir."

"The Manatee you were stroking is a Bull."

"I didn't know that. I am sorry Sir, I didn't know."

"So, you didn't know the Manatee you were stroking is a Bull. A male Manatee."

"No Sir. I don't know how to tell the difference between them."

"When you were stroking that Bull, you didn't feel anything odd? Nothing protruding from around it's belly button?"

As Boner sits on the dock box, he tries to think what the Officer can be talking about.

Several of the locals are now coming up on the decks of their boats to watch the day's new entertainment.

"It has bumps, like what I find on some of the hulls I clean."

"Son, that isn't a bump. It's his penis." And with that the FWC Officer breaks out into laughter.

Boner is now turning a deep shade of red with embarrassment. "Oh my God, what's my dad, the kids at school going to think when they hear this?"

Looking down at Boner, then glancing around the dock, the Officer sees everyone is interested in what is going on.

Taking a seat beside Boner on the dock box, the Officer lowers his voice and presents an air of understanding.

"You haven't spent a lot of time around these Mammals have you son?"

With tears in his eyes, Boner tells the Officer "No Sir."

"Well look, I don't think you knew what you were doing. And not knowing about Manatees, I can understand it. So I'm not going to write you up and if anyone asks I'm just going to tell them I though you were harassing him. I won't tell anyone what really happened."

"But son you have to do something for me."

"I'll do anything Sir!"

"Two things. One if anyone asks, tell them I was mistaken, that you were just pushing the Mammal away from you."

"Yes Sir. That is what I will tell them, even my dad. Yes Sir."

"Next, I don't want to ever see you in the water with another one. If there is a Manatee in the water you stay out. If you are in the water and one comes around, you get out. Is that understood?"

"Yes Sir. Yes Sir. Thank you."

Just then Boner's dad hearing the loud voices and seeing people on their decks, comes out onto the dock. Its not often he sees a water cop talking to his son.

As White Boots gets about halfway down the dock the water cop is standing up shaking Boner's hand.

When White Boots arrives at the Morgan, the FWC Officer is boarding his boat and untying his dock lines to leave.

His dad asks "What's going on Boner?"

Boner, still a little shaken by the FWC Officer. He tells his dad "He thought I was harassing the Manatee."

"The Manatee?"

"Yes Sir. There's a Manatee somewhere in the basin. And he thought, with me in the water, that I might be harassing it."

"So you didn't get a ticket again for not having your dive flags down?"

"No Sir. I have two dive flags out since that last time. I make sure I always have them out."

"He just told me I can't be in the water while the Manatee is also in there. So I guess I won't be able to finish the Morgan until tomorrow."

"That's ok, I think both of us may have done enough work for today. Why don't you go get cleaned up. Have you thought about where you'd like to go for dinner?"

"The Hogfish."

White Boots chuckles turning to go back to the houseboat. "Hogfish it is. Now put your equipment away and get cleaned up."

Chapter 8

Once cleaned up with the salt and sea urchins washed away, Boner meets his dad on the dock.

"Dad, are we walking, driving or taking the dingy?"

"I think we'll drive over. That sun took it's toll on me today."

Without having to open the door, both climb into their Conch Cruiser. A nineteen seventy-four Volkswagen Thing. The cruiser has no windows or doors.

The Thing looks more like a World War Two Jeep made into a low rider. The Thing's roof left during one of the past hurricanes. And the stick shift no longer has fourth gear, nor will it go into reverse.

It is only a short ride over to Front Street and down to the Hogfish. Boner usually walks over at night to listen to whomever may be playing music.

As they walk in, most of the other locals know them and they all share greetings of the day. Few tourists know of the Hogfish. But those who do, not only share the information but come back often.

And each year it seems more and more of the tourists sharing the sights and sounds are raving about the Hogfish's food. Which brings more and more tourists.

Arriving around four-thirty, they are able to get a good table as the band is just starting to setup. White Boots picks a spot, not too close to the band, as he wants to be able to talk to his son.

As their bodies melt and descend into their chairs, Bait is already putting their drinks down in front of them.

If there is one thing Bait is known for, its knowing her customers. She only needs to serve you once and she remembers what you drink.

But that is not the only thing Bait is known for at the Hogfish. No one knows where Bait comes from but they all are sure glad she came.

Standing five foot seven with one hundred and six pounds attached to a frame of a runway model, she's a Dixie Bell with a sultry walk, arousing the desire of all of those near and far.

Just as the commercial fishermen bait their traps and lines so does the Hogfish.

With her ever so slight southern drawl, she asks "Captain, what can I get you?"

"It's Boner's Birthday, so whatever he wants."

Pulling out one of the spare chairs at the table, Bait slides in next to Boner. Crossing her long legs and moving her shoulder into his "Ok birthday boy, what would you like?

Bait knows her moves and charm will bring out even the shyest of creatures.

Without moving his head from looking at the menu, White Boots raises his eyes and smiles at Bait. He sees she is going to put those southern charms to work tonight.

Some say Bait was a former Miami Dolphin's Cheerleader. Others see the moves of an exotic dancer who keeps EMTs on standby.

Boner's words are stumbling from his blushed face. "I think tonight I'll have the Stock Island Mixed Grill."

Bait still has her shoulder fused to his. "Humm, you're going to like that. I'll make sure."

White Boots can not help but grin, seeing how flustered his son is getting.

"And I'll have your Famous Lobster Pot Pie." White Boots tells Bait, in an effort to give Boner a moment to gather himself.

"I can do that for you Captain. Can I help you with anything else right now?"

Trying to hold back his laughter White Boots tells Bait "No Ma'am. That's all for now."

Placing her hand on Boner's knee and ascending it slowly up his thigh as she raises to go, she looks at Boner "I'll be back to check on you in a bit."

Once Bait is away from the table, Boner remains speechless. His eyes affixed to her sexually exciting walk, gratifying every person at the Hogfish. Him being no exception.

"Boner." White Boots utters, with no respo se. "Boner, hello Boner. Earth to Boner." His dad calls out to him.

"Yes dad, I'm sorry. I didn't hear you."

"I can see that." His dad says laughing.

"Boner, I know I've asked you this many times, but now you're eighteen and you'll be graduating soon. Have you decided what you want to do?"

"Yes Sir. I have some of it figured out, I think."

"Well, you going to keep it a secret or you going to share it with me?"

"I'm sorry, yes Sir I'll share it with you."

"I've been saving a lot of the money I earn from the bottom cleaning and the tips people give me for helping with their dock lines and what not."

"I want to go to college, but I know we can't afford for me to go to some big four year school."

"So, I thought I might get a car and maybe start taking classes over at the Community College. Maybe get a degree in Management and then later I can transfer to the University of Florida."

"That way I can walk, ride a bike or drive to school. It's only on the other side of the Overseas Highway."

"So you have been thinking about it. That's good son. I'm proud of you."

"Yes Sir I have been thinking."

"Hey, look whose playing tonight! Its Raven Cooper and Caffeine Carl."

"You like them son?"

"Sure. It's Blues, in a Trop Rock Reggae sort of way."

"What about Lady Gaga or The Black Eyed Peas?"

"I like Jimmy Buffett and Zac Brown. Its just that with Trop Rock and the Blues, I feel at home. It's the music you feel in the islands."

His dad knows the feeling. "You mean like the light salt spray in the air?"

"Sort of. Its as though you can shut your eyes and feel the water and know you are in paradise."

"I know how you feel son. There's nothing like the smell of the air here in the Florida Keys. Sometimes I'll even take a little longer on the traps, just to enjoy the clear water and the feel of the ocean's swells."

"Dad, have you heard Loren Davidson or Steven Youngblood?"

"Sure son. I think everyone from Key West to LA has, I hope. They're pretty good. Are there any other ones you like?"

"I like ones like Kelly McGuire and Howard Livingston."

To some people in the Keys it is fishing. For others it is diving on the wrecks. For Boner it is the music.

As Bait serves White Boots and Boner their dinners, she turns and smiles at Boner and kneels beside him. "So, its your birthday. Guess that makes you legal now."

In her sweet southern tone. Bait tells Boner "I guess, you don't have to sit in the back anymore."

While White Boots watches, he does all he can to hold back the laugher. He had talked to Bait several days ago, letting her know its Boner's birthday, today.

Bait said she is going to try to make this night special for Boner.

When Boner sneaks out, it is the Hogfish, where he will often go. Bait knows Boner as a quite respectful man. It isn't until talking to White Boots that she knows his age.

Bait is a mystery to those who know her. No one knows how old she is, but they guess somewhere around twenty-three or twenty-four. When the men look at her, age is the last thing most are thinking.

Leaving the table she tells them "I'll be back. But if you need anything just let me know."

And as if on cue, as she walks back to the server area, the temperatures rise as every head turns to watch her walk.

Boner's dad asks "How's Macky doing?"

"Since he's not allowed in school anymore, I haven't been able to spend much time with him."

"Yesterday, he tore up my knapsack and one of my books."

"Well son you need to spend time with him."

"I know. I won't be starting college for a few months after graduation, so I'll get to spend more time with him."

"I know he gets frustrated not having me around. So, I know I can't blame him, I guess."

As the band starts, Caffeine Carl is telling the customers the song they are getting ready to play is a protest song. Carl tells the crowd "Look at what's happening, condos popping up on every square inch."

Carl, Cooper and Jeremy Gill start picking and plucking, belting out their Protest Song for the crowd.

Boner starts to sing along with the words coming from the stage "I don't like big cities."

White Boots, looking over at Boner, tells him "He sure can pick those strings."

"Yes Sir. I like the bluesy feel he has when he plays the guitar. The way he plays, makes all their songs fun. And Raven's voice is, I don't know, different. But a good different."

"Son, you're eighteen now. So you don't need sneak out to come listen to the music."

"You know?"

"Of course I know, I'm your dad. It's my job to watch over you. So now you don't need to hide where you're going."

"Boner, I know you need space. I know how hard you work on those boat bottoms, while still keeping your grades up."

"I'll tell you. Had you not been keeping your grades up, I'd have said something. But Boner I'm real proud of you."

White Boots seldom talks this way. And when he does, it catches Boner by surprise.

"I guess the only thing I'd wish you'd do is spend more time with Macky."

"I will dad. I guess he needs me, the way I need you."

Now that catches Boner's dad by surprise. White Boots, for one of the few times in his life, is at a loss for words.

Looking at Boner, White Boot's expression goes from dumbfounded and amazed to grateful and blessed.

"So do you have any bottoms to clean tomorrow?"

"No Sir. No more bottoms until next week. Although I still need to finish the Morgan."

"Next week, lot of the snowbirds are heading out for a while and they will want their bottoms cleaned just before they go."

As the band breaks into "Happy Birthday", Bait is bringing out the cake.

Chapter 9

The traditional birthday cake of true Conchs. A four layer Citrus aurantifolia cake. With the bottom layer being three feet in diameter. Ascending to the top layer with a diameter of twelve inches across.

Only a true Conch understands the meaning of the Citrus aurantifolia cake. its unique flavor brought to the Keys by the descendants of Englishmen, Wreckers and Pirates of the Caribbean.

Like the King cakes of New Orleans, the Citrus aurantifolia cake also contains a small trinket. Except with the Citrus aurantifolia cake the trinket sits atop the cake as a symbol to all.

Bait slowly rolls out the bar cart with a cake large enough to feed the entire bar and still have half leftovers for days to come.

Boner watches this sultry siren pushing the cart towards him. When his eyes finally settle on the cake, he sees it. A rush of crimson floods his body from his neck up his face and forehead. His eyes unable to move. Affixed in a stare of horror. How did they know?

There it is, adorning the top of the Citrus aurantifolia cake.

Hand carved. Sanded and polished. Stroked and massaged by the artisan's hand. Tranquil as it lays across the top layer of the cake, it provides an embarrassment no one knows. Or do they?

There it is, in front of him. A hand carved, sanded and polished figurine of a Florida Manatee.

Flashes of the Fish and Wildlife Officer, the Manatee, the ridicule that will come if they know. "Do they? Do they know?" Boner's mind races. Tears start to flow.

"What's the matter son? I know this is a big night for you, but there's no need to cry."

"This is the cake all the ancestors of the Wreckers and Pirates of the Caribbean have when they turn eighteen."

Just then, Boner hears a whisper in his ear. "No one knows Boner. Its ok." Its the Fish and Wildlife Officer wishing him happy birthday.

Boner looking up meets his eyes. With the Officer squeezing his shoulder, he again tells Boner "Its ok." And walks away.

Fear is now exchanged with delight as Boner starts to grin.

"Look at that, even FWC wishes you a happy birthday. Go ahead and take your Manatee. It's a symbol of good luck for a Conch."

Boner takes the Manatee from atop the cake. Slowly wiping away the pieces of frosting. He turns it as he wipes, making sure it is totally smooth, with no bumps.

Boner looks at his dad and tells him "Thank you."

"Bait, will you serve everyone a piece of my cake, please?"

"Sure Boner, anything for the Birthday man."

"Son, I still have something for you back on the boat."

"Would you mind if we stayed for another song or two?"

"Not at all son. This is your birthday. We can do what ever you want."

"Thanks dad. This is the best birthday ever."

"Well, like I said, there is still something waiting for you on the boat. So its not over yet."

As Carl, Cooper and Jeremy Gill start another set, Boner lets his mind travel, getting lost in the blues being carried through the air.

"Dad its been a great night, but I can barely hold my eyes open."

With the cake served to everyone and the rest cut, packaged and placed in the walk-in freezer, it is time to call it a night.

White Boots paid the tab in advance and left a large tip for Bait. Boner and his dad get up from their table and start heading for the door.

Just as they start going to the door, Bait catches Boner by the arm. Boner feeling his arm being held, turns, and comes face to face with the goddess he knows as Bait.

"You can't leave without a birthday kiss."

White Boots continued towards the door to wait for his son and watch the developments from a distance.

Taking Boner into her arms, caressing his tall lanky frame, she slides her hands up his arms, taking his face into her hands. Drawing his face to hers "Happy Birthday Boner." Then she puts her moist lips onto his.

Slowly, she releases his face separating their lips and looking into his eyes. Boner appears to be in a state of shock. Speechless. Unable to move his feet let alone his mouth.

She tells him "Umm, you stay safe now." After another moment of looking into his eyes, she turns and takes that slow sultry walk that she is known for so well, back to the bar.

Boner remains motionless as he watches Bait return to her work station. Minutes feel like hours.

White Boots walks back over to Boner. "You ready to go son?"

With a smile in his voice, his dad asks him again "Son. Are you ready to go?

The cobwebs of fantasies clearing, Boner tells his dad "Yes, yes Sir. I'm sorry."

His dad says, with a tone of laughter "Nothing to be sorry about son. Come on, lets go home and get some sleep."

Climbing into the Thing for the drive around the canal, it appears this night has drawn Boner and his dad closer.

Chapter 10

Getting out of the Thing they can still hear the music as it drifts over the boats and the Mangroves. It is only around seven-thirty and the Keys nightlife is just coming alive.

Passing live aboards and cruisers in their slips, most are out on deck with Bar-B-Qs lit and cold drinks in their hands.

Walking down the dock to the houseboat, White Boots puts his arm around Boner, telling him "Son, you wait up here while I get your present."

White Boots is so excited on the inside, it is hard for him to contain it. While White Boots walks down the narrow finger pier to the crab boat, Boner sits on the dock box and pulls out his sculptured Manatee.

While Boner reflects on life through the Manatee, his dad is bringing a large rectangular shaped box out on deck and gently slides it up onto the finger pier.

Climbing off the crab boat, White Boots picks up the box and walks down the finger pier towards the dock and Boner.

Boner watches, as his dad places the box down in front of him and the dock box.

Putting the Manatee back into his pocket Boner asks "What is it?"

Laughing, his dad tells him "Well son, you'll just have to open it to find that out."

The sanded and polished wooden box appears to be made from new unused crab traps. It took White Boots weeks to construct it without Boner knowing.

Hinged on one side, Boner first admires the workmanship of the box, before he decides to open it. As Boner slowly opens the box, his expression goes from wonder to excitement.

The inside of the box, is covered with a light blue Sunbrella fabric that is both tucked and rolled, as though it is the upholstery of a nineteen-seventies Muscle car.

But it is what's in the box that has Boner again speechless.

Looking at his dad in amazement "We can't afford this dad!"

"Son, this is my gift to you on your eighteenth birthday. I hope you like it."

"Oh dad, I more than like it. I love it!"

"Well maybe you will be able to use it and not have to clean so many bottoms later on. Who knows."

"Oh dad, thank you so much. I don't know what to say."

"Don't say anything. I'm just glad it makes you happy."

"It does. I can't tell you how happy it makes me. I love it. Thank you so much!"

Boner now has in his hands, the gift his dad is so proud to be able to give him. The gift he was able to buy in the Pawn Shop.

Boner now has what he dreamed about for years. But he never thought he could afford to have one. When he watches others with theirs, he will shut his eyes and see himself.

In his hands is something he sees, but never touches. But this one is his. He holds it, as though it is a new born baby. Admiring the classic lines. The hi-gloss two-tone sunburst finish.

In his hands, he is holding a full size dreadnought acoustic Fender Starcaster guitar. As guitars go, it is what most will call a starter. But to Boner it is the greatest gift in the world. He runs his finger slowly across it's Rosewood fingerboard.

"It also has a built-in tuner Boner."

"Dad it's beautiful. I don't know what to say!"

White Boots squeezes Boner's arm. "Happy birthday son. I'm going turn in. I've got to get some sleep. Just do me a favor. Start spending more time with Macky, ok?"

"Yes sir, I will. Thank you so much for the guitar dad. Thank you!"

"Your welcome son. Please, try to keep the sound down. We don't need people complaining. Good night son."

"Good night dad. I'll keep it down and I may turn in shortly myself."

Boner has a hard time sleeping. He can't wait to show Red Stripe his birthday present, his new guitar.

Chapter 11

On Sunday mornings you will find Red Stripe on White Boot's crab boat pulling traps or plucking and lowly singing the blues, just outside the marina.

The same spot where he sits to wait for one of the Captains to provide him work for the day. Seems like Red Stripe has been sitting on those traps since anyone can remember.

Quiet and soft-spoken, Red Stripe doesn't say much. He just sits and sings the blues or some of the older Buffett tunes he likes.

Boner rises to the sun lighting his bunk. Quickly dressing, he still tries to take time to talk to Macky.

Boner holds up the new guitar for Macky to see. "Hey Macky, look what dad gave me."

Boner sits down on the couch holding the guitar across his thigh. As he runs his fingers across the strings, Macky still remains silent.

"Do you like the sound?"

Still no reply as Macky simply looks at the guitar and Boner. Boner lays the guitar back into it's hand made case, closes the lid and secures the snaps.

It is only seven in the morning, but Boner just can't wait. He wants everyone to see what his dad gave him. It is hard to tell who is prouder of the guitar, Boner or White Boots.

Then as Boner gets ready to leave the houseboat, he remembers, the Morgan. He stopped cleaning the hull and is suppose to finish it today.

He knows the guitar will just have to wait. White Boots has instilled good work ethics into Boner and Boner knows the Morgan must come first.

It takes Boner another four hours to setup and complete the hull cleaning of the Morgan, put all of the equipment away and clean himself up.

No Manatee….

Now approaching ten in the morning most weekenders are already out sailing, fishing or heading up towards the sandbar. The marina is quiet now, at least for a while.

Getting his guitar from the houseboat, Boner heads towards where he hopes to find Red Stripe sitting on his traps.

Inside himself, Boner is a little dishearten, as there is no one around for him to show off his present. The boaters are out and gone for the day. Bruce is way down the other end of the docks filling the gas tank of one of the last boats heading out.

Most Sundays, Boner and his dad head up to Mangrove Mama's for brunch. But not today. His dad has already left, knowing Boner has the hull to complete and that Boner wanted to show Red Stripe his present.

As Boner turns heading out of the marina he can hear Red Stripe's guitar singing out the blues.

His excitement is expressed in the fast paced strides he is taking to reach Red Stripe.

"Morning Red! You have to see what my dad gave me for my birthday!"

In a slow drawl Red Stripe tells him "Slow down son. I'm not going anywhere."

"I know. I'm sorry. I just want you to see it!"

Boner takes a seat on one of the old crab traps. He doesn't know Red Stripe already heard about the present from White Boots. But he doesn't let on, so Boner can share the excitement of his gift.

"You have got to see this!"

Boner sets the case on the ground and unsnaps the clips of the case. Lifting the top and setting the hinge so it remains open, Boner gently lifts the guitar from it's rest.

Boner, still holds the guitar with both hands as though it is a new born baby. He asks Red Stripe "Would you like to hold it?"

Boner isn't asking what he really wants, yet. What he really wants is for Red Stripe to help teach him how to play it.

Red Stripe sits down his own guitar. "Sure son. Let me see what you have there."

Red Stripe can see the pride in Boner's face. Showing the same care and reverence as Boner, Red Stripe takes the guitar from Boner. With Boner's guitar sitting across his thigh, he starts to tune the strings.

Red Stripe knows the guitar may only be a starter, but he also knows most any guitar can be made to sound good and this one is no different.

E, A, D, G, B, E he tunes each string with a slight strum, checking his hearing with the built-in tuner on the guitar.

"Has anyone showed you how to keep it in tune?"

"No Sir. I am hoping you will have time once in a while to help me learn."

Smiling Red Stripe tells him "Of course I can help you learn."

With the guitar tuned "Lets see how she sounds." Red Stripe says knowing the boy will want to hear if the new guitar is good.

Red Stripe decides to play an Eric Clapton and Duane Allman song, "Mean Old World" It gives him a chance to hit the strings with some taps, hammers, pulls and slides. It's a song that if done right, will show Boner his new guitar can perform.

Boner just watches in amazement as Red Stripe works the strings and makes the guitar come alive.

"Wow, that's great Red. You think I can do that one day?"

"Sure Boner. It just takes a lot of practice, that's all."

Knowing how much Boner likes music and the trop rock sound, he asks "Is there anything you'd like to hear, to see how it sounds on your guitar?"

"Will you play something by Jimmy Buffett?"

"Sure son."

Red Stripe tells Boner "Always make sure your guitar is in tune when you start to play. Otherwise the notes will sound like crap."

Boner listening to every word says "Yes Sir."

Once Red Stripe has the guitar in tune, he starts playing the chords slowly, allowing Boner to watch his hands and hear the notes.

Playing the chords D, G, A, D, Dsus, D, Dsus, D, Red Stripe starts to sing the Trop Rock song with a faster bluesy shuffle feel, as he is entering into Jimmy Buffett's world of "Margaritaville"

"Nibblin' on sponge cake,
watchin' the sun bake.
All of those tourists covered with oil.
Strummin' my six string on my front porch swing.

Smell those shrimp--

They're beginnin' to boil."

"Is that what you are looking to hear?"

"Wow, that sounds great Red. Will you teach me. Show me how to play like you do?"

"Boner, I'll show you how to play. But as far as like me. You have to play like you. Develop your own style. Your own feel for the music."

Boner knows the value of money and is hesitant when asking "How much do you charge?"

Laughing, Red Stripe says "Charge. I can't charge you Boner. You're like family. You wouldn't charge me to clean the bottom of my skiff, would you?"

"No Sir. I wouldn't charge you. But I live with my dad."

"That's true son, but you still need money as much as I do. In fact I hear you may need it more. What is this about you going to college?"

"Dad says if I learn how to play, I may be able to earn money playing instead of cleaning boat bottoms. And playing music may allow me time to go to the Community College."

As Red Stripe laughs in his deep mountain tone he tells Boner "Well then we need to get started then don't we."

"Boner, you do know this guitar has a built-in pickup and preamp, don't you?"

Boner didn't know, as Red Stripe can see the boy's smile growing.

Red Stripe never had a son and Boner is the closest he has ever gotten to having one. Like Boner's real dad, he has always tried to look out for him. That is one reason he is always sitting on the crab traps, each day when Boner gets off the school bus. Ever watchful.

"The first thing you will want to know is how to tune it."

So Red Stripe shows him how the built-in tuner works. And at the same time, he is showing him the names each of the six strings. E, A, D, G, B, E.

"Boner, I have to ask you. Do you want to learn how to play any song or do you want to learn how to play a song?"

"I don't understand."

"Well son, think of it like this. You can learn how to cook fried chicken and mash potatoes or you can learn how to cook anything. And by learning how to cook anything, you will also learn how to cook fried chicken and mash potatoes."

"What's the difference?"

"If you just want to learn how to cook fried chicken and mashed potatoes, you can learn that in a day or so. Kinda like learning one song. You can learn one song in a day or so. If that's what you want."

"I want to play like you and the bands at the Hogfish."

"Ok Boner, how about I show you some chords and scales. Then you practice them. Once you feel you can play what I've shown you, I'll give you more."

"I like that. Thank you Red. Can we do some today?"

"Sure Boner. Lets first learn the parts of the guitar. How's that?"

Over the next couple of hours Red Stripe and Boner sit on the old crab traps. Red Stripe explaining each part of Boner's guitar and Boner listening to every word.

"Red, what's the difference between my guitar and yours?"

"I guess I've had this one for going on thirty some years now. It used to be my dad's, then he gave it to me."

"No, I mean it looks like the hole in your guitar is covered up. Mine's not."

"Mine, is a old National resonator tricone. My daddy gave it to me. It was his when he played back in the thirties. Over the years you'll play several different ones. Then one day you'll find one guitar that just fits."

While Red Stripe shows Boner the different parts of the guitar, he also explains how the guitar hooks up to an amplifier.

Over the next several months Red Stripe shows Boner many chords and scales. And Boner, well Boner although he still goes over to the

Hogfish once in a while, he is spending less time there and more time on the dock practicing his chords and scales.

In turn, he is also spending more time with Macky. As Macky listens to Boner strum the guitar, he too is enjoying the time Boner is around him. Macky seems to be coming out from his shyness.

Chapter 12

The graduation from Key West High School although exciting for most of Boner's graduating class, is not all that exciting for Boner.

Boner is not one of the ones who hangs out under the bleachers, know as bleacher creatures. Nor is he one of the "in people" at school. Boner is one who understands the life around him. He is already looking forward to starting classes at Florida Keys Community College in the Fall.

Red Stripe is showing Boner more chords and scales. Every other day or so Boner will sit with Red Stripe, strumming the chords and playing the scales he's practiced.

Each day he is getting better and better. So much so, that when Boner has time to go over to Hogfish, to hear the bands, Red Stripe invites Boner to sit in with them on a song or two.

It's a humid fall morning and Boner is only a few weeks away from starting college. White Boots and Red Stripe are out pulling crab traps and Boner is sitting on their dock box, playing songs from people like Buffett, j.j. Cole, Tim Charron, and others.

As Boner sits on the dock box, the marina is coming alive with activity. A Poker Run out of Miami is arriving and filling up most of the marinas on the Ocean side of the Island. Go-Fast boats of all lengths are rumbling through the waters of Key West and Stock Island.

Keeping his guitar case beside him on the dock box, Boner is able to set his guitar down whenever boaters arrive. As the boaters arrive Boner puts the guitar down and helps them with their dock lines. This way even as he plays his guitar, he is still able to earn some tip money for helping them.

Sitting there, once all the thundering engines have shut down, his blues and trop rock sounds fill the air surrounding the docks.

It is a time he shares with Macky. Macky also learns the words to the songs Boner plays and often, one can hear Macky interjecting words into and after the song.

Tying off one of the last of the boats, Boner takes up his position on the dock box, retunes his guitar and starts playing a rendition by Dave Workman.

Red Stripe introduced Boner to the songs and style of Dave Workman. And one of Boner's favorite songs Workman plays is titled "Slip Away" and Boner has practiced it almost daily.

Boner also is taking time to practice the Keys standards such as "Margaritaville" and "A Pirate Looks at Forty" from Buffett and Eric Stone's "The Legend of the Lost Soul"

As he strums his guitar, the sound of the strings, lift into the air, the Key's Blues known as Trop Rock. Boner's mind wanders among the clouds with the songs and escapes from the reality of the marina.

Bruce, the Dock Master calls out from the door of the Dock House "Boner."

"Hey Boner!"

Boner is lost in his music, and does not hear Bruce's calls.

Leaving the Dock House, Bruce walks down to where Boner is sitting.

As Bruce reaches him, he touches him on the shoulder saying "Good morning, Boner. Sounds like you are getting a handle on how to play. You're sounding pretty good."

"Thanks Mr. Bruce."

"Look I've got a 52 foot Carver arriving in a little bit. I may be at the fuel dock, will you help him with his dock lines?"

"Sure Bruce, I'll watch for him. Do you know the boat's name?"

"Its called Aesculus glabra. And it is scarlet and gray. Thanks Boner, I really appreciate your help. And the music."

"You like the music?"

"I do and nobody is complaining so I think others are liking it also. Thanks Boner. Here hold on to this VHF radio, so you can hear them call when they arrive."

As Boner sits on the dock box, playing songs, the docks are being filled with his notes as he tries to mimic the sounds from the Hogfish, Larry Baeder, Chris Duarte, and even Fremont John.

Listening to his notes, he keeps an eye out for the Carver. He has cut back on the bottom cleaning, but helping with dock lines still earns tips.

Entering the marina basin, Boner sees a scarlet and gray power boat. Thinking to himself "This must be the boat."

Boner turns up the VHF to hear the Aesculus glabra call the marina. The marina monitors channel 16 and channel 10. So Boner put the VFH radio on Dual to hear broadcasts on both channels.

Watching the Carver making it's way in, Boner can tell this owner has money. He can see a radar arch spanning across the entire beam of the boat. And mounted on the arch he sees a satellite TV antenna, antennas for a satellite phone and Internet connects. Along with eight foot antennas for SSB, VHF radios, GPS and a Furuno 25kw 72 mile radar dome. This boat is loaded.

Boner hears the Captain of the Aesculus glabra hailing the marina on channel 16.

Boner responds to the hails "Motor Vessel Aesculus glabra, please switch to channel 10."

"Motor Vessel Aesculus glabra, I'm standing by for your dock lines Captain"

"Roger. I see you. I will be bringing my starboard side, beam to beam on your dock, if that is ok?"

"Yes Captain, please make sure your lines are ready and your fenders are out."

"Roger. Everything is set. I will be using my engines and my bow thruster for berthing."

"Roger Captain. I'll be taking your Starboard Bow line to tie off first. Please makeway to the dock at idle speed."

Chapter 13

Boner is standing by with the dock pole to grab the lines. The Captain approaches the dock, sliding the boat's beam sideways reducing the distant between the boat and dock an inch at a time.

Macky is watching this with great interest. He has never seen a boat move sideways coming into a dock before.

Once beam to the dock, a huge hulk of a man, appearing more like a Grizzly Bear standing on two legs, comes onto the deck tossing Boner the dock lines.

Grabbing the forward line and tying it off to the cleat, Boner walks down the dock to grab the aft dock line and tie it off to the cleat. Boner also checks the fenders, to make sure each one defends the boat from the dock.

With a sound of glee in his voice Boner greets the Captain "Good morning Captain. How was your passage?"

"We came down on the outside of the reef. Had a few three to four foot swells, but other then that, it was fairly uneventful."

"Where are you coming in from Captain?"

"We stayed in Marathon, Boot Key last night. They have a nice harbor with a good mooring field. They even have a water taxi service, so we didn't have to use the dingy."

"Yes Sir, Marathon is nice. A little different than here, in Stock Island and Key West."

"That's what we have heard. Is there some place nearby were we can get breakfast?"

"Yes Sir. There is the Hogfish across the way or Mom's up around the corner."

"Which one is where most of the locals eat?"

"A lot of locals eat at the Hogfish. Most of the deckhands eat at Mom's. Mom's got great food and doesn't cost much."

"Deckhands?"

"Yes Sir, you know, the guys who work on the fishing boats."

"That sounds like our type of place."

"Just go up to the end of the street, turn left, can't miss it. And be sure to tell Babs, Boner says hi"

"Babs?"

"Yes Sir. Babs is the owner and a great cook."

"Well I'll be sure to tell her hi for you. Look I will give you twenty dollars, if I can get you to wash down my deck while we are gone?"

"Yes Sir, I'd be happy to."

"Ok, give us a half an hour or so to get cleaned up and we will meet you on the dock."

Boner always is looking for ways to earn some extra money around the docks. Lately, he is sitting in with several of the bands playing his guitar to earn a few dollars. He is paying for his own college, so money is tight.

Walking back down the dock to his guitar and Macky, Boner takes a seat on the dock box and starts to play. He gets to sit in with the band tonight and he wants to have every note down right.

About forty minutes pass and he sees the man from the boat, walking down the gangplank with a woman. It must be his daughter, she is so young, Boner is thinking.

As the Man approaches Boner, he asks Boner again "You said Mom's is down the road and turn left?"

Standing up, Boner tells him "Yes Sir, you can't miss it. Mind you, the deckhands sometimes make for a smell, if you are not used to it."

"I understand. We should be a few hours as we like to do a little exploring."

"There's not much to explore on Stock Island. At least not as most tourists expect. We are mostly old Florida, not like being down in Key West."

"That's exactly what I am looking for son. We are not really into the tourist thing."

As the man and woman leave for Moms, its heard.

"Nice Bottom. Bone er"

The man and the woman abruptly stop and turn around. You can see the anger in the man's face and the woman is speechless.

"What did you say?"

Yelling, the woman wants to know "What is wrong with this kid JR?"

"How dare you talk like that about my wife! You want to bone someone, I'll bone you kid. What in the world is wrong with you?"

Jumping to his feet. "No Sir, I wouldn't…"

"Do you always talk about a women's rear end that way? Son, you don't yell out about a woman having a nice bottom and that you want to bone her. What is wrong with you?"

The man is enraged, to have his wife talked about, in such a manner.

The man keeps yelling about how Boner is talking about his wife, "Is this how you people treat ladies?"

"Sir, Sir! It wasn't me. I didn't say anything!"

"Boy, we both heard you say you wanted to have sex with my wife!"

"No Sir, no Sir, that wasn't me, I swear!"

"There is no one here but you, do you think I'm stupid?"

Then they hear it again.

"Nice bottom. Bone er."

Both men are in shock, as they turn their heads to look at Macky.

"Nice Bottom. Come on Bone er." Macky repeats as the two men stare.

It seems like minutes that the angry man just stares at Macky.

Then, without warning it happens. The man can not hold back his feelings. He can not hold back his emotions.

With one large exhale that can be heard throughout the marina, the man, bursts out with laughter.

"The bird. You're kidding me. Really?"

The man is now laughing hysterically. "The bird wants to have sex with my wife?"

"No Sir. No Sir. My name is Boner and he was saying your boat, your boat has a nice bottom. I clean hulls. Really Sir, he wasn't talking about your wife."

The man and his wife are now both laughing.

"Sir, I'm sorry. Sometimes he just blurts stuff out. He doesn't mean anything. Honest Sir. He doesn't mean anything."

"Slow down son. Its ok, I understand. Its ok."

Boner now turning red from embarrassment, does not know what to say. This has never happened before as Macky seldom talks.

Macky is a Scarlet Macaw that Boner has had since it was a baby. Boner spends many a day and night hand-feeding Macky. And when Macy does not receive the attention he wants, he will tear things up, like Boner's backpack.

Although most Macaws poorly mimic the spoken word, Boner took time with Macky. Training him to talk and act as the guard for the boat.

"I'm so sorry Sir."

"Son, that's ok. I have not laughed so hard in years. You take care of our boat and I will settle up with you when we get back from Breakfast."

Chapter 14

Boner and his dad, White Boots, try to eat at Mom's most everyday before they start their day.

A run down shack, weather beaten from the salt air and passing storms. There is only a small wooden sign near the highway letting people know Mom's is there.

With dust raising from the coral and gravel parking lot, you know something is going on, seeing the ancient trucks with fishing poles and crab traps rattling in and out of the lot.

JR looks at his wife as he holds the door for her to enter the restaurant. They can smell the slight aroma of the crab traps. But it is nothing you would not expect from a working man's café.

Off to one side, JR's wife sees a table against the wall and nudges him. Making their way past the crabbers, fishermen and dock hands there is a mixture of Spanish, Mexican and broken English spoken between those they pass.

The chairs are old metal chairs. If there is a restaurant in the Keys that can be called a greasy spoon this one is it.

JR starts telling his wife "Honey I really feel bad about yelling at that young man."

"I know. That bird sounded just like a person, didn't it?"

JR tells his wife "I have never heard a Macaw with a voice like that before. He must have spend a lot of time training that bird."

"I just can not believe I spoke to him in such a way. I need to find a way to apologize to him when we get back."

While Babs is taking their order, JR tells her Boner said hi.

"You know Boner?"

"No not really. We just came into the marina down the road. He helped us with our dock lines. I asked him where there was a good place to eat and Boner sent us here."

"Well that boy will treat you right."

Once Babs has their orders, she goes back to the kitchen.

And shortly after, Babs returns with both their orders. Setting down the tourist's plates, she smiles while telling them if they need anything, just call out to her. Then Babs leaves their table heading back into the kitchen

"Honey, what is the matter?"

"I ordered the special JR."

"And?"

Turning the food over with her fork. "Well look at this. What is this?"

"Have you tried it?"

Well, no."

JR laughs "So try it."

JR's wife sits turning the food over and over. She ordered Huevos rancheros a classic Mexican breakfast consisting of fried eggs served upon lightly fried corn tortillas topped with a tomato-chili sauce and refried beans.

While JR has Cuban toast and some remarkable Cuban coffee.

Slowly JR's wife raises her fork to her mouth, as a person would approach something with fearful regard.

Watching his wife taste her food, JR starts laughing. With him continuing to laugh he draws the attention of Babs. Babs isn't used to having tourists in the restaurant.

"Sir is everything ok?"

JR looks at Babs and then back at his wife. Wiping his mouth, he tries to control himself while covering his mouth.

"Yes. Yes everything in fine. I don't think my wife has ever tasted a Mexican breakfast before this morning."

"Oh Miss, I'm sorry. Can I bring you something else?"

"No. In fact this is rather good. I like the mixture and the different textures. We are from Ohio and seldom enjoy real Mexican food."

"Thank you, Miss. Boner and his dad have it almost every morning."

"Sir, you are one of the few tourists I have seen drink a large Cuban coffee."

"I fell in love with Cuban coffee years ago."

"I have to get back to the stove. It was nice meeting you."

With Babs returning to the kitchen, the restaurant is starting to empty out.

"JR, Boner must have a pretty hard life from the looks of those in here this morning."

"I know and after the way I yelled, I really want to do something for him. Maybe Babs will know something we can do. Lets finish breakfast and after everyone leaves, I will ask her to join us for a minute."

Two by two and three by three the workers leave for their jobs. Some to work on the docks shoveling the fish while others head to small repair shops and other under the table jobs.

Catching Babs eye while she is at the register with the last customer, JR motions for her to come over.

Closing the register and tying up her apron, Babs makes her way over to the table where JR and his wife are sitting.

Standing, JR asks Babs to please join them for a minute.

"Certainly Sir. Is everything alright?"

"Yes Babs, the breakfast was excellent."

"Oh yes it was delicious. I must admit I was a little afraid to begin with but once I tasted it, I could not stop. Thank you, you're a great cook."

"Thank you Miss."

"Babs, I hope you don't mind but I'd like to talk to about Boner, the young man back at the marina, if that is ok. Is that ok, Babs?"

"I don't like talking about my customers. Most are like family."

"I understand Babs. He seems like such a nice young man I wanted to see if there is anything I could help him with."

"I know he and his dad work real hard on his dad's crab boat. And when he is not working on his dad's boat he either works around the dock or helps me clean the restaurant when he has time."

"So you know him well then?"

"Yes Sir. He and his dad have been coming in since we opened, years ago."

"I take it the fishermen and crabbers are making good wages?"

"They earn enough to get by. Some seasons are good and well others, they aren't so good. Now like I said Mister, I don't like taking about my customers and Boner and his dad are like family to me."

"Yes Ma'am, I understand."

Raising from the table, Babs asks "I can get you folks anything else?"

"No, just the check, please. And thank you for talking to us."

"That's fine son. This time it's on the house. You pay next time you come."

Chapter 15

On the walk back to the marina JR and his wife slow their pace to see the side of life seldom seen by the tourists from the cruise ships.

JR's wife looks at him saying "Honey I just can not imagine people living in these conditions. These trailers are no bigger than our living room."

"I guess I understand, looking them, why they keep their washers, dryers and freezers outside."

"Yes love, and you notice the freezers. They all have locks on them. I bet it is a hard life to us, but it is all they know."

"Do you think they like it JR.?"

"Well, as I said, to some people it is all they know. For others, maybe they just became tired of today's world and want a simpler life."

"JR what do you think Boner wants?"

"Here is the marina, why don't we sit with him a few minutes and find out."

As they turned into the marina, they can see Boner down by the boat playing his guitar.

"Do you think people live on these smaller boats JR?"

"Yes honey. They too may just want a simpler life. I have known for people to live on boats as small as twenty-three feet."

"But they look so small."

"Just like the trailers we saw on the road. Sometimes I too think maybe a simpler life will be better. Lets see how Boner feels."

As they get closer to Boner, they now hear the sweet music from the guitar he is strumming.

Seeing them coming towards him, Boner stops playing and starts to stand up to greet them.

"No no, please don't stop. We would like to listen for a while if that is ok with you.?"

Laughing, Boner says "No Sir, I don't mind playing if you don't mind me messing up some."

With all three setting down, Boner asks "Is there anything you'd like me to try and play for you?"

"Just play what is in you son. Just play what is in you."

"I can do that Sir."

Now mid-day, the heat of the sun is being broken up with the cool breezes of the Islands. The clanging of loose rigging can be heard from a distant mast, as Boner tunes his guitar.

Boner starts to strum and pick at the guitars strings. As he strums, he sings a Patsy Cline song, in a folksy blues tone, "I go out walkin' after midnight

In the moonlight just like we used to do;

I'm always walkin' after midnight searchin' for you.

I walk for miles along the highway"

JR and his wife listen in amazement.

Upon ending, JR holds up his hand "Son, how long have you been playing the guitar?"

"Only a year or so. Red Stripe has been teaching me chords and scales. And some of the local bands are showing me different songs."

"I hate to ask but do you play any jazz?"

"Yes Sir. I really enjoy the blues, jazz, and the trop rock they play here in the Keys."

"I know you might be busy, but will you play some jazz for us?"

"Sure Sir."

And with that, Boner slides into some smooth jazz one can picture on a sunset evening in the Keys. As he settles into playing 'Breezin' by George Benson, JR and his wife close their eyes. They can feel the trees sway and see Tiki bar lights on the distant shore.

As Boner plays the last note, both JR and his wife stand and applauds his talent.

"And you said you have only been playing for a year or so?"

"Yes Sir."

"Well you sure do not sound like it. You really enjoy playing don't you?"

"Oh yes Sir. Very much so."

"Let me ask you son, what plans have you made for your future?"

"I don't understand?"

"Well you play very well. With the way you play, are you going to keep working on the docks? Are you going to keep working on the water with your dad. In others words son, what do you want in your future? A year from now. Three, four five years from now? What do you want for your future?"

"Right now I'm saving money to go to college After that I don't know. I'd like to be able to play music while going to college, rather than smell like crabs all the time."

"You don't want to work the crab pots with your father?"

"No Sir. I mean I love the water and I love my Dad. But I want, I don't know. Not more. Just something different I guess."

"Have you talked about it with your father?"

"Oh yes Sir we talk. He knows the crabbers and commercial fishermen around here are disappearing slowly each year."

"So you are going to college?"

"Yes Sir. As soon as I can save enough money and support myself."

"Do you remember the name of my vessel?"

"Yes Sir. It's the Motor Vessel Aesculus glabra."

"Do you know what Aesculus glabra means?"

"No Sir."

"Aesculus glabra means Ohio buckeye. Ever heard of the Buckeyes?"

"Yes Sir. My dad and I watch football all the time. Everyone know of the Buckeyes. But I don't understand."

"Earlier, before breakfast I really jumped on you for nothing and I'd like to make it up to you."

Laughing Boner tells JR "Yes, I'm sorry about Macky. He may not talk much but when he does, seems like I'm the one who gets in trouble."

"No son there is nothing to be sorry about. I have never heard a Macaw mimic the human voice so well. I lost control and as part of the Buckeyes I'd like to make it up to you."

"Ok"

"We decided to eat at Mom's and Babs told me to tell you hi. I must say the Cuban coffee was great."

"Babs is almost like my mom."

"That's what she said."

"We will be going into Key West for the day. So if you could watch over the boat I would really appreciate it."

Even knowing he really wants to find Red Stripe to learn another song or two, Boner tells JR "Yes Sir. I didn't have anything planned for the day."

Macky and Boner stay on the dock most of the day watching the weekend boaters come and go. He sits thinking of the songs he is playing, while drifting off to another shore.

He dreams of what life must be like off the rock. But his dreams never really start, as the rock is all he knows.

Boner's dreams are filled with only the stories he has heard from cruisers around the marina. He hears stories of other people's lives. The lives they are escaping.

Walking up the dock is JR and his wife coming back from Key West.

"Hey Boner, how is it going?"

"Good Sir. I washed your boat off again."

"Well that's real good of you Boner. We will be leaving early in the morning, so I hope we don't wake you."

"Oh no Sir. We get up fairly early around here. What with the fishing boats and tourists coming and going."

"Well if you happen to be up, maybe you can help me the dock lines."

"Yes Sir. I'd be happy to. Do you know about what time?"

"Daybreak. I am guessing around six-thirty or seven in the morning."

With his big smile beaming ear to ear, he tells JR "That's great. I'll be here Sir. You can always count on me Sir."

JR turns and with his wife board their boat while Boner returns his concentration back to his guitar.

The nights in the Keys are always alive with sounds. The music from the waterside bars. The loose rigging from the many sailboats dotting the harbors and marinas. The Palm fronds dying and pealing away from the tall palm trees. The sound of the Gulf and ocean waters lapping the Mangrove dotted shorelines.

It is the reason so many wayward souls make the Keys their home. Be it for a Day or two like JR and his wife or the ones from the mainland who want to escape.

Boner's fingers are becoming quicker with double and triple picks on the guitar strings. But as he sees the Dock's lights being replaced

with the moon light, he knows it is time to stop playing for the night.
He too will take in the sounds that lull the Keys to sleep.

"About time you came in son. How was your day."

"Good dad. How are the traps?"

"Missing three. I guess someone hit them with a prop or rudder.
Two balls were missing but the lines were still there so I was able to
re-attach them."

"Seems like Macky is doing better now that you are trying to spend
more time with him."

"Yes Sir. Funny how he picks words to speak."

"Is he learning something he shouldn't?"

"Oh no Sir. Just the way he puts some of them together, that's all."

"The man and his wife at the end of the dock want me to help him
with their dock lines in the morning."

"Ok, I'll get you up when Red Stripe and I head out in the morning.
Good night son."

"Nite Dad. See you in the morning."

Chapter 16

The sun isn't up, but as with everyday, the marina is coming back to life. As things change in the Keys, things also remain the same. The low rumble of the boats diesel engines, the churning props being tested by the Captains.

The start of the marina's day is filled with dinghies being raised and lowered from their davits, small outboard engines with their buzzing sound filling the waterways into and out of the marina basin.

White Boots smiles, as he sees he remembered to turn on the coffee maker the night before.

Pouring that first cup of coffee he looks out the pilot house's side window and sees Boner too is up stirring around. Taking his first sip, he gains a knowing smile. His son makes him so proud.

A few minutes pass and White Boots hears the sliding Glass door of the Houseboat open and sees Boner shutting it behind him.

Boner pulls the dock line and the crab boat drifts slowly toward the finger pier. Boarding the boat White Boots greets his son with a cup of coffee "Good morning. I see you made it through the night."

White Boots Hands a cup of coffee to Boner "Yes Sir. And I see you didn't forget to turn the coffee on."

"Yep, it makes for a better morning." Laughs White Boots.

"Red Stripe going out with you today?"

"Ya, he should be here shortly. Engine is warmed up. Just need to stop by the fuel dock and we're gone."

"What's your plans for today son?"

"The big power boat at the end of the dock is leaving this morning and he asked me to help with the dock lines. After that, I don't know. With the cruisers and weekenders going out for the day, there is not much bottom cleaning to do."

Hearing the knock on the boats hull, Boner and White Boots turn and White Boots motions Red Stripe to come aboard.

White Boots greets Red Stripe "Good morning Red. Ready for some coffee?"

"Always ready for a cup of good coffee."

"I didn't say it was good."

"Trust me, I know. I know."

"You coming out with us today Boner?"

"No, I've got to help the large power boat at the end of the dock."

"I think you're going to miss a good time on the water today."

"It should be. I've already checked NOAA's weather report and it looks like the seas should be almost flat."

Later that morning as JR and his wife get ready to leave, JR hands Boner two one-hundred dollar bills for watching the boat And he again apologizes to Boner for getting angry with him.

"Hey Boner, I was thinking, I might have some pull with the University. If I could arrange it, would you like to attend the University?"

"Are you kidding, I'd love to but I could never afford that Sir."

"Son, I'll worry about that. I just need to know, if it was arranged would you leave the island and come to Columbus?"

"Yes Sir. After it all it would only be for four years, right?"

"Well that is how long it usually takes to complete a four year degree."

"Then, yes Sir. But I still don't see how."

"Like I said son, that is my problem. Let me see what I can do for you."

And with that, JR and his wife power away from the dock, waving good bye making way out of the Marina's basin.

With part of the two hundred dollars, Boner buys a small amplifier for his guitar. Then puts the rest into savings.

That evening Boner is again with Red Stripe. More songs to be played. More songs to learn. Once Red Stripe completes his picking of the song, Boner starts talking to him about life..

Red Stripe stops his playing and sits his guitar down "How you doing today Boner?"

"I really like that song. Who is it?"

"That was a Billy Ray Charles song. He calls it Johnny Walker Red."

"Red, I really like learning from you and sitting in with some of the bands."

"But?"

In a sad tone, Boner replies "But I also want to go to college. I don't want to have to struggle. I don't want to barely get by like so many Conchs do."

"And?"

"And. And I don't know how to do it all. I mean, I want to play the guitar. I want to play music, go to school, and still be able to help my dad. Crabbing is down and the marina is looking to fill the slips with cruisers and tourists instead of commercial fishermen. I just don't know how to decide on what I should do."

"Wow, that's a lot for someone so young to have to be thinking about Boner. No wonder you're looking a little down"

With a consoling voice Red Stripe asks Boner "Have you talked to your daddy at all?"

"No Sir. I tried talking to Miss Babs. But she would just say things will work out. And that didn't help me much."

"Boner, you told me what you want. So now you need to make a plan to get where you want to be."

"I've saved enough to pay for my first semester of school."

"But isn't that only three or four months? What are you going to do after that?"

"I know. If I go to school during the day and keep working at night and helping Dad, I don't see when I'll have time to study. I know people do it. Going to school at night and working during the day, but there aren't no day jobs around here that pay enough."

"Well Boner, maybe right now isn't the time for you."

"I know Red, but dad really wants me to go to school. He keeps saying how he wants me to have it better then he did."

"And you will Boner. Your daddy is working hard to make life better for you. And it will happen. Maybe just not tomorrow. Don't rush life. Enjoy it."

"I do Red, but I don't want to disappoint my dad."

"Boner, your daddy is awful proud of you. Don't you know that?"

"Yes Sir, I guess I do. And that is why I want to do something where he sees all his hard work is paying off. That is one the reasons I want to go to school."

"I understand son, but you need to understand there is a time for everything. And rushing will only cause you stress. You don't want stress do you?"

"No Sir."

"Well then slow down and enjoy life. That's what your daddy really wants for you. To be able to enjoy life."

Chapter 17

So for the next month or so, Boner does just that. White Boots gave Boner the summer off and has Red Stripe helping out on the boat.

Boner is spending most of his time learning more songs, listening to the local bands and helping out at Mom's Restaurant.

It feels odd to Boner not having to get up and ride the bus from Stock Island and down to Key West for school. And now, every morning he wakes up, there is that slight grin knowing those twelve years are behind him.

Bruce, the Dock Master is grinning inside himself as he waits to see if Boner notices the letter addressed to him. But Boner does not even look at the mail in his hand. And after a few minutes with Bruce, Boner returns to houseboat.

Once at the houseboat, Boner starts looking at the mail he has in his hand. Boner receives a letter from the University.

Somehow Boner has won a scholarship to the University due to his grade point average and Musical Accomplishment, so the letter reads.

The scholarship papers state all of his studies will be paid for, along with his housing. He will be a member of "The Best Damn Band In The Land."

Not wanting to wait to tell his dad, Boner calls him on the VHF telling him of the news.

In the weeks to come Boner is planning and dreaming. Fears are offset by the adventure of leaving the island and not knowing what might lay ahead for him.

Knowing he will be leaving the rock, Boner decides to take a long walk around the island. Seems like every street holds different memories.

Courtesy of Chris Rehm

As Boner walks south on Roosevelt Boulevard he passes Sears on his left and Sigsbee Park to his west. There are many great times to remember on the island.

The Sears parking lot is almost empty compared to a few months back. A lot of RV'ers try to park there for the night but get run off. He never really understood why. After all they are tourists spending money. And most of the campgrounds are either full, closed or being turned into condominiums.

Stopping by Bayview Park Boner sees that a lot of the snowbirds and tourists have left the humid heat for the cooler climates.

Instead of taking a right and turning down White Street heading towards NAS Key West, Boner decides to walk along Truman Avenue towards the waterfront.

Passing the bike rentals on Truman he sees most of the bikes are still in their racks and the Vespas are all on their stands.

As Boner reaches Whitehead Street the feeling of being home comes over him like a cool breeze through his hair, on his face and in his heart.

Walking down Whitehead in the early morning, barren of the night's waves of island music, there is an aroma of Cuban Coffee and the sweet whiffs of the islands imported tobacco buds.

Boner stops to enjoy the morning's sun spilling down on Hemingway's old home. As the Keys change some things remain the same. Hemingway's old home remains.

While some people dislike the old narrow streets and the city fathers want to make changes, Boner and the rest of the conchs have told the city not to touch their homes.

Courtesy of Chris Rehm

As Boner turns to leaves Hemingway's house, he walks up on a Key West Police Officer making an arrest. Curious Boner asks the Officer "What'd he do?"

The Officer acting as a Marshall in the style of John Wayne and Rambo rolled into one tells Boner "Move on, he's under arrest."

"I can see that Sir. What did he do?"

"What did he do. You're asking me what he is being arrested for?"

"Yes Sir I am. Why are you arresting him?"

"Son, it's none of your business. But if you must know, I've arrested him for destruction of public property."

Boner is mystified. This is a public street and sidewalk but Boner doesn't see any damage anywhere, even down the street.

"I'm sorry Sir but what did he damage?"

Raising his voice, just a pitch below yelling, the Officer tells Boner "Look there." The Officer points to the sidewalk several steps away.

Looking where the Officer is pointing he still doesn't see what could be damage to anything.

"Right there boy. He drew all over a public sidewalk."

Boner is still unsure what Officer Rambo is talking about.

"Boy are you as dumb as this drunk?"

The man starts yelling. "I'm not drunk. I'm as sober as you are."

"Boy you need to move on before I arrest you too."

Boner, not one for walking away, presses the Officer.

"You can't arrest me I haven't done anything but ask you a question."

The Officer now turning red in the face, places the man in the patrol car and turns back to Boner.

" Look right there, he's drawn all over the sidewalk with those squares."

"You're talking about the chalk drawn Hopscotch game? You are kidding right?"

"That is destruction of public property. We can't have people drawing hopscotch all over our sidewalks."

Boner bursts out in uncontrolled laugher.

The police officer looks at Boner, shakes his head, grits his teeth, turning away walking to the trunk of the patrol car.

"Get away from the evidence."

Still unable to control his laughter Boner starts backing away, as the officer retrieves his large digital camera to take photographs of the evidence. The chalk drawn hopscotch game.

Boner knows the Keys are changing but never would he have dreamed someone could no long play hopscotch on a public street.

Crossing Petronia Street, Boner looks back to see other officers have now arrived at the scene of the crime. He can't help but to chuckle as he has visions of an Arlo Guthrie song.

Walking past the Parrot, doors are open and the staff is getting ready for yet another keysie day in paradise. Boner is heading to end of Whitehead Street and the end of the island.

Boner seldom makes it to the end of the island. Just too many tourists during the season. And it seems everyone is trying to sell you pieces of plastic to remember your stay.

But today is different. Today Boner is hoping to get lucky. He is looking for just one thing. One thing to enjoy.

As he reaches the end, arriving at Mallory Square he can feel the turquoise blue waters of the keys filling his lungs. His nose is alive with the salt in the air. And his ears pickup the beat of the island he was hoping to find.

The cruise ships left hours ago and another isn't to arrive for several more hours. Boner and the conchs feel the cruise ships, although needed for income, spoiled the view provided by Mallory Square people enjoy.

There, just off the seawall is the sound he is seeking.

Chapter 18

Its not the sunset this day that brings Boner to the Southern most point of the United Sates. It's the tropical sounds being played by one of Mallory Square's fixtures.

Boner wants to see, talk and learn from one old black man. A man who brings a tropical sound to old forgotten favorites.

"Morning Mustafa. How's it going?"

"Its always good in the Keys mon."

Pulling up a piece of pavement, Boner sits down and crosses his legs.

"I've listened to you for years. Will you teach me just one song?"

"Well mon, the ships, they leave and time is free. What is it you want'n to learn?"

"You often play something about a gypsy woman."

"Oh mon, you talkin bout Calypso Blues."

"Wa-oo-oo, wa-oo-oo,
Wa-oo wa-oo wa-oo wa-ay...
Wa-oo-oo, wa-oo-oo,
Wa-oo wa-oo wa-oo wa-ay...

Sittin' by de ocean

Me heart, she feel so sad,

Sittin' by de ocean,

Me heart, she feel so sad...

Don't got de money

To take me back to trinidad.", tat the one you askin bout?

"Yes, that's the one. Will you teach me?

"Sure mon. tis an old Nat King Cole tune mon. Most people thinkin this an island song. They be surprised they knew it really Nat Cole did it. But me sure, I teach ya."

So for the next few hours Boner learns the Calypso Blues Lyrics and chords.

As Boner thanks the old man, he stuffs a ten dollar bill into his cup.

"Hey Boner. You be safe leaving the rock."

Surprised, Boner asks, "How'd you know?"

"Everyone knows things mon."

Boner, smiling turns and heads out of the square. Looking out the corner of his eye, there is Silverman having a heated conversation with Goldman. It appears both statues want the same spot for their gig.

Laughing as he walks out, Boner thinks to himself "Only in the Keys will you find two grown men painted head to toe and fighting over three square feet of concrete."

Walking up Front Street Boner heads to Fort Zachary Taylor. Growing up he spends a lot of time there, with his friends, when he can get to the park.

Walking over the white sand beach of the park, Boner starts feelings slightly afraid. There is a saying of the locals. Never leave the rock. But that is exactly what he is getting ready to do. Leave the rock.

Looking out over the turquoise blue waters he sees the times his father takes him out to the crab pots and the fun just being on the sea.

A Conchs life is not an easy one. But Boner knows he will miss every bit of it. Tourists come and go. But Conchs are suppose to stay. But as more development comes in, it also pushes the Conchs and the locals out.

Boner starts to have some sadness, replace his fears. He sees more and more of the old conchs heading North off the rock. Lack of berths for their fishing boats, along with higher and higher property taxes are driving them out.

But there are a lot of the locals who won't, can't give up. Many are taking their boats and lives into the Mangroves. They use the Dingy docks to get to and from their fishing boats and their houseboats. As they live scattered among the hidden canals of the Keys.

Heading up a few back streets, Boner makes his way over to Flagler. He wants to stop by the High School on his way home.

Looking over the seawall on Roosevelt the sadness is still there. And then he sees his dad's boat making way, coming in from checking the pots. Boner is thinking. "Man Dad, we sure have fun out there."

By the time Boner makes his way back to the marina, his Dad is already docked, tied up and is washing the salt spray off the boat.

"Hey son, how about we get some dinner at Moms tonight?"

"Sure, I'd like that. How are the traps?"

With a huge smile, White Boots tells Boner, "All are accounted for today. Didn't even have one out of position. Must be an omen or something."

"I didn't see Red Stripe. Is he around?"

"He's already gone. He was out of here almost as soon as we touched the dock.", White Boots replies.

"I was hoping to show him the new song I learned today."

Smiling White Boots tells Boner, "Oh he'll be around later. He said there is something he must get done and almost ran up the dock."

With that Boner boards the houseboat. He picks up his guitar and Macky. Then comes back out on the dock, takes a seat on the dock box and starts to slowly strum the chords he was shown.

Once his dad finishes washing down the boat he comes over and sits down on the dock box beside Boner.

"Well son you sure have a big day tomorrow. How do feel?"

"I don't know."

"You know its ok to be a little afraid. After all you'll be moving over thirteen hundred miles away."

"I know dad. Its not the moving I'm afraid of. It's the leaving. You've said never leave the rock and that's what I'm doing."

With a pat on the back White tells his son, "Son, its not like its forever. The rock will be here when you get back from Columbus."

"Now that the boat is clean, I need to get clean. If you want, we can talk after my shower."

"I'll be fine dad. Really."

"Ok, see you in a few and we'll head out for dinner." White Boots tells Boner heading to the marina's showers.

Leaving, getting into the Thing, with White Boots driving, they head to Moms for dinner.

Chapter 19

Boner exclaims, "What in the world! I've never seen Moms this packed!"

"Yep looks like we'll have to park over by the old broke down truck."

Laughing, Boner affirms, "Yea, broke down alright. I can't remember when it ever ran."

"I think its been sixteen seventeen years or so.", laughs his Dad.

"You'd think they were giving away free beer with so many people here this evening."

"Free beer, in the Keys. Yea right Dad."

White Boots opens and holds the door as Boner enters Moms.

Then it hit him. It's a going away Party. A party for him.

As Boner stops at the doorway everyone starts yelling. "Boner! Boner! Boner!"

Turning red with embarrassment he is speechless.

"Get in here Boner. This is your party. Come on in here!"

As Boner looks around, there is Red Stripe, John Saterday, Ziggy Wilson, the boys from the Green Parrot and locals from Schooner Wharf as well as Bait, and most of the bands from around the island.

With it being Boner's Going Away party, it gives a lot of them a reason to party. Even though Conchs and locals never need a reason to party in the Keys.

The Drag Queens are there and some of the locals from Tony's even came up for the party. Babs cleared out some tables for the bands to setup and that night the music flows.

Band members have come down from as far as Big Pine and No Name key. Even Marathon, Grassy Key and Tavernier. All coming to wish Boner well.

Everyone in turn, comes and shakes Boner's hand and gives him a hug. He is one of theirs. Seems like everyone on the island is there for Boner. And yes, even an FWC Officer shows up to see him off.

When the FWC Officer gets his turn to shake Boner's hand, he leans into Boner's ear and asks, "They don't have Manatees in Ohio do they?"

As Boner again turns red, the Officer tells Boner, "I just had to son. You'll be fine.", then he keeps laughing, as he heads for the door.

Bait comes over, grabs Boner's arm and escorts him and White Boots towards the stage setup in the rear. To the left of the front of the stage, Babs has a platform setup with a table and two chairs. From here Boner has a front row seat of the Stage and view of all those around him.

"Boner, look.", his dad is pointing. Pointing to the beer kegs setup all around the room. "There must be ten beer kegs."

Laughing Babs tells them, "Ten, no not ten. How about twenty-three full kegs. You once said there is no free beer in the Keys. Well here it is."

"You're kidding.", Boner says in disbelief.

"No Boner, I'm not kidding. We wanted you to have the best send off we can give you. Oh you thought all these people were here for you. You're funny.", Babs says laughing as she walks away. "Yes, Boner, its all for you darling."

Babs setup the stage with lights and a sound system. The only thing the bands did was bring their voices and instruments.

As some of the boys from the Hogfish leave the stage, all the lights go dark. As a minute passes by, they can make out shadows going off and on the stage. People rushing back and forth.

Then on cue, two baby spot lights shine down on two of the Drag Queens and then a blue spot pierces the smoke from a small dry ice machine. Through the smoky haze the outline of a slender female form.

As the light grows brighter, the soulful smokey sound is heard from the stage throughout the restaurant.

"Mississippi in the middle of a dry spell; Jimmy Rodgers on the Victrola up high.

Mama's dancin' baby on her shoulders.

The sun is settin' like molasses in the sky

The boy could soon know how to move everything,

Always wanting more, he'd leave you longing for.

Black Velvet in that little boy's smile.

Black velvet in with that slow southern style."

"Its Bait!" Boner exclaims, "Its Bait!"

Yes it is Bait. Dressed in one of those slinky clingy satin black gowns. The side shows a slit three–quarters the way up her thigh and a plunging neckline almost to her belly button. Yes it is Bait singing, in the style of Alannah Myles the song, "Black Velvet"

Its one of Boner's favorite songs and he plays it often on his guitar. But never like this. Boner can't move. For a second time tonight he is speechless.

Boner can not believe what he is seeing or hearing.

Bait, as if floating off the stage, extends her left hand out to Boner's cheek. She gently caresses it downward, as she sings the final words slower, putting hot night flashes through Boner's veins.

"Black velvet in with that slow southern style. A new religion that'll bring you to your knees, Black velvet, if you please." Then Bait takes both her hands drawing Boner's face to hers and presses her moist lips on to his.

For Boner it seems forever. When Bait releases him, everyone erupts with clapping and laughter. She wasn't just putting on a show. She is the show.

Every couple of minutes another band or musician takes the stage for their tribute to Boner's success. See it isn't everyday one of their own makes it and when they do, they are all proud.

Chapter 20

With the sun raising over the Atlantic, it allows it's light to sift into the marina. White Boots has been up for hours and Boner is starting to stir.

"Come on son its time for breakfast. Lets go.", White Boots yells into Boners room.

Although Boner is not a drinker, tossing down a few at the party is leaving him in a fog as he sits up.

His Dad tells him as he sits down the plates, "Glad to see you could join us."

"Thanks Dad. Was that your idea last night?"

"No son. That was a lot of people. People who care about you and want to show you how they feel."

"Well tell them thank you. That was great."

"You thanked them all last night. You don't remember?", his Dad asks with laugher.

"No Sir. I don't remember a whole lot. At least not yet anyway."

"Do you have everything packed?"

"Yes Sir, I did that a few days ago."

"Eat up then. You have a long drive ahead. You sure you still want to take the Thing?"

Boner laughs. "Sure Dad why not. As long as it makes it there I'll be fine."

"It'll make it there. I just had everything checked. I mean it looks like its half dead and been run through the surf, but she runs fine."

"No. I mean are you going to be ok riding the Vespa?"

"Boner, its no different than a bike. And beside if I need something else, I'll just get another conch cruiser for a few hundred bucks. As long as it can go ten or twelve miles at a time. I'll be fine son."

"Need any help with putting the boxes in the Thing?"

"Naw Dad, I got it."

"Ok then, I'll get theses dishes clean up while you're loading."

Boner plans to stick to the Interstate even though the Thing will not go much over sixty. And not having been off the rock before he doesn't want to get turned around and lost on some country back road.

He's already mapped it out. Taking the Overseas Highway to Alligator Alley and up Interstate Seventy-five, crossing to the North side of Cincinnati, where he will take Interstate Seventy-one into Columbus and the University.

Giving his Dad a hug goodbye, Boner starts up the Thing and leaves Stock Island. He doesn't know if it the fear of where he is a heading or leaving the rock, but his stomach is in a knot. Can't be the party the night before he thinks breaking out in a small laugh.

With the snowbirds and tourists gone its an uneventful drive up the Overseas Highway. Every so often he catches the turquoise blue water while crossing the bridges out of the Keys.

It is one hundred and twenty-six miles to Florida City and the Interstate. Boner will be crossing some forty-two bridges and passing over the one hundred islands making his way up the Keys.

The more north he gets, he can see the change in the color of the water. The more North he goes, the more the water loses it turquoise blue color and changes to a bluest green.

It has been two hours and he still is not yet out of the islands. He hears it sometimes takes eight even twelve hours to leave the island if there is a wreck on the eighteen mile stretch or somewhere on the Overseas Highway. But not this time.

Ninety-six degrees, sun shining and the breeze of going sixty-three miles per hour on Interstate Seventy-five. For Boner, life is great. Hugging the right hand lane watching cars, motorcycles, and life pass by.

Chapter 21

It is an early Wednesday afternoon when Boner arrives at the campus of the University.

Searching the through the Thing, Boner can not find the address where he is suppose to check-in. As he is looking under the seat, a co-ed approaches.

While Boner is looking he is also talking to himself. "Why am I doing this? I have a good life."

Hearing Boner's conversation the co-ed asks "Sir are you ok?"

Boner without stopping, tells her "I'm lost and I think I need help."

"I understand, I was lost coming here also."

Boner raises from the Thing. Questioning the red haired stranger "You mean I'm in the right place?"

"Yes, you're here. Why don't you come with me and let us both see how we can help you.", the co-ed says extending her hand.

Boner shakes her hand and follows the path the co-ed gestures to, by her body movement.

Walking up to building number one hundred forty-four on Neil Avenue the stranger asks Boner "Have you been here long?"

"I just arrived. Where are we going?"

"Well first, we are going to get you checked in, that's ok with you right?"

"Sure. That's what I want to do."

The red haired stranger tells Boner "Well then, that is what we will do first.", as she opens the door.

"My name is Debbie. What's yours?"

"I'm Boner, Boner Morgan."

With a hint of laughter through her smile she asks "Boner. Is that your full name?"

"They call me Boner. But my full name is William R. Morgan."

"Well, I like Boner. So that is what I will call you, if that's ok with you."

"Yes, I'd like that. Boner is fine."

"Ok, well lets go get the Boner checked in."

"Susie, this is Boner. Will you please give him a pass to enter."

"Yes Debbie. For how long should I make it?"

Debbie looking at Boner, turns and tells her "Lets give Boner a week and see how he fits, shall we."

Boner standing in front of the security desk is in awe with his new surroundings. Chrome and glass makes him feel as though he is at the Lower Keys Medical Center.

Looking slightly down at Debbie, Boner asks her "What should I do with my stuff?"

"Your car, that was a car wasn't it.", she laughs.

"Yes."

"Well your car will be fine where it is. But don't worry, I'll take care of it for you."

Boner can not get over the greeting he is receiving. Everyone seems so nice and these building are like something out of a dream or a movie.

"Thank you Susie, OK Boner why don't we go upstairs and set up some of your testing. That's ok with you right?"

"Testing?"

"Yes Boner, we have to make sure we place you in an area that you are best suited. You want to be in a place where you fit in, don't you?"

Hesitantly Boner replies "Well, sure. I want to fit in."

"Well then lets get started.", Debbie says while pressing the up button for the elevator.

Upon arriving at the third floor Debbie guides Boner out of the elevator and into the open hallway.

"Debbie, is this where I am suppose to be?"

"Yes Boner. Lets check in and we can get started.", she tells him, while gesturing toward the Duty Station.

"Ms. Grip, this is Boner. I mean William for check in. He will be with us for some testing. Will you please take his information and I'll be back shortly."

"Boner, Ms Grip will get you registered and I'll be back in a few minutes.", Debbie tells him, turning and walking away not waiting for a reply.

Boner takes a seat in the standard aluminum waiting chair and precedes to disclose his entire life's history to Ms. Grip.

"Ok, Ms. Grip are we all set up?", the Doctor asks upon his arrival.

"Yes Doctor, Mr. Williams is all checked in."

"Great. I understand you like to be called Boner. Well then Boner please come with me and we will start your testing."

"Doctor, are you sure I am in the right place?"

"Certainly son. You want to get checked in and start your testing and studies don't you?, the Doctor asks him.

"Yes Sir, but…"

"No buts son. We are here to help you through the testing and we now have you registered, right? That is what you want, to get checked in right?"

"Well, yes Sir I guess I do.", comes Boner's again hesitant response.

Walking Boner down the hallway and around a far corner, Doctor Woody opens a unmarked door and gestures for Boner to enter.

To Boner it looks like one of the small exam rooms he's been in, in the keys. Desk, two chairs and what appears to be a patient's bed. With his mind spinning, Boner is now questioning himself. "What in the world is going on."

"Doctor."

"Boner, its ok. It is all part of making sure we put you into the right programs. You do want to be in the right program, don't you?"

Without waiting for Boner's reply, the Doctor tells Boner, "Ok, there is a gown over there. Go ahead and get undressed, put the gown on and I will be back in a few minutes or so." The Doctor then turns the door handle and leaves the room.

Sitting on the patient's bed Boner is in shock. What is going on. He knows he never did this for high school. Is this what college is going to be like. If so, Boner does not like it one bit.

Boner does not understand why he has to get undressed as part of the admissions process. But as usual, Boner does as he is requested.

Pulling off his tank top and removing his Cargo shorts and boxers. As well as removing his fisherman sandals.

The room is cold and sterile. And Boner is freezing, sitting in nothing but a hospital gown. Minutes tick by, then ten minutes and then a half hour. After an hour Boner can not stand the cold sterile environment of the room any longer.

Opening the door he slowly peers out into the hallway. He now sees it's bareness. Empty of people. It too feels cold. His bare feet step into corridor and he slowly walks to the corner they had turned from when the Doctor brought him here.

Again bright harsh light, a hallway empty of people and even wall hangings. Fear slowly enters Boner's mind. Boner never knew what people meant by paranoid till today. Something just does not feel right.

Making his way down the hall he hears a voice behind him. Turning, it is Doctor Woody in a white lab coat.

"Where are you going? Come on back and lets see how you do with your testing.", the Doctor tells Boner motioning with his out stretched hand.

As if in a daze, Boner turns and starts making his way back.

"That is good, come on. You'll be fine. And it will all be over with shortly.", Doctor Woody assures Boner.

Taking Boner back into the same room he had just came from, the Doctor opens a second door leading Boner into the testing room.

"Doctor Woody I'm sorry but I don't understand what is going on. This isn't at all what I expected."

"Its ok son. Everyone gets a little nervous. Just take a seat and you will be able to start. It really will not take long. Go ahead take a seat.", the Doctor tells Boner nodding to the single chair in the center of the room.

Boner's mind is spinning. He is freezing and afraid. All he can think is this isn't right.

As the Doctor guides Boner into the chair, the hypodermic needle presses into Boner's neck. And within seconds Boner becomes fully dazed.

With Boner sinking down into the chair, Doctor Woody presses the buzzer for the Intern to come in.

"Debbie, please take Mr. William's gown off and connect the external probes. Then join me in the observation room."

The Doctor and his Intern, Debbie, quietly watch and wait for Boner to regain his functionality.

"Doctor, why do people volunteer for this research?"

"Most do it for the money, I have very few do it for the research itself. Looks like he is coming around."

Boner slowly regains his senses and can not believe it.

"What the hell! Hey where am I. What's going on?", Boner yells.

"Do they often behave like this Doctor?"

"No. In fact I don't think I have had one so upset. Let me see his chart."

All the while the totally nude and exposed Boner struggles to free himself from the restrains he is in. "Hey! Someone. Anybody. Help!"

"Something is not right. This is not Mr. Williams. He signed the permission as William Morgan.", the Doctor says.

Pressing the room to room microphone Doctor Woody tells Boner "Mr. Morgan, Boner, settle down. Please Mr. Morgan we are so sorry but there appears to have been a, shall we say a misjudgment."

"Misjudgment! What the hell are you talking about! Get me out of here! You people are nuts.", Boner is yelling while still struggling to free himself.

"Yes Mr. Morgan we are coming, but please relax. It will be ok."

"Debbie, I want you to go in there and calm him down before we undo the restraints."

"Me? Why me? I didn't put him in there."

"No but you were the one that brought him in here and you can calm him down. Now please go in there and get him to relax. Tell him there must be a misunderstanding and that I will be in shortly. Please, now get in there before he hurts himself."

"Where's my clothes. I want my clothes! And get me out this thing!", Boner yells as Debbie enters the room.

"Mr. Morgan, we are so sorry and embarrassed. Please, take a deep breath. I have already sent for your clothes and the Doctor will be here shortly."

Debbie, a new Intern, never worked with Doctor Woody or with this research before today. In fact Debbie herself is new to the campus and only took the internship for a class credit.

Boner looks up into Debbie's eyes, but finds her looking somewhere else. "What are you looking at? Get me out of this thing, NOW!", Boner demands.

Embarrassed and turning a deep shade of scarlet she tells Boner, "Yes Sir, the Doctor will do that. He already knows of the challenge."

"Challenge! You call this a challenge!", Boner yells while stressing his restrains.

"Now starting to cry, the Intern tells Boner, "Sir I am so sorry. I never knew something like this would happen. Please."

Boner stops struggling and looks at Debbie. He sees it has been an ordeal for her as well as him. "Miss It is ok. I don't know what is going on, but I don't want you to cry either." He tells her.

Through her tears she tells him "Boner I am so sorry. It is my fault. I thought you were a volunteer. I messed up Boner. I am so so sorry."

"Its ok. Can you get me out of this chair and all these wires?"

"I can start removing the wires. Well I'll remove all but one."

Looking down, Boner starts to laugh telling her, "No that's ok, I'll remove that one."

The straps are removed and Boner now has his clothes back where they should be, on his body. As quickly as he can, he's making to the elevator and exiting the building.

"Debbie, go after Mr. Morgan and make sure he is alright, please.", Doctor Woody tells her.

Chapter 22

Finding Boner outside, she walks up to him asking, "Boner, are you ok?"

"Ok. You're asking if I'm ok? I've just been strapped down nude to a steel chair, in a freezing room with wires attached to my, well you know where they were attached. Am I ok? Tell me Debbie, should I be ok?"

"No Boner. You should be mad and I am terribly sorry. It is my fault and I am sorry.", she tells Boner while again starting to tear up.

"Debbie, look its ok, I'll shake it off."

He can see what she's thinking.

"No, silly girl. I'm not shaking IT off.", he tells her with him too starting to laugh.

"What the hell is that all about anyway?"

Pointing to the Building entrance sign, "They do all sorts of interdisciplinary research."

Boner was so amazed by the building's architecture, He didn't notice the entrance sign. Had he seen the sign, he would have known, he entered the building for Cognitive and Behavioral Brain Research.

"They do all sorts of interdisciplinary research in there."

"Interdisciplinary what? Girl what are talking about?"

"This is where they do Cognitive and Behavioral Brain studies Boner."

"And people volunteer to be strapped down and tested? Really?"

"Sure. They have all sorts of studies going on around campus. It is how a lot of students earn credits and sometime money."

"I can think of far better ways to earn money, then having wires attached to my..."

Laughing Debbie stops Boner. "Ok. I was there remember."

"Well at least my car is still here. You still want to help me?"

"Anything.", Debbie replies.

"I still need to find the Admissions Office and the Band Building."

"The band? Why the Band?"

"Because the University gave me what they call a full scholarship to play in the band. So It might be good for me to know at least where the band is located."

"You are in the Band. That is great. What do you play?"

"I play the Guitar."

"You play what?"

"I play the Guitar? You sound like you've never heard of it. You know, you hold it in…"

She stops him. "I know what a Guitar is. I have just never seen one in a University band before."

"I guess that makes us even. I have never been strapped to a chair before. Now if you will please take me to the Admissions Office."

"I can do that. But we will need to take your, well your car. If that is ok?"

"Hey, its not much but it got me here from Stock Island."

"Stock Island. Where is Stock Island?"

"Most people think its part of Key West. But really it is just outside of Key West."

"Wow, the Keys. I love the Keys.", she tells him.

"It's the only place I've known. Lived there all my life."

"Ok Boner from Key West, lets get you to the Admissions Office."

"Great, think you can help me backing up?"

"Backing up?"

"Yeah, I don't have a reverse gear so it needs to be pushed."

Laughing Debbie tells him "Sure Mr. Key West. Lets push."

As they jump in the car Debbie asks "Where do I put my feet?"

"Put your feet?"

"Yeah, there are big holes over here."

"Well most people don't put their feet through the holes.", Boner tells her as he releases the clutch and starts through the parking lot.

Three and a half hours later Boner is registered and enrolled in the next semester's classes.

JR made arrangements for Boner to live in his summer home while he attends the University.

Chapter 23

Once he is registered for classes Boner now sets out to locate where he will be living. Using his GPS it does not take long for Boner to find JR's summer house.

Boner is tired and frayed from all of the days activities. After several trips back and forth between the Thing and the house, Boner throws himself on the couch and quickly enters into a sleep of coma like status.

Boner is usually up before the sun but not today. No alarm clock. No boat bottoms to clean and no diesel engines idling. This is one of the few times Boner is able to just let his body recover.

Eleven-thirty A.M., with the sun shining brightly through the living room window, the knocking starts. He can hear it in his dream. A knock on the boat's hull. In a daze his mind is confused. How can there be knocking on the hull. "I'm not on the boat. Am I?", he questions in his sleep.

It won't stop. "Why is someone knocking on the hull. I don't have a bottom job to do. What if something happened to Dad."

He is out of his body, thinking inside his dream, trying to force himself to wake up. It feels like hours go by, while he forces himself to pry one eye open then the other open.

His mind is spinning "That's right I'm not on the houseboat. Did I really hear knocking or was it part of the dream.", he is thing to himself.

That answer comes as he is thinking.

Knock Knock. Knock knock knock.

Rolling over putting his feet on the floor, Boner places his hands on the couch to steady his body, while the day creeps in between the cracks in his eyelids.

Knock Knock Knock.

"Ok. Ok. I'm coming. I'm coming, hold on."

Boner did not take notice of his surrounding when he arrived. Only enough to find the living room and the bathroom. He did not even see the bedroom, crashing on the couch in exhaustion.

Again the knocking starts. "Ok, hold on!", he yells.

Boner opens the front door to see Debbie standing there.

"Debbie?"

"What. Did you forget you wanted me to show you around today?", Debbie giggled as she entered through the open front door.

"I guess I did forget. I'm sorry."

"Quiet Boner of Key West. Here this should get you going.", Debbie says, pushing a twenty ounce cup into his hand.

"What's this? Strong coffee I hope"

With a smiling grin Debbie tells Boner "No silly it's a Venti Green with Pumpkin Spice."

"It's a what? Please, have a seat while I try to wake up."

"Crap, this isn't coffee. What the heck is this?", Boner cringes as he tries to swallow the remaining drops of something tasting like warm beer and stale pie.

"I'm sorry. I just wanted to welcome you. I mean, I want to make up for yesterday."

Laughing, Boner tells her "Stop. Just stop. Yesterday was yesterday. Let me take a quick shower and then you can show me where I can get some coffee. Real coffee.", he says, as he starts toward his overnight bag.

"I see you have moved in already.", Debbie says looking around.

"I don't think move in is how I would put it.", he responds, over his shoulder going into the bathroom.

While Boner is taking a hot shower, Debbie looks around taking inventory of the living room.

She knows expensive taste and this room is overflowing with it. Art work from renown Artist and grand New England furniture.

"Ok, I'm ready. Now. First lets get some real, strong coffee. You know like the Cuban Coffee found in the Keys."

"Well Mr. Boner of Key West, I've never had Cuban Coffee but if you want strong coffee, we can make that happen."

Pulling the side door shut as they leave, Debbie looks at Boner's car. "I know. Help you push it out of the driveway, right."

Boner laughs. "You catch on quick."

Driving out onto the road, Boner tells her "Ok, just tell me where to turn."

Gleefully, Debbie says "Lets go to Starbucks. You can get a Grande Bold Quad Latte macchiato style."

Laughing and shaking his head. "A what. That doesn't sound like Cuban Coffee."

"It's not, but you said you want it strong, right?"

"Well yeah."

"Ok, then that is what you will get. A strong coffee."

Once they order and start to pay the cashier, Boner is in shock.

"You're kidding me right?", he asks the young lady with her hand out.

"Sir, that will twenty-six seventy-four."

"Wow. Ok.", handing her two twenties."

"Thank you Sir. Please come again."

Placing their drinks on the table, "I have never paid that much for coffee in my life!"

Debbie giggles. "Welcome to the real world, Boner of Key West."

"Surely there is some place with a cup of coffee where it doesn't cost a days pay."

"I'm sure we can hook you up Boner of Key West."

"Stop that. Please stop calling me that. Just call me Boner."

"Ok. Ok, I'm sorry."

"And stop saying you're sorry."

"Ok, I am sorry."

"Debbie."

"You're right. Ok, so where would you like to go today, I only have a few hours."

"A few hours?"

"Yes, I have cheerleading practice this afternoon."

"So you work at a whacked out psych house and you're a cheerleader also?"

"It is not a whacked out psych house. And yes. I am a Cheerleader and a Alpha Artemis. You're surprised?", Debbie says with a big smile.

"Debbie after yesterday, I don't think anything is going to surprise me here."

Handing Debbie a piece of paper, "Here is a list of places where I need to know how to get to."

Taking the paper from Boner's hand, "Oh this is easy. Lets see, Coffee, we've been there."

"No we haven't. I want real coffee at a price I can afford."

"Ok. Lets see, Sears, that is at the mall. Campus book store. Bars with live music."

"Bars with live music?"

"Yes. Bars with live music. I want to see if I can get a job playing somewhere."

"Well we have a large selection of night clubs here."

"Night clubs? What is the difference between a night club and a bar?", Boner asks, having never been in a night club.

"Its easier just to show you. How about you pick me up around nine tonight?"

"Sure, I'm game."

For the rest of the morning Debbie shows Boner where he can find all the locations. Including where his classes are located.

Once back at the house, Debbie tells Boner she will be ready at nine and to dress like he is going out to a nice dinner, not the shorts and a tee shirt from Sloppy Joes.

Chapter 24

Getting his first real look at the house, Boner is dumbfounded.

The Living room appears to be from one of the magazines he read at school. It looks like something out of Architectural Digest. An eighty-four inch LCD flat screen TV, stone fireplace, even a wet bar.

"My own bar. You're kidding.", he laughs to himself.

Walking past the wet bar into the master bedroom, he stops at the French doors. "Wow, they are kidding, right?"

The bedroom is equal in size to his entire houseboat plus some.

Against one wall is a full king size bed with more pillows than he has ever seen on a bed. Another set of French doors leading somewhere. A mahogany dresser running the length of one wall. And above that, yet another large flat screen TV. Three panel windows starting at the floor towering almost to the ceiling with shear drapes.

Looking back to the bed, Boner spots an envelope. Walking closer he sees the envelope has his name on it.

Pulling a letter out of the envelope, Boner starts to read.

Dear Boner,

Welcome to our summer home. My wife and I will be cruising for the next few years or so please use our home as yours.

The bar is stocked and as I know you are not a drinker, I took the liberty of having the house service stock up on your Arizona Ice Tea.

Please do not worry about any bills or upkeep for the house. Everything is taken care of through my Trust Account.

The Band Director and the Jazz Club have openings set aside for you and will be expecting you once you have registered for the Fall Term.

You have my phone number and I am reachable anytime you may need me.

Best wishes,

JR.

Putting the letter back into the envelope Boner turns to see more of the room. He did not see it before. A small sitting area and yet another set of French doors leading to the master bath. Master bath, this could be bath house.

Coming out of the bath, he opens the set of French doors to the outside. "Wow, what a wonderful view." Before him, is an in ground pool, bordered by brick walkways that lead down to a seventy-five foot dock on a beautiful looking canal.

Boner is thinking "I must have died and gone to heaven."

Walking into the kitchen, he can't believe it. "Babs would die to have a kitchen like this."

The kitchen contains two double ovens with warmers, a huge double door refrigerator, a walk in cooler, an eight burner stove top, even a four foot by twelve foot prep island.

Boner is thinking to himself "JR, this is your summer home?"

It takes Boner all of twenty minutes to unpack his boxes and getting his new place setup.

Once done with the unpacking Boner decides it is time to relax and play some music. He opens his guitar case. Then taking the neck of his guitar in his hand and grabbing a few picks he leaves the mansion through the rear French doors and heads to the back dock on the canal.

Walking down to the dock he passes the Olympic size pool, the outside kitchen and a lot of the properties water features. He walks slowly taking everything in. "I've never seen anything like this except in movies", Boner is thinking.

Sitting down on the dock, he hangs his legs over the edge. He tunes up the guitar strings and starts to play some of his favorite songs that his mind brought with him.

He can hear the sounds of people far down the canal. And he hears the occasional chirping birds that surround him.

He starts with some soulful blues and gradually leads into the Trop Rock style he has grown up with on the rock. Seems Columbus is being invaded by the Conchs of the Florida Keys.

For Boner, it will be his own three hour concert. He never notices the small regatta of boats who have pulled up near the dock and dropped their anchors. Their own music systems lay silent and all of their engines are shutdown as they drift up to listen to Boner play his guitar.

Completing one of Buffett's songs and starting to tune his guitar strings, clapping and hoots start coming from the concert goers, from their boats.

Startled, Boner whips his head to where his ears hear the sounds of all the clapping. "Wow, you're kidding. What the heck.", Boner mumbles.

"Don't stop!", exclaimed one boater.

Others still clapping are also shouting, "We love it."

Still others are yelling, "More! Please don't stop.", as they continued to clap and show their appreciation for Boner's music.

Laughing Boner asks, "You really want more?"

Everyone is yelling they want to hear more. Boner tells them to hold on, that he will be back in about five minutes. Going back into the house Boner grabs his twenty watt amp and heads back to the dock.

For the boaters who stayed, the wait is over. Boner plugs in the guitar's amp, takes a seat and sets about re-tuning the guitar strings.Once the amp is set and the guitar strings are tuned, Boner starts with some down home southern blues. As more applause comes, Boner goes back to several of his favorites, including "Calypso Blues" Trop Rock style.

As Boner looks at the setting sun he knows it is time to pack it in up and get ready to leave to pick up Debbie.

"Thank you all. This has been great. Thank you.", Boner yells out.

The clapping intermingles with some hoots and yelling.

One man with a balance problem stands up to show his appreciation. As he stands, his canoe tips first to one side then to the other. The man tries to recover one way, the canoe goes the other, as Boner watches, in slow motion the man is tossed into the canal leaving the canoe upside down.

Boner watches the man falling like a bonefish. Several other spectators go to the man's rescue, righting his canoe and bringing him aboard their boat, so he can get back to his boat.

Even in the excitement other boaters are still yelling, "Who are you?"

"I'm Morgan, but people call me Boner."

"Boner, you're great!"

"Boner, play some more!"

"I'm sorry folks I have to go. But thank you."

"Where are you playing. How can we hear more?", came the questions as Boner packs up his amp and microphone, grabs his guitar while waving to his new fans and returning to the house.

Chapter 25

Boner never plays solo for people. In the Keys, he is always sitting in with one of the bands. "This is great. I think I might like it here. Oh well, time to go. Now lets just hope I can find the sorority house.", he tells himself.

Not only did Boner find the Sorority House, he arrives fifteen minutes early. And as he sits in the Thing, he starts to wonder, "Should I go up and ring the bell? Maybe I should just wait and see if someone comes out. Crap."

Ten minutes go by. Boner can see people are looking out the windows of the Sorority House.

"Ok, they're looking at me, but no one is coming out. Guess I need to go ring the bell."

While Boner is climbing the steps to the house, the front door opens and a stately woman in her fifties comes onto the porch with her arms folded.

"May I help you?", she asks as a prison guard might ask a question of an inmate.

"Yes Ma'am. I'm here to pick up Debbie."

"Pick up. Son, our ladies do not get picked up, as you say."

Taken back, Boner asks, "May I see Debbie?"

"First you say you want to pick up one of our ladies and now you want to see one. Son did you mistake this Sorority House for a Brothel?", she asks in a demanding manner.

"No Ma'am. No, I didn't mean that.", Boner stutters.

"Then what is it you meant young man?", the stately woman asks, taking one step forward.

Boner backing up a step of his own, trips falling backwards doing a summersault on to the lawn.

Laughing now, the woman asks Boner "Son would like to try this again?"

"No Ma'am. Falling like that, one time is enough."

Seconds pass as the woman eyes this strange young man. Then as if she is only kidding, walks down the steps and offers her hand to help Boner to his feet.

"Thank you Ma'am."

"Son, please stop calling me Ma'am. I am Miss Gentry. And what is your name?"

"I'm Boner. Boner Morgan. Debbie told me she lives here and I'm suppose to pick her up."

"Mr. Morgan. What did I tell you about picking up our ladies?"

"I'm sorry Miss Gentry, but I don't know how else to put it."

"Mr. Morgan, are you going to escort her to a function tonight?"

"A function?"

"Yes, Mr. Morgan, a function."

"You are not from here, are you Mr. Morgan?"

"No Ma'am, I mean Miss Gentry, I'm from Key West."

"Key West. You are a long way from home Mr. Morgan. Do they have manners in Key West Mr. Morgan?"

"Yes Miss Gentry."

"It appears then, either you may be lacking those manners or Key West's manners are different than they are here in Columbus."

"Mr. Morgan you may come up and take a seat while I announce you are here."

"Announce me?"

"Yes Mr. Morgan. Announce you. Please have a seat.", the lady replies, as she walks in and closes the door.

Boner can hear voices and giggles behind the door. Out of the corner of his eye he can tell people are still peering out the windows at him.

Boner is thinking "What the heck. Maybe I should just leave."

Suddenly the front door opens. "Miss Rehineheart. Mr. Morgan.", the stately woman says, introducing Debbie to Boner.

"Thank you Miss Gentry."

"Please remember Miss Rehinheart. You must return from the function no later then eleven-thirty.", Miss Gentry tells Debbie, while looking Boner over again from top to bottom.

Chapter 26

Noticing Boner's sandals, Miss Gentry can only shake her head and return inside closing the door behind her.

"Who the heck is she. Is this like a halfway house or something?"

"No silly. This is a Sorority House and she is our house mother. I guess you can say she runs the house. In your terms, she will be the Captain of the boat."

"So you're a deck hand?"

Laughing and taking Boner's arm, "You're funny. Come on we only have a few hours. And what is going on with you wearing sandals?"

"What's wrong with sandals? There're clean."

"Ok, whatever Boner. Now do you want to go to a Nightclub or a Dance club?"

"There's a difference?"

"Yes, there is a difference. But you know that don't you.", she replies as more of a statement than a question.

"Debbie, I'm from the Keys. We have a lot of things but I'm sorry, I don't really know the difference."

"Ok. A dance club is just that. It is a club where they play music and people do of all things, dance. And a night club is a club where people gather at night, listen to music, dance some and talk some."

"Which one has live music?"

"That would be the night club."

"Then lets make it the night club. I'd like to hear some live music."

"Then live music it is.", Debbie says, while trying to sit in the Thing, without falling through the any of the holes in the floorboard.

"I'm glad you parked on the street.", she tells him.

"Whys that?"

With a devilish sort of smile, she tells Boner "Well at least I don't have to help you put this thing in reverse."

Arriving at one of the downtown night clubs, the Valet doesn't even come over to their car. One Valet nudges the other and then another until all the Valets are looking and laughing.

From a distance one of the Valets calls out "You can't park that here."

Already out of the Thing, Debbie asks, "This is for Valet Parking, isn't it?"

"Yes. It is valet parking, not junk car parking.", the man laughs. "Now, please remove that thing from our property."

"Would you rather we arrive in a Bentley?", she replies sarcastically.

"That would be nice. Now get that junk out of here, we have others waiting."

Debbie gets back in the car and Boner is too embarrassed to look in her direction. "Now what?"

"Well we surely are not staying here with that reception. Go ahead and drive I'll tell you where."

Four blocks down Debbie, not taking a chance this time tells Boner to find a parking place. She's not going to be laughed at again tonight.

Then she remembers about the reverse. "Boner park in an end spot please. That way you can use us as the reverse gear."

Her relaxed attitude starts to rub off on Boner. "Ok boss lady."

Boner is able to pull into an end parking space, right behind a car just pulling out. "Well that works out good."

"Yes it does Mr. Boner." Debbie says with a smile. "The club is up on the corner. So yes, you did good."

Walking up to the club, Boner takes in some of the sites around them. Buildings twenty and thirty stories tall. Sidewalks wider than the docks and streets, he is used to in the Keys.

Approaching the entrance of the club the Doorman holds up his hand signaling them to stop before going into the club.

"I'm sorry but we can not allow you in tonight."

Debbie is now getting frustrated. "And just why is that?"

Responding to the question, the Doorman points to a sign reading "Proper dress required."

"And just what is wrong with my dress?", Debbie asks.

"No Miss not your dress. It's the gentlemen's footwear. We can not allow you to enter with those Sir."

Surprised, Boner asks "Why? What is wrong with my sandals?"

"Sir it is policy. I am sorry. If you would care to change into appropriate footwear…"

"Appropriate footwear!", Boner interrupts. "Just what is wrong with my footwear? They're clean and my feet don't stink."

"Sir, I am sorry it is the policy. Please, step aside so other parties may enter."

"Thanks for nothing.", Debbie tells the Doorman, taking Boner's arm and leading him back towards the car.

"Well, you sure have some nice clubs here."

"Boner, I am sorry. But this is Columbus and I guess we have different rules than Key West."

"Debbie, that's ok. But now its my turn."

"Your turn? Your turn for what?"

"After dropping you off, I drove by a place I'd like to check out. Come on get in. Show me how to get back towards the main street up by your house."

"Boner forgive me for asking."

"Forgive you for what Debbie?"

"I can not help but notice, but how can you afford the home where you are living?"

"The house?"

"No Boner the barn. Yes the house. How can you afford to live in a such a beautiful and spacious home. Most of the people in that area are multi millionaires."

"It's a family home. A summer home. I'll be living there at least until I finish school."

Once back on the main road, Boner knows where he wants to go. He wants to see High Street.

Chapter 2 /

"Ok, the place is only a few more blocks. Keep an eye out for somewhere to park.", Boner tells her.

"Yes, I don't want to play reverse again.", she laughs.

Passing by the bar, Boner points to it. "That's the place. Pete's Jazz and Blues Club with live music."

After locating a parking place Boner and Debbie walk the half block to Pete's.

"Are you sure about this?" she questions Boner while increasing her grip on his arm.

"Sure. Why?"

"Well. The neighborhood." she says looking around.

Boner being around the many alleyways and narrow streets of the keys replies, "The neighborhood? What's wrong with it?"

"Nothing, I guess. Just please don't leave me alone in here."

"Don't worry. It's a Jazz and Blues club not a knife and gun club.", Boner tells her while thinking "at least I hope it isn't."

Inside the lights were not turned down to pitch black. You can see people and the band on stage playing an upbeat jazz tune Boner doesn't recognize.

"There's a table over there, lets get that one.", Boner suggest.

"Yes, that will be fine."

"See this place doesn't look that bad. Does it?, he asks.

"No I guess not. But the people seem a lot older than where I go."

"Older?"

"Yes. They must be thirty-five, forty and some in their fifties. You know, Old."

Boner laughs. "You say that like it's a bad thing."

As they are looking over the club, the waitress appears, asking for their drink orders.

"One white wine and an Arizona Iced Tea if you have some please.", Boner tells the waitress.

The waitress takes a moment to look at the couple, "Sure, coming right up. Will there be anything else?"

"The band sounds good. Are they here all the time?", Boner asks.

"We have different people and bands come in all the time."

Nodding towards the band. "This one will be here for the rest of the week. I'll be right back with your drinks."

"So, what do you think of the music?", Boner asks Debbie.

"Its ok. But I still can not get over how old these people are. Don't most people this old go to bed at nine?"

"Maybe some places here in Columbus, but in the Keys all age groups know how to have a good time."

Debbie doesn't know it but Boner has a reason to stop into this club.

From the stage they hear "Ok folks we're going to do one more before the break, hope you enjoy it."

That is just what Boner wanted to hear. You see, Boner doesn't want to hear the band, as much as he wants a job. A job playing music. Although JR is giving him a house to live in and the school is paid for, he still needs money to survive on.

As the song ends Boner excuses himself for a minute.

"Hi, you guys sound great.", Boner tells the band. "I know this is a strange request.", he starts telling the band.

"We've heard a lot of strange requests. What is it?", the keyboard player asks.

"My date and I just came in and I was wondering, could I use the stage to play some music while you're on break?"

"Play some music? You mean that new age Lady Gaga stuff?"

"No no. Nothing like that. Just some blues and maybe a little Trop Rock."

The band members look at each other. "Sure why not."

"Ok I know this is asking a lot. But could I use one of your guitars. I know I know, but I promise not to smash it or burn it in effigy."

"Sure, here.", one of the members tells Boner. "Use mine."

"Great. Thank you. Thank you so much."

The noise is starting to pick up with conversations. And the waitresses are delivering drink and food orders to the customers.

Debbie can see Boner with a guitar in his had, making his way to the stage. "This should be interesting.", she thinks to herself.

After a minute of adjusting the microphone and the amp, Boner says into the microphone "Good evening ladies and gentlemen. I've asked the band if I could entertain you with some music while they're on break. So I hope you don't mind."

No one is even listening to him. They are deeply enthralled in their own world now. No different than in the keys when the band breaks between sets.

The manager, standing to one side of the bar can only think "Oh great, here we go, amateur night at Pete's."

Boner decided to start with something that will bridge between the tempo and style of the song the band just ended with and to the songs he wants to play. So Boner enters onto Columbus's music scene with the Bob Marley rendition of Curtis Mayfield's "One Love"

It doesn't matter to Boner if the people stay with their conversations or stop to listen. He only wants to play.

Knowing there are a lot of boaters in Columbus using the Scioto River, Boner almost without stopping he goes into Buffett's "Son of a Son of a Sailor"

Debbie is starting to like this. Seems like with each verse the patrons are ending their conversation and turning to listen. A new sound and they seem to like it.

This time Boner pauses to check the guitar's tuning and the patrons start to applaud. "Thank you.", Boner says into the microphone.

He knows there's only time enough for one more song. So he starts playing and singing his favorite. "This ones for you Mustafa", he says, as he enters back into the world and lyrics Nat Cole's "Calypso Blues"

As Boner chants the ending "Wa-oo-oo, wa-oo-oo,
Wa-oo wa-oo wa-oo wa-ay...
Wa-oo-oo, wa-oo-oo,
Wa-oo wa-oo wa-oo wa-ay... ", and fades it to the end.

The patrons have quickly fallen in lust with the music.

Even the Owner standing by the bar, at the waitresses station likes it. "They love him. Where did you find him?", one waitress asks while ordering her drinks.

"Find him., the Owner laughs. "He found us."

With the band ready to come back, Boner tells the customers "Thank you. I hope you liked it as much as I did.", stepping away from the microphone and handing the guitar back to the one who gave it to him.

"Man, that was great. Where do you play?", asks the drummer.

"In my backyard for now.", Boner replies.

Bursting out in laughter, the keyboardist tells him " You can sit in with us anytime. Thanks for keeping them warmed up. Really, you're good. Thanks."

Going back to the table, Boner sees Debbie is smiling. Excited, he doesn't even feel the people patting him and leveling him with praise as he walks by them.

"Boner that was wonderful!", Debbie exclaims upon his return.

"Thanks. I guess that's why I'm in the University band.", he replies sheepishly.

"No, really. You are good."

No sooner then her words leave her mouth, a man comes to their table with a waitress in tow.

"Free drinks for the lady and the gentleman.", he states, gesturing for the waitress to set the drinks on the table.

"Thank you Sir but…"

"No buts son. You are great. The customers love it."

"May I sit with you a moment?", the owner asks.

"Sure, I guess.", Boner tells him while glancing at Debbie for acceptance.

"My name in Pete. Welcome to Pete's place."

"I'm sorry Sir, I didn't mean…" Boner starts.

"Stop son. Everything is fine. No need to be sorry about a thing. In fact I'd like to ask you a couple of questions if that's ok?"

"Yes Sir."

"Do you play like that often?"

"If you mean do I play on stage, no Sir. I sit in with some bands once in awhile. Mostly I play at home."

"So you are not playing anywhere now? I mean you're not playing at any other clubs or anything like that are you?"

"Oh no Sir. I just arrive a little bit ago. I'm going to school at the University."

"At the University?", now Pete can see dollar signs, getting in a younger more fun group who like to party.

"Well, how would you like to play here?"

"Play here? Boners surprised it is happening so quickly. "Play here, really?"

"It will only be Saturday and Sunday afternoons to start with, to see how you fit in. But it will give you a place to play and you will get paid for it."

Debbie leans slightly away from Boner to gage his interest and expression. She can see he is interested, but how much interest is the question.

"Look, don't decide right now. Go home think about it and if you'd like to, come on by in a day or two and we'll talk numbers. Ok?"

"Sure. That will be good. I'd like to think about it.", Boner says, all the while his insides are jumping for joy, Ruth, Martha and Mary.

As the owner stands to leave the table, Boner stands with him. Each taking the others hand.

"I hope to see you soon, Boner is it?", Pete confirms.

"Yes Sir, its Boner. And this is Debbie"

"Ok Boner, Debbie. The drinks are on the house the rest of the night. Please enjoy."

"Boner this is truly wonderful and everything, really it is. But please do not forget I must be back to the sorority house before curfew."

"That's an awful early curfew isn't it?", Boner asks.

"Yes, I guess so. But if we are not in by then, we get demerits from the house mother and end up having to do nasty chores."

"Demerits. Nasty chores?", what are nasty chores?"

"You know. Like scrubbing the kitchen floor. Dusting the parlor. And sometimes she will even make us even empty everyone's trash can."

Boner laughs. "I thought you said nasty. Like cleaning out the head with a sponge or something."

"The head?"

"Yes, you know the head, the throne, the toilet."

"Oh gross. Boner that is sick. She will never do something so mean as that."

"But please it is already getting close to time and I don't want to be late."

Laughing at how nasty Debbie has it, Boner tells her "Ok lets drink this last drink and I'll take the stepsister home."

"Stepsister. You mean like Cinderella don't you.", she laughs.

"Yes, Cinderella, now drink up."

As they leave, Boner waves goodbye to the man who gave them free drinks.

Leaving Pete's they head back to Debbie's.

"Boner, you really need to think about obtaining another car. Now if you will, please walk me to the porch", Debbie tells him, so people watching do not think she was out with a Neanderthal.

"Sure, I'm sorry. Yes let me walk you to the house."

"Here is my cell phone number. If there is anything else I might be able to do for you, please give me a call."

"I'd give you mine but I need to get one.", Boner laughs.

"Just please do not tell anyone about the Doctor's office."

"Lets just tell them we met in the campus bookstore. How's that?"

"That's great. Thank you.", Debbie says with relief.

Boner waits until Debbie walks up the porch and enters the sorority house.

Returning to the mansion, Boner again is exhausted from a long day. But this time he has a full king size bed to sprawl out in.

Chapter 28

No alarm clock. No cell phone and no one knocking on the door. Boner sleeps in till almost nine A.M.

Taking a quick shower, in a shower as big as his bedroom on the houseboat, Boner can not help but think "What do they do, have parties in here?"

Opening the refrigerator it hits him. He didn't get any food. So, grabbing his keys, he heads out looking for someplace for breakfast.

Meantime at the Sorority House Debbie is being quizzed by some of the sorority sisters, about her date the night before.

"First, it was not a date. I met him at the bookstore. He did not know where his classes or the building are located. So I decided to give up a day and show him around.

"But you didn't know anything about him. He could have been…", Sara started to say.

"I knew he was nice."

"Sure and they said the same thing about Ted Bundy.", Sara finished.

"No really. He is very nice and not at all full of himself."

"You mean like the ones around here.", Splender-sky chimes in.

"Exactly. He is very down to earth and polite.", Debbie says.

"You will invite him to the social next week. That way all us can meet him.", Splender-sky suggests.

"Yes, why don't you?, agrees Sara.

While the sorority girls are grilling Debbie, Boner is making his shopping list.

Shoes, large baking pan, coffee pot, mallet and black spray paint.

Leaving the house Boner is heading out to find a good Mom and Pop restaurant. And he is in luck. He finds one only a mile or so from the house.

Once in the restaurant and in his booth, the waitress arrives to take his order.

Once he orders coffee, Boner asks the waitress where is the nearest Sears store, she tells him "Sears is at the mall, but we have a Wal-Mart about 3 miles up."

Boner has never been in Wal-Mart. As the nearest one to Stock Island is all the way up in Florida City.

"Thank you for the information.", Boner says, as he pays his bill and heads back out into the parking lot.

Using his reverse footing, he backs the Thing out of the space and makes his way to the Wal-Mart.

"Wow. This place is better than the Sears store.", he thinks to himself. Grabbing a cart, he feels like he's in a different world.

Thinking to himself "This place has everything. Why would anyone need to go anywhere else. Well other than West Marine that is.", he laughs.

Not only does Boner pick up everything on his list, he is also able to pick up some groceries for the week so he will not starve.

Chapter 29

Boner knows he needs to get a cell phone. And decides to go ahead and buy one while he is in the store.

So many choices of cell phones. Pictures, video, ones with mp3 players, ones without. Ones with a front facing camera and ones with front and rear cameras. Text messages, email messages, voice messages, ring tones, contacts, and games. "Games, really?", Boner questions.

"Darn, I just want one that rings. Is that too much to ask?", he asks the non-existent counter person. "I just want one that rings."

Finally he decides the cheapest one should at least be able to ring. After all, that is all he wants.

"Do you need a minutes card for the phone?", the checkout clerk asks.

"A what?"

"A minutes card. This is a prepaid phone. You'll need minutes on the phone if you want to use it."

"Does it come with minutes?"

"Yes Sir. It comes with thirty minutes and then you have to add more to keep using it."

"Thirty minutes. That would be about one minute a day for a month or maybe ten or fifteen days in reality, till I will have to add more minutes?"

"Yes Sir that sounds correct."

"You can get a thirty, sixty, ninety or a one hundred and twenty minute phone card. And the card will guide you on how to put the minutes on the phone."

"Ok, let me understand. I buy a phone with not enough minutes to hold a decent conversation. So, I have to buy a card that will allow me to use the phone I just purchased. And then, to use the minutes I have to put the minutes on the phone myself."

"Yes Sir, that's about it. Do you want a ninety minutes card?"

"Doesn't sound like I have a choice, if I want to use the phone."

On his way home Boner is starting to realize living on land isn't a whole lot of fun. No wonder people are so cranky.

"I don't think I could live my life on land. Rules, rules and more rules. Everyone seems like they are trying to control someone else."

Once back at home Boner puts his groceries away and sets out to put the minutes on his new pre-paid cell phone.

While at the Sorority House Boner is still the topic of conversation.

"Ok, tell us all about last night.", Splender-sky, prods Debbie.

Debbie does not want to tell the girls how they were denied entry to the clubs, so she tells them about the Jazz Club.

"We went to a jazz club over on High Street. They even asked for Boner to play."

"They what? They asked who. Is that his name?", Sara started asking.

Cutting Sara off, Debbie says "That is his nick name. He said they started calling him that after some boating accident hurt his leg."

"I'm sure that is what is it.", Laughs Splender-sky. "Why did they ask him to play?"

"I don't know why. But I do know he is good."

"Are you going to start dating him?, Sara asks.

"No. I am more interested in John Jackson, the tight end."

"Great. Then invite him for the social next week and we can decide if he is a prospect.", Splender-sky tells Debbie.

"A prospect?"

"Yes Debbie, a prospect. You know. Like husband material for one of us.", she laughs.

Chapter 30

After an hour and half later, Boner is able to finally put the minutes on the phone.

His first call is to his dad to let him know he is in the house and that he is getting settled in to Columbus and school.

After checking in with his dad, Boner takes a walk around the spacious home and the property. He really enjoys the dock and the landscaping.

Going back to the house and getting his guitar and amp he sets up on the dock and starts thinking about the offer from Pete. It will give me spending money and will not cut into my studies or even going out at night.

Over the next couple hours Boner disappears into his music.

Now the fear starts to creep in. Playing solo. In front of a crowd of people for money. "What if I bomb. But then again, they did like me.", he keeps thinking.

During his own private concert, Boner remembers while leaving the Admissions Office he noticed a bulletin board with announcements of things going on around campus.

"Yeah, I think I'll make a run back and see if there is anything going on this week.", he tells himself.

Back at the Admissions Office and the bulletin board, Boner starts writing down local pubs and bars offering live music and some nightlife.

Seems like there are as many college bars in and around Columbus as there are in Key West. "Columbus may offer something for me after all", he thinks.

Using the desktop computer setup in the office off the foyer, Boner starts bringing up on the Internet, the bars and clubs he wrote down from the board.

Boner learns JR's home computer is connected to sound speakers throughout the home and the back yard clear to the dock. Learning this he keeps the computer on almost twenty hours a day. But this computer is not used for class work.

Boner keeps the home computer almost always turned on and logged into www.troprock1290.com . It is an Internet radio station out of Panama City Beach, Florida. The station provides Boner the constant music from the likes of Bob Marley, Howard Livingston, and Chris Rehm.

Going out to the garage, attached to rear right side of the home, Boner finds a full array of tools and small equipment.

"I wonder why JR has all these tools when he has a lawn and pool service doing all the work around the home.", Boner thinks looking in the garage.

Boner brings with him, to the garage, the large baking sheet, mallet and spray paint. As he starts looking around he searches for metal cutters or some type of hacksaw.

Gathering all the tools together he places everything on the work table. And using the tools, he starts cutting and filing and trimming.

Finding a tape measure, he uses it to obtain the measurements he will need to complete his project. Returning to the garage he keeps cutting and filing to get the shape and size he needs.

So as not to get any paint overspray on anything, Boner takes a closer look around the property for a place to paint his newly formed metal.

With his newly formed and painted part, he takes it, along with the tube of fifty-two hundred sealant out to the passenger side of the Thing. Then using the sealant, he installs the new floorboard made from the baking sheet.

Boner decides to take a drive back to Pete's Jazz and Blues club, to see if Pete still wants him to play. Walking in the door it doesn't seem real busy. But then again its not even four-thirty yet and it is the weekday. Boner must keep telling himself, this is Columbus not the Keys.

"Boner! Hey how are you doing? I was hoping you would come back by.", Pete greets him.

"Hi Pete. Looks a little slow.", Boner stating the obvious.

"It's this way, most weekdays before school starts back."

"I hope you are here to talk about my offer."

"Yes Sir. That's what I'd like to talk about."

"Great, come lets sit."

Boner likes what Pete is telling him. Boner gets to play music anyway he wants. Any genre he wants, as long as it brings people in and the club makes money.

The downside is now Boner needs to find a larger amp and a small PA system. His music doesn't require any special effects. Only the backing tracks for the music.

Once Boner and Pete work out a deal, Boner heads back to the house to search for the equipment he will need. As he does a Goggle search for the nearest Guitar store, it hits him. The equipment doesn't need to be new. It just has to work.

Chapter 31

Searching Craig's list he finds several amps and a PA system already setup for playing backing tracks. It turns out they are all close by the Sorority House where Debbie lives.

Calling Debbie, he tells her he is not asking her out on a date, at least right now, but he will be in the area and wants to know if she would like to grab something to eat.

Thinking to herself "I know it is not a date Boner.", laughing she tells Boner "Sure I'd love to."

"Great, I'll see you in about thirty or forty minutes."

"Ok, I will be here."

"Who was on the phone?", asks Splender-sky.

"Boner. He is coming over in about forty minutes. I guess he has more questions."

"Well do not forget. Ask him to come to the Benefit Saturday night. I am sure all of us will like to meet him.", Splender-sky reminds Debbie.

As Debbie starts to get into the Thing she stops. "You fixed it!", she exclaims. "Well I am impressed. I don't have act like the Flintstones anymore."

"Laughing Boner tells her "I wouldn't go that far. There's still no reverse, remember."

"So, just don't park where you need to back up when I am with you."

"There is a great little lunch and dinner place on the other side of the University. Keep going straight, I'll tell you when to turn."

Parking nearby, Boner and Debbie walk over to the outdoor patio and sit at a table near the street.

"This is cute. Almost reminds me of some of our restaurants in Key West on the side streets. I like this."

"I like it now. But once school starts back you have to wait to get a table. This is one of the better places around the University. You will see a lot of the Profs here when school is in session."

"Profs?"

"Professors silly."

While they eat, Debbie tells Boner which Professors are good, which ones are hard and how the University works.

"Boner, I almost forgot, the Sorority is holding a Benefit Saturday Night. It will be a good place for you to be seen and start getting to know people. We will expect you, say between eight thirty and nine. Ok?"

"Sure. But I'd like you to do something for me."

"And what will that be Mr. Morgan?"

"After we eat, I need to make a couple of stops and I'd like it, if you could show me the quickest way around the University."

"Where do you need to go?"

Handing Debbie the addresses, "I need to go by these three places. I'm hoping I can pickup an amp and a small PA system. Will you show me?"

"Sure. In fact all three are on the way back to the Sorority House. Now you are coming to the Benefit Saturday then, right?"

"Ok ok, I'll be there.", he replies with a laugh, "You should be in sales."

Boner is able to not only pick up the equipment he needs, he is also able to pick up a computer with all the backing tracks and software he will need for a long time.

Once he is back at JR's home, he can not wait to hook everything up and start practicing with the equipment. He does not have to be back at Pete's till Saturday of the next week, giving him plenty of time to pull his sets together.

Boner is lucky. Due to the massive size of JR's summer home, he is able to set his equipment up and play at a volume he will be using at the club. And with the home's size, the sound never leaves and disturbs anyone.

Boner practices four, five and sometimes up to nine hours a day as he looks forward to his first afternoon at Pete's.

Chapter 32

Friday afternoon Boner's cell phone rings. Not with one of those hip hop ring tones or the sound of some voice yelling for him to answer the phone. No, Boner's phone rang. It rang like one of the old black telephones in the movies.

Ring, ring ring, ring, ring ring. "Hello", Boner says, once he opens the flip phone.

"Hi. Boner.", the lady says, on the other end.

"This is Boner."

"Boner, this is Debbie. How is your week been going? Getting settled in ok?"

"Debbie. Yes, its a good week. I've been able to practice a lot and I've even been cooking. And how have you been?"

"I am having a good week also. Boner I just want to remind you about the Benefit tomorrow night. You do remember don't you?"

"Laughing, "Yes Debbie, I even have it on my calendar. Eight-thirty, right?"

"Yes, eight-thirty. Boner I was thinking, how would you like to bring your guitar and play some music. It will be fun and can work for all of us."

"I'd love to, but what do you mean it could work for all of us?"

"Well, we can always use more entertainment and you will get some exposure before you start at Pete's."

"You're right. That could work for everyone. Ok, I'll bring the guitar. But are you sure the people at the benefit will be ok with what I play?"

"I think we will just have to find out. What is the worst that can happen?"

"They can throw shoes at me or worse, rotten tomatoes."

Laughing, Debbie tells Boner, "Our shoes are too expensive to be throwing at someone. And Boner, we do not serve rotten food. We will see you at eight-thirty tomorrow."

Flipping the phone shut Boner can't help but think so far, "Leaving the Keys isn't so bad. What is all this about never leave the rock.", he chuckles to himself.

Arriving at the Sorority House you would think they are giving away free beer. Boner searches the first block to park. Then the second. And the third and the fourth. Finally about five long blocks up from the house he is able locate a parking spot.

The only problem. Boner will have to parallel park the Thing, with no reverse.

Thankfully for Boner the sun is down, there is a nice ten mile per hour wind and the heat of the day is gone for the most part. So after ten minutes of driving forward and pushing the Thing backwards parallel into parking space, success.

"Thank God she didn't ask me to bring the new equipment.", Boner said to no one, unless the trees are listening.

He did not noticed before, but the Sorority House has a Valet for the Benefit. Although he could not use the service, without having a reverse gear.

Boner just follows others around the side of the house to the backyard. They turned the backyard into a riverboat casino. This is amazing. He never expected something like this after meeting the house mother.

There is a banjo player and someone singing with a guitar on a stage that is setup towards the rear of the property. Lights are strung between the trees. Card tables, a roulette wheel and the cider is flowing.

On his way in, he picks up a flyer for the benefit telling him there is also going to be a silent auction to benefit the home for wayward Dachshunds.

"What?", he chuckled reading it one more time. "Proceeds to benefit wayward what?" No, he reads it correctly. "This should be interesting.", he is thinking.

There, talking to two other ladies is Debbie. She nods, showing she will be with him shortly. So while waiting, Boner, tries not to stand out. At least not as much as a tall lanky Conch would standout any where, he guesses.

"Well what do you think?", Debbie said greeting Boner.

"Its not what I expected."

"What did you expect?", she laughs.

"I don't know but this isn't it. And I have to ask. What is a wayward Dachshund?"

"You have never heard of the wayward Dachshunds? I thought everyone knew about them. But we can get to that later there are some people, well sisters, who want to meet you, come with me."

Taking Boner's arm, Debbie walks him over to Sara and Splender-sky for the introductions.

"Mr. Morgan, I would like you to meet Sara Brooks of the Zaleski, Ohio Brooks and this is Splender-sky Bonito of the Napa Valley Bonitos."

"Nice to meet you ladies. Looks like you have a nice turn out this evening. That's a different name, Splender-sky. Is that a family name?", Boner asks, not knowing he is about to walk into the spider's den.

Splender-sky tells him "Why yes it is Mr. Morgan it is."

"Oh please, everyone just calls me Boner."

Giggling, Sara blushes and Splender-sky glances down Boner's lanky frame.

Boner quickly understanding, tells them "It's a nick name I got after I hurt my leg in a boating accident."

"Oh I see Mr. Boner", came Splender-sky's response while still smiling.

"Where is your house mother, I think that's what you call her?".

"She is just starting her two week vacation before classes start back. We are on our own for two full delightful weeks.", Sara responds.

I didn't know mothers can just take off." laughs Boner.

"She is not our real mother silly.", Debbie tell him.

Sara, letting her feeling be known states "No, she is more like a warden and we are in a prison."

"Enough of talking about us Mr. Morgan, Boner. Come let me show you around.", Splender-sky tells everyone in ear shot. As she takes Boner's arm she glances back smiling at the two girls shaking their heads and laughing.

Chapter 33

The girls know, from the past, what Splender-sky is doing.

It seems Splender-sky is in the habit of trolling for some man meeting the qualities her mother has set for her, as husband material.

"You remember one of the last strays you brought home?", Sara asks Debbie.

"Oh I remember. That is why this time I did not tell Splender-sky everything. She almost destroyed the last one."

"Debbie she is our sister. She should know what you know."

"No, not this time. I really did like the last one she cast aside. I think it is wrong how she gathers them in and then devours them like they are some sort for meal for her."

"Ok. You are right. I will not say a word.", replies Sara.

"Boner, I hope you do not mind, but when you are around Debbie or with one of the Alphas, will it be ok with you that we address and introduce you by William Morgan rather than Boner?"

"Sure, I guess its ok. Why?"

"William seems much more respectful, don't you think? Of course you do. Tell me William do you like art?"

He thinks of all the Art Studios in Key West. "Sure I like art. Doesn't everyone?"

"No. Some people find Art boring or wasteful. I am happy you like art. Columbus has many nice showings every week. Maybe we will be able to take in a viewing.", Splender-sky suggests, seeing if she is able to tempt her prey.

Nibbling at Splender-sky's bait, Boner tells her "Yes, I'd like to see more of the city."

"What is that you are carrying William?"

"Oh. This is my guitar. Debbie ask me to play a set for the Benefit."

"A set?"

Boner laughs. "Sure, you know a set. A group of songs."

Not really knowing what a set still means or just what to expect. she replies "Oh certainly."

Dangling more of her bait. She tells him "William, I believe I am available most of next week. I will check my calendar and see which days there are showings, if you would like?"

"Sure, I'd like that.", he responds, setting down his guitar case. "Here let me give you my new cell phone number and you can call me."

"Oh William that is so nice of you. But Alphas do not call men. It just would not be proper. Here is our Sorority House phone number.

You will call me, say Tuesday afternoon, at four O'clock and we will make plans then, ok."

"Tuesday afternoon at four, ok."

"Oh there you are Boner. Are you enjoying yourself?"

Splender-sky tells Debbie "Please, let us show some respect for William and use his proper name. You do think William deserves that from us, don't you?"

"Certainly, what was I thinking." All the while thinking "I'll bet that is not what you want to show him."

While looking into Splender-sky's eyes Debbie asks "William, will it be possible to have you play some music for our guests?"

"Sure. This will be fun."

To make a point, while still in front of Splender-sky, Debbie asks Boner "Well then, let me take you to the stage. And tell me, how do you want me to introduce you?"

Thinking for a moment, Boner goes over all the ways she can introduce him, "I'm sorry Splender-sky, but Debbie I think just Boner. Boner Morgan will be fine. After all its my name. And that is what they will know me by at the club."

"Great. Boner it is.", Debbie says taking his arm and walking to him to the stage.

Debbie finally won one over Splender-sky. And they both know it.

Chapter 34

"Attention please. May I please have your attention. Ladies and gentlemen, I want to introduce to you a new Artist just coming onto the Columbus music scene.", Debbie tells the crowd.

Debbie tells the crowd "Will you please put you hands together and give a big welcome to Boner, Boner Morgan. Mr. Morgan is from the Florida Keys and brings with him some unique sounds. Mr. Boner Morgan everyone!"

Clapping her hands, she moves aside to let Boner have the microphone.

"Hi. I hope everyone is having a great time this evening."

Boner is thinking to himself "This is great. I can play the set I am going to do next Saturday and see how it works."

He starts with his old standby "Son of a Son of a Sailor" Then, with only a slight pause he goes into "Southern Cross"

Now the people, who are playing the games are stopping, leaving their card and roulette games and they are gathering around and near the stage.

Upon completing "Southern Cross" Boner takes a little longer pause and the crowd greets him with the applause of approval.

"I see we must have some boaters here tonight."

And from the crowd, "Lots of us." And "Parrot Heads too.", comes the replies.

So Boner starts the next one in the set. And tells the crowd "Ok, this one is for all the Parrot Heads here tonight."

As Boner starts strumming the song "Fins", he laughs saying "And its also for all you sorority ladies who may come to the islands one day."

Boner is singing "Fins" He makes a slight change to Buffett's words and sings "She came down from Columbus Ohio. It took her three days on a train."

The crowd loves it and Boner is a hit.

He plays six or seven more songs during the set. As he finishes the last song, Boner tells the people "Thank you for listening tonight. If you'd like to hear more I'll be at Pete's on High Street every Saturday and Sunday afternoon starting next Saturday. Thanks everyone."

Leaving the stage the people at the benefit keep applauding and asking "Please, one more. Just one more for us Parrot Heads."

"Ok. Ok, I'll play one more. But this one isn't done by Buffett, John Reno or even John Patti."

"This one, is a favorite of mine. It's a rendition of a Nat King Cole song. It's called "Calypso Blues" I hope you enjoy."

Debbie and Splender-sky meet Boner as he comes off the stage.

As people at the benefit clap and voice their praise, Debbie tells Boner "They really like your music Boner."

Splender-sky tells Debbie in a scolding undertone manner "Please, Debbie, call him William. Remember, respect."

"Yes, William.", Debbie acknowledges.

"William you are wonderful." Splender-sky tells him. "You are just wonderful."

"Thank you. I had fun doing it. Seems like your guests liked it."

Splender-sky taking Boners arm, tells him "Yes, well they seldom listen to your style of music, so it is a treat for them."

"I am starving William. Will you join us in getting something to eat?", she asks while moving him towards the buffet area, setup towards the house.

Splender-sky tells Debbie "William is going to take me to a few of the Art Studios next week."

"You are?", Debbie questions Boner.

"I guess I am." Boner replies, looking at Splender-sky. "I guess I am."

"You two should have fun. Columbus has many studios to visit."

Looking at the table, Boner says "This is an interesting buffet."

"Interesting. Interesting how, William", Debbie asks.

"Well for one, the snails are still in their shells and the fish is raw instead of grilled or even cooked."

"Snails?" questions Splender-sky.

"He is referring to the escargot.", Debbie tells her.

"Do people here really eat raw fish?"

Splender-sky giggles, "William, now you are being silly."

"No, I'm serious. Does everyone here eat their fish raw? We cook ours in the Keys. Grilled, Baked, fried and even blackened. But never raw."

Splender-sky tells him "Some people call it Sushi but it is really Sashimi. Try some, but be sure to use one of the dipping sauces."

Boner mumbles to himself "Raw fish and wayward Dachshunds."

Splender-sky hears him mumble "Excuse me?"

Boner tells them "Oh nothing, just thinking out loud."

"I'll try your food if you will try the cupcakes I brought with me.", Boner tells the girls.

"Cupcakes. I didn't see you with cupcakes.", Debbie replies.

Pointing to the end of the buffet table. "There, it looks like there are still a few left. I had just set them down before you saw me."

"This is good. You like art, play music and you cook too. William, you are not gay, are you?", Splender-sky dared to ask him.

Boner laughs. "No. "Everyone from Key West isn't gay."

"Oh no, I didn't mean anything by the question.", she quickly responds.

Motioning towards an empty table and changing the subject. "Here, let us sit down." Debbie tells them.

"I hope you like them. There're Key Lime"

"Key Lime? I thought Key Lime was a pie or a cake or something.", Debbie says.

"Oh no. You can put Key Lime in anything. They're just a little tarter than regular limes and a little smaller too. I have a lot of recipes, I created using Key Limes."

"It is delicious William. These are very tasty. I hope our guest are able to enjoy some." Debbie tells him.

Looking back at the table "Oh, I think your guest have enjoyed most of them." Boner replies seeing there are only two left from the four dozen he brought with him.

"William I am so happy Debbie invited you tonight. I hope you are enjoying it as much as I am. I mean we are.", Splender-sky says, supposedly catching herself.

"I have enjoyed this very much. But I do need to go."

Splender-sky quickly responds "Well William, let me walk you out."

"Sure, if you'd like. Debbie, thank you its been fun."

"I am glad you had a good time Boner. If you need anything give me a call."

"Oh I'm sure William will be fine Debbie." Splender-sky says, while taking Boner's arm and turning him towards the side of the house where he came in.

While walking Boner to the front Splender-sky uses another test close on Boner in order to get him to take her out on the date.

"William I had so much fun with you tonight. You will you be calling me Tuesday at four P.M., correct?"

Laughing, Boner agrees. "Yes, you're correct, you said to call you at four. So, I will call you at four."

"That will be good. I will take your call at four on Tuesday."

Leaning into Boner, Splender-sky kisses Boner on the cheek. "I am so happy you came."

"So am I." Boner tells her as he turns to walk towards the street. When Boner turns and looks back, Splender-sky waves goodnight and returns to the backyard.

Chapter 35

Over the next few nights Boner goes into a few of the clubs he's seen while driving around. It seems there are some very wide tastes in music around Columbus.

From Jazz and Blues, Country, a few Hip Hop and Dance Clubs. But he still has not found one that has his Trop Rock Island style.

But Boner's music isn't just Jazz, Blues and Trop Rock. He too plays several of those Country songs that are always party favorites.

Meanwhile back on the rock, there is bad news on Stock Island.

The commercial fishermen at the marina are starting to receive notices. The marina is not going to renew their slip leases.

Red Stripe meets White Boots at the boat for the mornings crab trap run. "White Boots, what is this I am hearing about the marina not renewing the slips?"

"I don't know. I checked the mail yesterday and I haven't received my letter yet. Why, what are you hearing."

"The guys are saying the owner isn't renewing anyone's lease once they're up."

White Boots tells him "Well that's something I didn't need to hear."

"That's going to either put a lot of people out of work or many will have to move away, just to survive."

"I know Red. I've been dreading this day. But we all knew it was coming someday."

"Yeah, but with the spill and the housing market, I didn't expect it to happen this soon.", Red Stripe tells him.

"I know Red, but what are you going to do?"

"How long do you have on your lease?"

"I just renewed mine a couple months back. So I guess I've got almost a year to decide my next move."

"Guess we'll need to squeeze a few years crabbing into one."

White Boots laughs. "Maybe its time for some of us to retire and enjoy the good life that's always been talked about."

"You mean this isn't the good life?", came Red Stripe's joyful reply."

"Well Red, it has been for a good number of years. Go ahead and cast us off, will ya."

Idling the boat slowly out of it's slip, White Boots guides the boat through the still water of the marina to the sea. It will still be another hour or so before the sun is up.

"Looks like everyone is out this morning Red."

"Yes Sir, sure does. Guessing those letters are making a lot of people nervous.", came Red Stripe's response. barely heard over the rumbling diesel.

Back in the pilot house with White Boots, Red Stripe tells him something he had not heard. "You know that developer, the one up in Marathon who is buying up everything?"

"Yeah, I know the one, why?"

"I hear he bought the land next to your marina, a few weeks back."

"Really. Guess that's why we're getting the notices."

"Well, it gets better. The other day I heard the State Attorney hired one of the developer's, shall we say, close relatives."

"That doesn't surprise me any. Its always been them against us. Maybe that old saying is true."

"What old saying is that boss?"

White Boots laughs. "You know, save the Keys, blow the bridges."

Laughing with him "Boss they should have done that years ago. I think its too late now."

"How's that boy of yours doing? Have you heard from him yet?"

Checking his trap chart overlay "He called just the other day. Seems like he's getting settled in and even been meeting some people at the University."

"Sure do miss him being around."

"So do I Red. So do I"

Red Stripe laughs. "I'll bet Babs misses him too. She's now stuck doing all those dishes by herself."

"Yeah, I wonder if she's heard the news about the slips yet.", Red Stripe says, thinking out loud.

Concerned, White Boots tells him "I know she won't be any happier than us. I'd think most of her business is from the locals."

"I don't doubt it. Guessing we'll all be looking to retire. Given any thought about where you might go?"

"Yeah Red, I have. I've been looking for a couple years now. I'm thinking I might like it up around the Peace River in Charlotte County, just north of Fort Myers."

"That's Charlotte Harbor isn't it?"

"That's the place. I've been there several times and it feels the way the Keys felt years ago. And seeing as how I never want to really leave the Keys, I can always take that high speed ferry from Fort Myers to Key West in about three and half hours. Sure beats driving.", chuckles White Boots.

"Peace River." .

"Yep, the Peace River. Have you ever been up that way Red?"

"No Sir, can't say that I have."

"I think you'd like it. Charlotte Harbor is full of restaurants and bars. It has as much if not more music than Stock Island and Key West. Great fishing, with access right into the Gulf or just about anywhere in the harbor."

"I see you've been doing a lot of recon on the area."

"Well Red, I knew once Boner goes to school and is out on his own, I'd be able to finally give up this hard labor and enjoy life. I won't be worrying about having enough money to provide for him."

"Don't get me wrong Red, I miss the hell out of that boy. But its been time I retired for a few years now."

"I know you miss him. There's a lot of us that do. I sure hope he does alright for himself up there."

White Boots laughs. "I'm sure he will Red. He's always had a good head on his shoulders. Better than his old man anyway."

"If you move to the Charlotte Harbor area, you going to take the boats?"

"Take the boats?"

"Yeah, you going to take this one and the houseboat up there with ya.?"

"No. I'd just as soon sell the boats and find something up there. I don't need much. A place to lay my head. Maybe something big enough to fish from once in awhile. As long as I have the sunsets I'll be happy."

"Why'd you ask? You want to buy them? I'll make you a good deal Red."

Red Stripe laughs. "No, not me. When you own things you have responsibilities. I don't want no responsibilities."

"I'm sure I'll find someone to buy them. But I've got a while until I really need to start looking for someone."

"Hey Red, why don't you join me for breakfast over at Moms tomorrow morning?"

"Sure boss, I'll even pay for my own breakfast."

"You can pay for mine too if you want."

"Well if the boss pays me well today, I'll be happy to."

"Yeah sure. Start grabbing those lines and lets see those crabs."

"Oh man, what the heck it this?", White Boots asks Red Stripe.

"What? What's the matter boss?"

Pointing off to the starboard, "Looks like we have a visitor.", replies White Boots.

Chapter 36

Red Stripe turns his head to where White Boots is pointing. "FWC, must want to inspect our haul."

"Yeah, well with all the low hauls this year, I guess some people are cutting corners and keeping the small ones." Replies White Boots. "I rather have them keep people honest than to kill the crabbing industry all together."

"Well the good thing is that is the last trap of the day." Red Stripe tells him.

"Thanks Red. You're a hard worker. I couldn't do it with out you."

Red Stripe laughs. "Just put it in my pay boss, just put it in my pay."

The Florida Fish and Wildlife Officer with blue lights flashing, slowly glides up along side the crab boat and ties off.

"What can we do for you today Officer Jimmy?" White Boots asks the Officer.

The FWC Officer raises his hand to let White Boots know he will be right with him, as the Officer responds to his radio.

"Hi Mr. Morgan. How are you doing today?"

"I'm fine Jimmy. What's up?"

"Oh this isn't an inspection or anything. We hear a lot of the crabbers and commercial fishermen are receiving notices from the marina their slip leases are not going to be renewed. We just want to advise everyone if they decide to leave the area that they must pull all their traps."

"Oh that's not a problem Jimmy. If I can't sell them, I'll run them up to Everglades City. I've got some old friends up there can always use traps."

"I didn't think you would be one of the ones to leave them. But we were told to get the word out."

"Thanks Jimmy. Anyone who abandons their traps should be arrested or at least fined." White Boots tells the Officer.

"I know you and your people care. But there are some who don't put out a lot of effort after the canes."

"Yeah, there are a few. But most of us care about the sea and the environment Jimmy. That's one of the really nice things about the Keys. People Care."

"Hey Mr. Morgan, do you know the difference between a catfish and a Developer in the Florida Keys?" The FWC Officer asks him.

"No Jimmy, don't think I do."

Laughing, the FWC Officer tells him "One is a bottom-dwelling, scum-sucking scavenger and the other is a fish!"

White Boots laughs with him. "Yes sir, you got that one right."

Untying his boat and turning off the flashing blue lights, the FWC Officer tells him "Ok, that's all I needed Mr. Morgan. You and Red have a great day."

"Thanks Jimmy, you be safe out there today."

Pushing off from the crab boat, the FWC Officer waves as he slowly starts to power up his thirty-three foot triple tail Contender.

White Boots tells Red Stripe "Ok lets head for the docks."

Chapter 37

The next morning while Boner is making his breakfast, White Boots and Red Stripe are having breakfast at Mom's. Debbie, Sara and Splender-sky are having breakfast on Pennsylvania Avenue.

And of course the topic of conversation on Pennsylvania Avenue this morning is Boner.

"I always like having these Sunday morning breakfasts.", Debbie says.

Sara, pulling out her chair responds. "Yes a very nice way to start the day."

Then Debbie turns to Splender-sky asking "So, tell us why did you snatch Boner up?"

Laughing, Sara chimes in "Yes Splender-sky. Why him, after all the ones you have caught and tossed back?"

Splender-sky tells the girls " Mother always tells me the right one will come along."

Mockingly, Debbie says "Boner is the right one."

"Mother always says you do not know if you like it, unless you try it."

"So, that is what you are doing.", Sara replies.

With Debbie interjecting "You are tasting Boner? She laughs.

"Splender-sky, just how many do you have to taste, before your taste buds are shall we say, quenched?"

Splender-sky laughs. "Oh now, you are just being funny."

"Oh yes, funny." Debbie giggles. "How many was it last year five, six?"

"Keeping score now are we?", Splender-sky asks.

Sara tells her "I don't think I could ever capture as many as you do."

"Its not capturing. Its more like test driving. You want to make sure it rides nice and that it looks and feels right."

"Maybe you should try a different dealership.", Debbie quipped.

Giggling, Splender-sky tells Debbie "Oh the dealership is just fine. And it has a wide variety to choose from too."

"Ok teacher, just how do you manage to get your hooks into so many?" Sara asks her.

"Do you really want to know?" Splender-sky asks them.

In unison, both Debbie and Sara tell her "Yes!"

"Yes, we really do want to know." Sara replies.

"Mother tells me everything in life is sales."

"Sales?"

"Yes Sara, sales. Mother says it does not matter if it is grapes or wine from our vineyard. It can be potatoes, cars or even church. It is all sales." Splender-sky tells them.

"Church?"

Laughing, Splender-sky tells them "Yes even church. Think about it. The Pastor is selling the people on tithing, giving money to the church. He or she is selling them on the need for being in the church and giving the church the money needed to keep the church running."

"You are serious?", Debbie replies.

"Certainly. What happens if the people did not feel a need for that particular church? The people will leave, right? And what will happen if the Pastor can not move the people to give money to the church? Yes girls, everything is sales in one way or another."

Sara tells her "That's blasphemy"

"No, not at all. Each church is providing a message. But it is the Pastor that must sell the people on the message, in order to survive. No people, no money no church."

"So, everything is sales." Debbie responds.

"Yes. Everything." Splender-sky says.

"Ok, lets say we can see your point, that everything is sales." Debbie laughs, asking Splender-sky "What are you selling?"

"And how do you know when they are interested in buying what you are selling?", Sara asks.

"Oh honey. You have to make the man interested. Just like selling a car."

"Like selling a car?" Debbie questions. "I do not understand."

"Ok, lets take William. Debbie, you told me some of what he likes."

"I did?"

"Yes, you did. You told me he likes music. That he is from Key West and that he lives in a huge house."

"Ok, yes, I did tell you about Boner. But I'm not getting it."

"It is all about prodding. Learning about your prey."

Sara laughs. "So now Boner is your Prey?"

Splender-sky giggles. "I guess I could have said quarry."

"When you go to a car dealership, the salesperson asks you all sorts of questions. Like what type are you looking for. What type of work do you do. Do you live nearby."

"Ok, yes they do."

"So they ask you all these questions to learn about you and how to sell you." She tells them. "And Debbie, you provided me with enough answers to help sell William."

"You tell me he is from Key West. Key West is full of Artists and Art Galleries. You tell me, he likes music and lives in a huge home. And then last night I learn how much he does like music and how polite he is. It is hard for polite people to say no to someone, when the question is asked correctly." Splender-sky laughs.

"Questions? I just want to know which questions got him to take you out."

By now Splender-sky is the center of attention and she is loving it.

"Well, first I make sure any question I ask, will be answered with a yes. Once you get them saying yes to you, you now have your prey trapped."

"Trapped. Prey, quarry. It sounds more like you are going hunting." Sara giggles.

"Look we all are looking for Mr. Right, correct?"

"Well, yes I guess. But hunting just sounds so primitive."

"Well then Sara, what would you call it?" Splender-sky asks.

"See it is hunting. Look, I just told William I hear he is from the Keys. And he said yes he is. Then I told him I know there are a lot of Musicians and Artists in the Keys. And again he tells me yes there is."

Smiling, she continues. "I keep asking him questions or telling him things I feel he will say yes to. As I said, once you get a polite person to start saying yes, they are all yours."

"But that still does not tell us how you got him to ask you out."

"Oh silly girl. He didn't ask me out, as much as he selected which day."

"I told him about the Art Studios Columbus has around town. And then I said I will be happy to show him. Before he can respond, I just ask him which day will be better for him, giving him the choice of two different days."

Trying to control her laughter, Sara tells her "Oh you are so bad."

"I don't know if your Mother taught you well. But you sure are learning what she is teaching." Debbie tells Splender-sky.

"Well you do not expect me to just wait to be asked out, do you. I mean after all, you never know when the right one may come along."

Hoping to now learn something from the master, Debbie asks her "Once you have caught your prey, how do you make sure the prey wants to keep you?"

"Mother told me never to tell anyone. But we are sisters. So I will tell you, but you must never tell anyone I told you."

"Mother says there are two ways to get Mr. Right to marry you. You can either stay around other couples that are very happily married or you can use a puppy dog close."

"You want to give him a puppy?", Sara asks.

Laughing, Splender-sky tells her "No silly. You are the puppy dog."

Debbie is confused. "You want us to be a puppy?"

"Let me ask you a question. If either of you are given a puppy dog to take home for the weekend, will you want to give it back on Monday?"

Thinking about the question Debbie replies "No, I guess not. I mean it will be hard to give up something after becoming attached to it."

"That's just it. You close the sale, of him wanting you around all the time, by letting him see how nice and attentive you are while staying together, say over a long weekend."

"Attentive?" Sara questions.

"Sure, attentive. Either sexually, cooking or anyway that makes his life fun."

"But that sounds like deceiving him.", Debbie tells Splender-sky.

"Is it deception if you want or like what you are doing? You do like to have fun don't you? So you are sharing, not deceiving."

"And your Mother teaches you all of this?"

"That and so much more. Now you know how I get to go out so often. And after playing or toying with the prey for a while, you will know if you want to capture or release." Splender-sky tells them while giggling at her own statement.

Chapter 38

The next morning, while the Alpha Artemis girls are still discussing mother's teachings, Red Stripe and White Boots are placing there usual orders at Moms.

"Morning boys. Glad to see you this morning." Babs tells them.

"Thanks Babs, wouldn't want breakfast anywhere else." White Boots tells her.

"Looks a little slow this morning." Red Stripe says.

"Times are a little hard." she replies.

"I hear your marina isn't going to renew the slips, is that true?"

"Yep. That's what the letter said. Got it late yesterday."

"Seems like the whole island is changing. Soon the only commercial boats will be out of Key Biscayne, Everglades City or Fort Myers." Babs tells them.

"I told Red, I've been thinking about retiring and moving up toward the Peace River." White Boots replies.

"Peace River. Charlotte Harbor area. I hear its nice up there. What about you Red?"

"I haven't thought much about it."

"How about you Babs? How's things with you?" White Boots asks her.

She laughs. "Oh you know. Things could always be better. But then again, they could always be worse too."

"No, I mean with business slowing and all the marinas being turned over to development and condos. You going to be able to keep Moms open?"

"Don't know boys. The land and the building are paid for. So are the ten acres behind it. But the property taxes are taking everything I have."

"I'm sorry to hear that." Red Stripe tells her.

"I am too. But what can you do. Business gets much slower and I'll have to sell out. Those developers haven't offered a whole lot but don't look like I got many choices."

"I'll be back in a few minutes with your breakfast boys."

"I guess you aren't the only one feeling the pressure boss."

"These developers have deep pockets, enough time to ride out the storm." Replies White Boots.

"Development in the Keys is both good and bad. Its good because more people will be able to enjoy them. But its bad cause it runs a lot of the locals out, cause they can't afford to live here."

"Yeah, I know Red. But at least I've got some time to think about it."

"Well, I guess knowing is better than not knowing."

"I was thinking about going to Matlacha next week or so." White Boots tells Red Stripe.

"Macramé. Boss your hands have a hard time baiting the traps. What are you going to macramé?"

"Not macramé. Matlacha. Up on Pine Island outside Cape Coral, the Fort Myers area."

"Why are you going to macramé in Cape Coral?"

"No Red." White Boots now laughing. "Not macramé, Matlacha. Matlacha. It's a place."

Red Stripe laughs. "Ok, ok I get it."

"Maybe you'd like to ride up with me?"

"That's at least a weeks trip isn't it?" Asks Red Stripe.

"Not by boat. I'm going to rent a car and drive up."

"That's still a two day trip isn't it? Where we going to stay?"

"I'm sure they have motels Red. They say its like the Keys only different."

"Ok boys. Here ya go. And some more coffee too." Babs says setting down the plates. "Here ya are, let me fill those cups up for you."

"Thanks Babs."

"Hey have you heard from that wayward son of yours?" Babs asks White Boots.

"Sure have. He got him a cell phone and called just the other day. He tells me Columbus has a place called Wal-Mart. He said its bigger than our Sears and they have more cashiers than we have bartenders." White Boots says, laughing at the thought.

Babs laughs, "More cashiers than bartenders in the Key West."

"He said Wal-Mart is like a city. That they have everything from clothes and fishing gear to more food than Albertson or Winn-Dixie. He tells me some people have gotten lost for days inside there."

"You know there is one up in Florida City." Babs tells them.

"Florida City. I can't see driving all the way to Florida City when we have everything right here on the rock." Red Stripe says.

"More cashiers than bartenders." Repeats Babs.

White Boots tells her "Well if anyone should know, its Boner. After all he did sit in with a lot of the bands between Duval and Front streets."

"I do miss that boy." She tells them.

"Yes ma'am, we all do." Red Stripe tells Babs.

"You tell him Babs says hi next time he calls."

"I will Babs. Thanks for a great breakfast." White Boots tells her, getting up and leaving the money on the table.

"Thanks boys. You be safe out there today." Babs tells them as they walk out the door.

Chapter 39

Monday morning Boner drives over to the campus book store to pick up his course books. Even though he only needs three books and the University was picking up the tab, he is shocked at the prices.

"Wow, you're kidding me two hundred and ninety-three dollars for a book?" Boner comments to the clerk stocking the shelves.

"Lets see which book you are talking about." The clerk says as he walks over to Boner.

The clerk laughs. "Oh, you're taking introduction to computers. You are one of those guys."

"One of those guys?" What guys?"

"You know, the smart guys." The clerk replies.

Laughing, Boner tells him "Smart, no not me."

"Than why are you taking a computer course. You know there is a lot of lab work with those courses, don't you?"

"Yeah, but the University said if I took the course, they will give me a laptop. So I'll be able to set my own lab times at home, instead of having to actually be in the lab."

"See, I told you were smart. Yep two hundred ninety-three dollars."

Boner chuckles, while walking to the register. "Thanks, but it is lazy people like me, who find ways to get things done with the least effort."

Boner knows the less time he needs to spend on campus the more time he can play his guitar.

Being Monday night in Columbus, Boner already knows where he wants to be. Back on High Street. Everyone is telling him not to miss a Monday night on High Street. The same street where he will be playing, starting the following weekend.

This time he is on High Street to listen to a Columbus legend. Once a teacher and mentor, he now brings his Jazz Orchestra to life.

Boner wants to spend hours listening, but he knows he has a full day and can not forget his four O'clock phone call with Splender-sky the next day.

"Do you think he will call on time?" Sara asks Splender-sky.

"I think if he is late, he will not be late twice."

"What does that mean?" Debbie asks her.

Splender-sky tells them "It means, if a man will be late the first time, he is not worth pursuing. Mother says you can tell a lot about the quality of a man by how punctual he is."

"Mother says a man should always arrive early, call on time and never be late."

"What if there is an accident or something that blocks his way or delays him." Debbie asks her.

"Mother says a man should always be prepared and make allowances."

"So the man should make allowances but the woman should not make allowances for the man?" Sara asks her.

"Correct. I have seldom known Mother to be wrong."

Splender-sky tells them "Now when William calls, I do not want him to think I have been waiting for his phone call. So please let him know you will see if I am in."

With the rest of the sorority sisters going about their afternoon duties, Debbie's duty is to monitor incoming phone calls.

Then shortly before four O'clock the house phone rings. And on the third ring Debbie picks up the receiver, stating "Alpha Artemis House, this is Debbie, how may I help you?"

"Debbie, hi its Boner. I was suppose to call Splender-sky at four. Is she there?"

"Hi Boner, I will have to see if she is back yet from the Cooling Center."

"Cooling Center?"

"Yes silly, the Cooling Center. When the temperatures get this hot, the city opens Cooling Centers."

"Ok, but what does a Cooling Center do?"

"A Cooling Center is where people can get out of the heat, play games, watch television, listen to music and get cold drinks."

Boner laughs. "In the Keys we call places like that bars."

"Boner, you are funny, using bars as a place to cool off. What a silly thing to do. Let me see if she is back yet, hold on."

As Boner waits, he can't help but laugh at the idea of Cooling Centers. Thinking to himself "Guessing they should change Sloppy Joes to Joe's Cooling Center. Maybe the Chamber of Commerce could put out a Cooling Center Guide listing all of the Key West bars."

"Hello, this is Splender-sky." The greeting comes from the other end of the phone.

"Splender-sky, its Boner. You said to call you at four."

"Yes William how are you today?"

"I'm doing good. Did you decide which gallery we will be going to?"

"Yes, we will be going to the Short North Art District. It will be fun. We can see the studios, and we can take in the sites with an early dinner and the art districts light show. You will love it, I'm so excited."

"I think I've seen some of it during the day. You're talking about up on High Street, right."

"Yes William. It is located off and on High Street. It is where the arches are across the road. Now I will be free both Thursday or Friday. Which day is better for you, Thursday or Friday?"

"How about Friday?"

"Great Friday it is. Please remember to call Thursday afternoon at four, just to confirm the time to pick me up on Friday."

"Yes, I'll call you at four on Thursday."

"Great William, I will talk to you then. Have a wonderful evening. " Splender-sky tells him and hangs up the phone.

Chapter 40

In the following weeks Boner spends more and more time with Splender-sky. Giving her the opportunity to mold him into an acceptable young man. One meeting her mother's standards.

All the while his father, White Boots, is exploring the South West Florida areas of Charlotte Harbor, Punta Gorda, Matlacha , and Englewood. Looking for the place to relocate to for his retirement.

"I see you didn't spare any expense on the rental car.", Red Stripe tells White Boots.

With a chuckle, White Boots replies, "No. I figured if we were going for a long drive off the rock, we might as well be comfortable in doing it.".

Driving up to Lee County, where the Burnt Store Marina is located, is an uneventful trip. Up the Overseas Highway, over the same islands and bridges Boner takes getting to and from Columbus.

Across Alligator Ally and up Interstate Seventy-five with little traffic as the snowbirds have yet to arrive.

"Red, put some music on will ya.", White Boots asks.

"Sure boss. I don't think I've listened to a radio station, any station for years. Well other than Channel sixteen on the VHF."

"Well find something we grew up with. I want this to be a fun trip."

Red Stripe laughs, "Not a problem, as long as I can figure out how to operate the thing.".

Finding a station after hitting buttons for twenty minutes, he asks, "How this Boss?"

The station he found is Ninety-four point five.

"That's the one Red. I like listening to the sound we grew up to."

"It is nice to take a break from Trop Rock. At least every once in a while.", Red stripe laughs.

"You do know where we are going right?"

"Yes Red I know. But with it getting so late, lets stop at one of the motels on Forty-one, for the night. And go over to Burnt Store Marina in the morning."

"Works for me. Shoot, you can't see anything at night anyway."

So as they come off of Interstate Seventy-five and head toward U.S. Forty-One they start looking for an inexpensive place to stay. Of course everything in Lee County is inexpensive with you compare it to the Florida Keys and Key West.

Lee and Charlotte Counties are one of Florida hidden gems. As when most people think of Florida, its either Orlando, Miami or the Keys.

After getting a good nights sleep, both men wake to another morning of their search for peace and relaxation.

And knowing little about the area they head to where they know. It is breakfast at the Waffle House.

"So Boss, what do you know about the Burnt Store Marina?"

"I know it is suppose to be one of the best live aboard marinas in South Florida. It has something like five hundred slips and direct access to the Gulf of Mexico."

"Boss just do me one favor."

"Sure Red, what's that?"

"Because we are in a strange county and a rental car, lets make sure we drive like we are taking a driver's test."

"Oh believe me Red, I won't be speeding and I'll be stopping at every stop sign."

Laughing, Red Stripe says, "Good, I'm just saying."

"Oh I understand. Seems like cops everywhere always look for the out of towners. At least we have Florida tags."

"Yeah Boss, but its also a rental." Red Stripe laughs.

"Ok, here we are."

"Hey look boss. Burnt Store Marina is gated with a real guard and video surveillance."

"I am liking this place already."

After signing in at the guard station they start moving slowly down the marina's road. White Boots is sure to stay at or below the speed limit of twenty miles per hour.

"Wow, there sure are a lot of nice homes in here.".

"I know. And when I was looking at the area online I also saw how inexpensive they are here.", White Boots tells him.

They follow the signs through left hand turns and curves till they see the marina's main building.

Standing in the parking lot both men wanted to just take in the area before walking up the stairs of the entrance. As they looked around they could see a well maintained landscape, a large cover area with ten to twelve picnic tables.

"Boss, so far this is looking better than the Keys."

"I know. Maybe we should have gotten off the rock earlier. Lets find the Marina's Dockmaster."

"You know we could have came up on the boat.", Red Stripe tells him.

"Yes Red, I know the Lat and Long by heart. Latitude twenty-six point forty-five point seventy-one by Longitude eighty-two point zero four point twenty."

"Dang boss, I guess you do."

"Told you I've been doing my research."

"Ok, here's the dock office."

Entering the Dock Office they are greeted by the staff and Ian Fowler the Harbor Administrator. Both men are taken back at the greeting they receive.

As one staff member starts bringing out every piece of information they have available.

The Harbor Administrator is telling them how Brunt Store Marina is a sheltered deep water harbor with a waterfront restaurant, deli, swimming pool, fuel docks, pump-out, and even suites for accommodations.

White Boots and Red Stripe feel as if they have died and gone to heaven. The marina even has a large facility for the boaters. With showers, laundry and much more.

"Boss, I don't understand."

"What is it you don't understand Red?"

"This place is more like an Island Resort than most of what they have in the Keys. At least for us non millionaires. Why do they offer so much for so little. I don't get it."

"Red, the reason is most people don't know about these places. Everyone in the world knows about Key West and the Florida Keys."

What they didn't know is the history of the Keys and the area around Burnt Store Marina are similar in a way. The area around the marina used to be Indian lands many many many years ago.

As Ponce de Leon and others moved in, they forced the locals, the Indians out. A few remained, but most left the area. In a similar way the Conchs, the locals of the Keys, are also being forced out. As the millionaires develop the Florida Keys, the locals like Red Stripe and White Boots leave for more peaceful areas. Lee and Charlotte County.

"Boss, can you believe this place. Not only are there over five hundred slips, but it also has twenty-seven holes of Golf, an Athletic Club and tennis courts."

After White Boots and Red Stripe spend an hour or so talking to the marina staff they decide to look around the marina itself.

Looking at White Boots, Red Stripe asks, "So?"

"So what?

"So what do you think about the marina?"

"What do I think."

"That is what I asked. What do you think about the marina?"

"I think living here, be it on a boat in the marina or in one of these beautiful homes, you just can't go wrong. That's what I think. I can't believe I waited this long."

As they drive out of the marina, both men are still awestruck.

As the guard gate raises and they leave Burnt Store Marina, they are now heading to Fishermen's Village.

They decide to go North, coming back the way they came, White Boots decides to go a little slower because he wants to see more of the Counties he may be living in.

After stopping at a stop sign, White Boots continues on looking at the area. As he is leaving the stop sign he sees the Deputy Sheriff's car off to his right.

White Boots taps Red Stripe on the leg, "You see that?"

With a slight laugh, Red Stripe replies, "Guess he is looking for stop sign runners and speeders. Good thing you stopped."

"I'll say. I don't want or need any tickets."

"Yeah, but watch. He is going to pull us over anyway I bet."

"Now how can he pull us over? I'm not doing anything wrong."

"You just watch."

And sure enough. The Deputy pulls out from where he is sitting and starts following them. Red Stripe knows what is going to happen because it happens to him all the time. The police see someone with long hair blowing in the breeze, dark sunglasses on and they always want to check it out.

Sure enough, Red Stripe is right.

"Well he is pulling in behind us."

"I knew that was going to happen boss. But its ok, you didn't do anything wrong. He looked at me with my long scraggly hair and these shades and just had to pull us over.

Red Stripe is laid back until he runs into a police officer who acts like you are nothing and must bow to his power because he has a badge. Most officers are real people but Red Stripe sees they are all alike until they prove otherwise.

There is a saying in the Florida Keys. "Come down on vacation. Go home on probation."

"Yep, there's his lights."

Both Red Stripe and White Books are chuckling over getting stopped. Then after a minute or so the Deputy gets out of his car and approaches their car.

"May I see your License and registration?", asks the Deputy.

"What did I do Officer?, White Boots asks

"You didn't stop at that stop sign.", the officer tells him.

Red Stripe knows darn good and well his boss stopped. "Yes Officer, he did too stop."

"I'm not talking to you.", the officer tell Red Stripe.

Never taking being wronged laying down, Red Stripe tells the Officer, "Well as a witness, I'm talking to you. And I'm telling you he did stop at the stop sign."

"Let me see your registration!", the officer state sternly.

Red Stripe is now upset with an Officer telling them they did something wrong, when both men know that they did nothing wrong.

Speaking up again, Red Stripe asks the Officer, "Do you want to get the registration out of the glove box?"

"Just give me your registration!"

"I asked you if you want to get it out of the glove box as there is a pistol in it."

"Sir, give me your registration!"

"Dude, did you not hear me or what? There is a pistol in the glove box, do you want to open the glove box and get the registration?"

During this exchange between the Deputy and Red Stripe, White Boots hands the Deputy his Concealed Weapons Carry permit.

"There is a gun in the glove compartment?"

"That's what I said. Do you want to get the registration?"

"Please get out of the car!", the officer now tells both of them while his hand rests on his own pistol.

Red Stripe gets out and steps back from the door while White Boots makes his way around the car to the passenger side.

Once the Deputy comes over to the passenger side, Red Boots tells the Deputy, "There is a Sig in the glove box and I am carrying a Glock on me."

"Where is the Glock?"

Red Stripe slowly lifts his shirt exposing the holstered Glock. He can see the Deputy looking at the weapon and almost wants to laugh. As it appears the Deputy is undecided how to remove the pistol from the holster.

"Do you want me to remove it?, Red Stripe asks him.

"Yes, if you would."

Red Stripe understanding the Deputy is also now concerned with his own safety, removed the Glock using only his thumb and two fingers on the grip.

"Do you want me to unload it. There is after all one bullet in the chamber."

Appearing surprised, the Deputy states "A bullet in the chamber.".

"Yes sir. Do you want me to unload it?

"Yes, unload it.".

So Red Stripe ejects the magazine and the bullet in the chamber and sets the weapon on the trunk of the car.

Once the weapon is unloaded, the Deputy opens the glove box and takes out the Sig 380.

"That one also has one in the chamber."

"Ok. I'm just going to set this one down. I won't unload it."

After a long discussion regarding the stop sign, the Deputy decides not to write White Boots a ticket. Even Red Stripe is starting to feel different about this Deputy. It is not at all what he expected after his dealings with those in the Keys.

"Ok you can go ahead and pick up your weapons.", the Deputy tells Red Stripe handing him back the bullet that was chambered.

"Well the only challenge now is getting the bullet back in the magazine. I don't have the auto-loader with me."

"You want me to do it for you?", the Deputy asks

"Sure, if you can. My hands just are not strong enough anymore to fully load a Glock magazine."

Putting the magazine into the Glock, and pulling the slide, Red Stripe loads one bullet into the chamber then ejects the magazine handing it and the one bullet to the Deputy.

Taking the magazine and bullet from Red Stripe the Deputy loads the bullet and hands the magazine back. Where Red Stripe inserts it back into the Glock and places the weapon into his holster.

As they are getting ready to leave, the Deputy says, "I do have to ask, why so many weapons?".

Laughing, Red Stripe tells him, "So many. You didn't see what is in the trunk.", making them both laugh.

Having found common ground the Deputy and Red Stripe shake hands. With Red Stripe telling the Deputy to be safe and the Deputy telling Red Stripe that the may have only been moving a little.

As they continue on their way to Fishermen's Village, Red Stripe tells White Boots, "You know, I may like it here. That Deputy was nice to us."

Laughing Red Stripe goes on to ask White Boots, "I mean where can you go where a Deputy will help you reload your pistol on the side of the road and not write you a ticket?"

"Oh Red, the world is full of surprises."

"All I know is, that is how I wish all Deputies would be. And if that is how the Police are up here, I am on their side already."

"Maybe we did spend too many years in the Keys. Here, it seems like both people and Deputies alike are real people. Kind of like the old Florida we grew up with."

"That and it sure is peaceful up here."

"Well now lets see how Fishermen's Village is compared to here."

Chapter 41

Meanwhile Splender-sky is meeting Boner for lunch at Katzinger's Delicatessen on third. Katzinger's Delicatessen is where all of the "in crowd" goes for lunch. And Splender-sky wants people to see she is with a man of means.

"William, why don't we have a party?

"A party? What kind of party? I don't know. I mean who will we invite, I don't know a lot of people here."

"Oh silly. I will take care of that. You do want more people to hear your music don't you?"

"Sure. I'd love more people to find out about Trop Rock."

"Great. We can invite the Sorority House and I will match them up with one of the better Fraternity Houses."

"But where can we have a party?"

"Well your place silly. I will have the girls setup everything, just like we did for the Benefit. People will learn about your Trop Rock music and you will get to meet a lot of nice people."

"I don't know. Strangers in the house."

"William, it will be just like the benefit. You remember how well that went. It will be fun. I know you play at Pete's on the weekend, so do you think a Friday night or a Saturday night will be better?"

"I guess a Friday night. That way I won't be exhausted for school on Monday."

"Wonderful. I will talk with the other girls and start working on the plans."

And while Boner and Splender-sky are enjoying their lunch, Red Stripe and White Boots are heading towards the next stop on their road trip.

Chapter 42

Exiting Interstate Seventy-five, they take State Road Seven Sixty-nine North and head towards Fishermen's Village.

As they drive down Marion Avenue the men can not help but notice the beautifully restored historical homes. Some from the early Nineteen Twenties and Thirties.

White Boots starts to drive slightly under the speed limit to be able to take in the beauty of the street and the restored homes they are passing.

Downtown Punta Gorda appears to be quiet and peaceful even on this Saturday morning. There are of course cars, tourists and locals. But there is a calmness you only feel before the start of the day. Yet it is already almost noon.

As they turn into Fishermen's Village they notice the dock runs the full length of the Pavilion.

Before they enter the Pavilion they want to walk the docks, as this could be where White Boots will be living.

Leaving the parking lot, they start walking towards the outside of the dock area, towards the harbor itself.

Stopping at the corner, they can see one part of the dock runs the length of the Pavilion towards the harbor. And to their right the dock runs for several hundred feet before turning left again heading towards the harbor.

As they go right they see another long dock connecting to theirs also running towards the harbor.

Once they located the dock office, they learn Fishermen's Village has over one hundred slips, a fuel dock, a Boater House with showers, large TV, mail service and just about anything a boater could want. They even have tennis courts.

Fishermen's Village, like Burnt Store Marina, is also gated.

They also have a dinghy dock so if people are anchored out in Charlotte Harbor, they are able to come to shore and enjoy all of Punta Gorda, the Yacht Harbor and Fishermen's Village.

Both Red Stripe and White Boots are impressed with all that Fishermen's Village Yacht Basin offers. It is far better than the marinas in the Keys and at a much lower cost.

"Boss I still can not get over the difference."

"What do you mean Red? Difference in what?"

"These marinas. They offer so much more than what you are getting in Key West and Stock Island, even the entire Keys for that matter, but here the cost is much lower."

"Like I said, most people still don't know about Charlotte Harbor. Its one of Florida's hidden gems."

"Red look, in the keys, Tourists come to feel like they are in the islands, drink at the Tiki bar, go fishing and diving."

"Boss I understand that. I'm just saying they can do the same thing here for less."

Laughing White Boots tells him, "Well, lets just hope the Tourists don't find out."

Still looking at Red Stripe, White Boots says, "Ok, lets go inside the Pavilion and see what else they offer."

Walking back to the front entrance, both men are still looking around. It is now mid-day and the parking lot is starting to fill in some. But unlike Miami or Key West it is still quiet. Noticeable absent is the noise of the City. The noises which sound like loud static.

Entering from the front, they are greeted with the low mellow sounds of saxophone player. Nothing like the loud rap, hip hop or rock of today. No, it is an old jazz and blues player, letting the sound just drift above their heads.

"Red, in case you want to look in one store and I don't, lets meet down at the end at Harpoon Harry's."

"Sure Boss, I can't wait for lunch I'm starving."

As they walk past the saxophone player, each man sees different stores they are interested in. It appears there are many boutiques to choose from for shopping.

Red Stripe's eye is caught by one of these boutiques. The Sea Spirit. With it's splashes of glittering glass and chrome, it's displays captivates most who walk past. And Red Stripe is no exception.

Inside Sea Spirit, Red Stripe engages in conversation with the owner. It turns out the owner and his wife searched far and wide for a location to start their business. From South Carolina to the Palm Beaches. And after seeing Punta Gorda they could not leave.

The shop carries crafted artistry from around the world. The dolphin figurines you find in the Keys, to one of a kind sculptures, gifts and jewelry.

It is the jewelry Red Stripe is most interested in today. The owner enjoying their conversation takes the time to show him around the store and aid Red Stripe in his search.

And then he sees just want he wants. It is a silver necklace with a single white pearl.

Having only taken minutes, with the owners help, Red Stripe is once again on the Pavilions walkway. But White Boots is now gone on his own sight seeing tour.

As Red Stripe passes the event center, he sees they have a lot of the Trop Rock stars playing on center stage. They have Fremont John, Paul Cottrell, Michael Hirst, and Jim Morris playing for the crowd. All on center stage, you don't even need to go in to one of the local watering holes.

But is not just music at the event center Red Stripe learns.

Fishermen's also has events for Fine Arts & Crafts, the Charlotte Harbor Regatta, Seafood Festival, a Bridal Expo and more. To Red Stripe this seems like a small city. But yet so laid back one will think they are in the islands.

Unlike White Boots, Red Stripe has been around the world. He's dined at Governor's Balls, sipped Martell Cognac along the Coast of France, and he gained shelter sleeping in the viaduct of an overpass.

There is not much Red Stripe has not seen. But, upon stopping, turning around and then around again, he is amazed with the Village. To Red Stripe and others, Fishermen's Village is a real jewel.

Turning to walk towards Harpoon Harry's, out of the corner of his eye, he see something. Sweet Treasures. He can only make out, there are bottles stacked on the shelves. Not what is in them. And not knowing, makes him curious.

Entering the store Red Stripe finds it is a small bouquet specializing in of all things, Florida wine. The shelves are stocked with everything. There are several different kinds of Watermelon, Mango, and Blueberry Wines.

As he is looking over the selections, both the owner and her husband come over to offer him assistance. Red Stripe is looking to see if they are carrying one Florida wine in particular. And the owner says she carries it.

She turns from him walks a few steps and retrieves a bottle from the shelve.

There it is, in the owner's hand. A bottle of Key Limen - Key Lime. Made from Key limes grown in Florida. Taking the bottle Red Stripe starts looking closely at the label. And then he sees what he had hoped to find.

The wine is indeed from Florida's Key Limes and it is bottled where he had hoped, St Petersburg. As he reads, his smile grows. This shop is great he is thinking. All Florida wines. Made from fruits, that when closing your eyes, you are taken to Islands.

After exploring the shelves, Red Stripe knows it is getting late and he still has not had lunch. Thanking the owner and her husband he leaves Sweet Treasures and heads to Harpoon Harry's.

Red Stripe steps up to the huge entrance. He sees one large bar on the left and pool tables, air hockey and other games on the right.

Walking through the first bar he comes out onto an open area which also contain a large bar area with what appears to be one television for each sports game.

To Red Stripe this place is huge. Then he walks out of the second bar area taking a few steps down onto the outside patio. Where every table has a panoramic view of Charlotte Harbor.

There he found White Boots already on his third dozen of oysters on the half shell.

As the two men sit and enjoy the view of the harbor from Harpoon Harry's patio, they see the dinghies darting back and forth.

Watching the water, they see one dingy dead in the water. And using their dinghies as most people use cars, the two men know what they are seeing. The dingy is either out of gas or spun its prop.

"I sure hope he's got oars on that thing.", White Boots says.

"Looks like he is still trying to start it.", replies Red Stripe.

As they watch the man in the dingy, both know how the guy is feeling. At least right then.

"Look Red, the guy is standing up getting ready to pull the rope to start the engine."

"Oh man. I don't think this guy knows what he is doing."

Just then, the man standing at the outboard, pulls as hard and fast as he can. And in seconds, the outboard's engine starts, not in idle, but with the throttle full open.

In a flash, the outboard engine twists itself off the transom of the dingy, flinging itself to a watery death. While the engine is falling into the marina's basin, the boater is still holding onto the outboard's starter rope. And is quickly pulled into water right behind the engine.

For a moment they just look at each other, speechless. Then it starts. First one person then another. Throughout the patio, those who watched the entertainment start to laugh. And for minutes the laughter fills the patio.

It does not take long for another boater to rescue the misfortunate man. And wanting to know what happened White Boots pays their bill and walks down to the dingy dock.

As the man is being brought to the dock, the man's wife is already there. It turns out the couple just bought a sailboat in partnership with someone else. Their partner is suppose to teach them about boating and how to sail their new boat.

Her poor husband looking so embarrassed, as he reaches the dock. But Red Stripe, in an effort ease his feelings, tells them it happens to everyone. Sometime the engine works itself loose and when running, it will twist itself off. It happens.

Even though the couple is now laughing at what happened, the wife tells them they have had enough. They own a business in North Florida and it turns out their partner does not have the time to teach them. It took them less then ten minutes to decide to sell their new boat and place a call to Boat Trader.

Neither White Boots nor Red Stripe is able to get the picture of the engine flying off of the boat and falling into the water, out of their minds. They continue to laugh while leaving Fishermen's Village heading toward the Navagator and the old Desoto Marina.

And Boner is finishing his lunch with Splender-sky.

Chapter 43

After lunch with Splender-sky, excited and nervous, Boner joins other students entering and taking their seats for the introductory course in music.

The course is not what Boner expects. There are no instruments in sight. No microphones either. Just desks for students and a fifty-two inch LCD screen in the front of the room facing the students.

With the Professor introducing himself, he tells the class this is an introduction to music class. Telling the class they will be learning the origins of music and it's progression through the centuries and how music has becomes a focal point today.

Boner starts thinking "What? What the heck is he talking about?"

The Professor tells the class "We will be studying the styles and genres of music and how they came into being from a historical point of view. In doing so we will discover new and interesting lives of Composers throughout history."

"What did he say?" Boner is thinking, trying to understand what this man is talking about.

Boner raises his hand.

"Yes, you have a question." The Professor states calling on Boner.

"Yes sir. When will we be learning about the guitar and amplifiers?"

"And what is your name?"

"I'm William, William Morgan. But most people just call me Boner, Sir."

In a stately and slightly appalled manner, the Professor tells Boner "Well Mr. Morgan. This is the School of Music. This not the School of Rock."

"This course involves exploring non-Western cultures where we will be concentrating on cognitive ethnomusicology." The Professor informs him.

Boner mumbles "What? Seriously. He's kidding right?"

Boner keeps his book closed, waiting for something. Anything that will tell him he is in the right class. But there is not one word coming from this man's mouth, that Boner understands.

Boner remembers JR's advise. It does not matter what you learn or even how your feel about a subject. If you want to pass, just give the Professor what he or she wants. You can have your own opinions, just keep them to yourself.

"Ok, take notes on what he is saying and just give him what he wants. I can do this." Boner tells himself "I can do this. I hope."

Boner is starting to take notes on only what the Professor is saying. And while he is taking notes, Red Stripe and White Boots are heading North to the Navagator and the old Desoto Marina.

Chapter 44

Leaving downtown Punta Gorda White Boots takes highway Seven sixty-nine North. Surrounded by a lot of open farm land and woods you will never know you are just minutes from the city.

Not knowing where the Navagator is they look hard for any signs. Then off of the right shoulder is a huge billboard advertising the Navagator.

As they start to pass the billboard there just off the road is a hand written sign measuring about two feet by three feet with the word Navagator and an arrow point to right.

"Well, looks like we are close", White Boots says, pointing to the hand made sign.

Laughing, Red Stripe tells him, "I guess we really are in old Florida now. Not too often you will see a sign made out of cardboard and crayons directing you to a well known landmark.".

Turning down the road and traveling about a half a mile, there it is the Old Desoto Marina and Navagator Grill.

The parking lot next to the Navagator is filled with high priced motorcycles and White Boots is directed to use the lot across the street. The lot is actually an open field with a dirt driveway to the marina's small cottages.

Leaving their weapons in the car, they walk across the street and around to the back of the pub/marina. On the backside of the main building they see your usual plastic table and chairs scattered around between the building and a stage.

Having arrived a little early for the start of the Two P.M. show there is a table right by the back entrance to the pub where they take their seats.

For White Boots and Red Stripe, the entertainment is not just on the stage but is performed by the people around them.

The Navagator is one of those rare backwater bars that used to be everywhere in Florida. Until development pushed them out.

From their table they are able to see the airboats come and go for "Gator Tours", servers carrying the famous Navagator Beer, the sound stage and a full view of all the locals.

You can tell a place has great live music when during the day the locals show up with their own lawn chairs and tents to enjoy the entertainment.

The men sat and listened to the sweet sounds of Latitudes, a husband and wife singing duo, who provide more sounds of the islands.

Before they leave White Boots needs to see the marina itself. The marina has a lot of local fishing guides and gator tours taking people into the Mangroves and history.

The marina provides everything from the Air Boat rides in search of gators, to pontoon boats for lazy days on the Peace River.

As the men are standing on the dock, looking at the Peace River, they are watching airboats gliding across the water ferrying tourists to and from the sights.

There are even cabins for tourists to rent. This is old Florida and only minutes from the city.

Having seen what he needed to see, White Boots and Red Stripe go back to the parking lot and start their trip back to Stock Island.

Chapter 45

In the following days, Splender-sky is again meeting Boner at their (her) favorite spot, Katzinger's Deli, to go over the details of the party.

"Now William, we will want to keep the party outside, just like we did with the Benefit you attended. That way people will not disrupt our, I mean your home." She tells him.

"Good. I'm a little nervous about so many strangers."

"Oh William, you are being silly again. We will only be inviting the top echelon of the campus."

"I am thinking maybe one hundred to one hundred twenty-five people or so."

"You are kidding right?"

"No William. That will allow us to include the best couples in Columbus. We want to show us, I mean you off. You do want more people to hear your music, don't you?"

"Well sure I do but..."

"No buts now. Remember I will be taking care of everything."

Little does Boner know, she will be taking care of everything. Including inviting the Editor and Photographer from the Society Page of the Dispatch, Columbus's main newspaper.

She wants the Newspaper to run the story before she takes Boner home to meet her mother. This way, Boner will already be on the inside of Napa Valley Society.

"Now I have talked to mother and she wants to meet you. I am thinking we can go out during Thanksgiving and then go to Key West for Christmas. Do you want to go to Key West for Christmas?" She asks Boner, again knowing his answer.

"Yes, I was hoping to get back down there for Christmas."

"Great, then I will tell mother we will see her during Thanksgiving, and we will go to the Keys for Christmas. Oh William, I am so excited."

"Now I know you have never flown before William. And there are a lot of new regulations and passenger screenings, people have to go through since nine eleven."

"Here is a pamphlet to tell you what to expect from the people screening the passengers." She tells him, handing him the TSA pamphlet.

"It says here, all pat-downs are only conducted by same-gender officers." Boner tells her, reading the pamphlet.

"Yes, William. Men check men and women check women."

"I don't get it, why?"

"To make the passengers feel more comfortable"

"What happens if I'm gay and would be more comfortable having a woman do it?" Boner asks her.

"William please."

"I serious. I have a lot of gay friends from High School who would be uncomfortable about another man touching them."

Splender-sky, not wanting to discuss the matter tells him "William, don't worry about it. It doesn't really concern you, now does it."

"I will call Mother to let her know our plans and I will let you know what she said."

She did not already call her mother. Splender-sky wanted to make sure William is agreeable to going before she talks to her mother about him.

Chapter 46

"Well it is about time you called. I have not heard from you in a week." Splender-sky's mother tells her.

Splender-sky starts to explain "Mother, I know and I am truly sorry. There is just so much going on this year."

"Darling you do not need to explain. Remember I am a Alpha Artemis also. So how is your week. The week I did not hear from you?"

"Everything is fine mother. It seems the classes are easier this year then last."

"Yes, each year becomes easier then the last."

"I have been seeing someone new."

"You have? Tell me about him. Is he from a good family? What is his major? How long have you known him? Is his family from means? What is his name dear and where is his family?" Comes her mother's questions.

"Mother, please."

"Now darling you know I only want the very best for you."

"I know mother. His name is William R. Morgan and his family is the Key West Morgan's."

"Key West Morgan's. William R. Morgan." Her mother repeats while jotting down the information.

"He is living in his families summer home while attending the University."

"Summer home, did you say?"

"Yes mother. Summer home. We are going to have a gathering for the Alpha Artemis and several of the Fraternities at his home. It is a mansion on the water."

"Really. And how long have you known this William?"

"One of the Alpha Artemis introduced us at a Benefit we hosted. He is not a drinker and he carries himself well."

"So his family is of means and the gentleman has manners?"

"Yes mother. I want for you to meet him at Thanksgiving, if you agree."

"Yes darling Thanksgiving will be acceptable."

"Thank you mother. I will call you in a few days to let you know how William responds."

Her mother laughs. "Oh I do not think you will have any challenges. After all I have taught you how to obtain your desires."

Once the call with her daughter ends, Splender-sky's mother, Nancy, starts doing her research regarding William R. Morgan of the Key West Morgan's.

Years ago, while Splender-sky is being prepared for the society life Nancy plans for her, Boner was scraping the weekly barnacles from his hands, watching his dreams through the picturesque sunsets of the Keys.

Nancy's father, Splender-sky's grandfather, is from old money in California's wine county. There are expectations to be upheld.

Nancy's father started the winery a few years before Prohibition, that put many of the Napa Valley wineries out of business. Supposedly Nancy's father changed from bottling wine to making jellies during this period.

Then, when Prohibition was repealed, her father still having the grapes, was a step ahead in his wine production.

Nancy helped form the Napa Valley Genealogical and Biographical Society. Afternoon teas and monthly socials with the Society, this is Nancy's world. A world she expects Splender-sky to join.

Nancy knowing appearance matters, makes sure Splender-sky is well groomed. In High School it is by sending her to etiquette classes to ensure she shows what can be described as Good Breeding.

While Splender-sky is learning to walk and talk with the air of high society, Boner is separating his time between his High School studies and helping his father on the docks, and scraping the bottom of their small fishing boat in the Key West marina where they live.

When Splender-sky tells her mother about William, her mother must know more. She needs to know everything about this new man in her daughter's life. She hires a private detective to learn what she can about William R. Morgan.

However, with all things Nancy did, she only goes far enough to make her feel better.

The Private Detective comes back with his first report.

The Detective tells Nancy, William's family owns a business much like her families. This pleases Nancy. And when he tells her William has a 4.0 grade point average, she appears to even smile.

In Nancy's mind, her daughter has caught a big one. And after all, that is the reason she pushes, pays and is sending Splender-sky to College.

While Boner studies at the University and plays guitar at Pete's, Splender-sky is with her sororities sisters holding fund raisers and hosting parties. And her grades show it.

For Splender-sky there is little time to study as she has a status to uphold and Parties to arrange.

Nancy is excited to meet this man. A man of family wealth. She is reading the first report from her Investigator. A brief report on William and his family.

She knows William's family owns a Seafood Business in Key West and that William is indeed living where Splender-sky says he is. She knows very few people receive a full scholarship to the University, especially in the area of music.

As Nancy is having William and his family investigated, Boner is sailing through the computer course.

Chapter 47

Seems Boner has a knack for understanding computers. The logic and thought process he develops from being around the dock and Key West bars is useful after all.

Boner is starting to stand out in class. While others in his class must wait for Computer Lab time Boner is spending many late night hours at home on his own computer systems.

Boner setup one of the bedrooms with a network of five computers. Each running a different operating system. He setup each computer with different programs and databases to test his knowledge.

He is even starting to design his own websites and learning several programming languages. Some days Boner is spending seven, eight even ten hours a day writing and testing his code. Where his classmates are only able to use the Computer Lab for one or two hours a day.

Several of his classmates are jealous of Boner. And the party at Boner's, only make their jealousy worse. They are having to form study groups to share ideas and their knowledge in order to just survive the class.

At Boner's party, they see Boner is computer smart, lives in a huge home, plays great music, appears to have money and all the girls want to be around him more than them. Every time they see Boner, the madder they get.

So while Boner is playing his guitar out on the dock entertaining everyone, they decide to play an old prank on him.

Sneaking into the house they plug a thumb drive into the USB port of his computer system. Once the thumb drive is connected, the drive downloads a program to Boner's computers.

Using a smart phone, the Frat boys, take a picture of Boner's Computer Desktop, with all of his icons.

Then using the computer program they loaded on Boner's computer, they hide his toolbar and load the picture of his desktop.. They make the picture of his desktop, his screen's background picture. Then rather than going back to the party, they decide it will be best to leave before anyone sees them.

The boys are hoping Boner will get confused. As when he clicks on the picture of the icon, nothing will happen.

But clever as the Frat boys are, it only take Boner about five minutes to discover the program and remove it. And other then that, the party goes off without a hitch.

Chapter 48

As Thanksgiving approaches, Splender-sky is making the arrangements for her and Boner to fly out on a United flight to San Francisco from Columbus.

Nancy, Splender-sky's mother will have her G-5 waiting to bring them to the Napa County Airport. Where Nancy's driver will bring them to the Vineyard.

Boner has never been on an airplane. Sure he has seen them takeoff and land at the Key West Airport but he never had a reason to actually board one. Let alone fly anywhere.

Arriving at the airport Splender-sky tells Boner what to expect when going through the screening process.

"So, let me get this straight. I have a choice. I can either go through a scanner or I can have some guy I don't know run his hands up my legs into my crotch. That's my choice?

"Yes William. The scanner only takes a few seconds and does not make you glow at night."

"How do you know?"

laughing, she asks him "William, have you seen anyone glowing at night?"

Boner tells her sarcastically "No, but you can't see air either. But its there isn't it?"

"Oh Boner."

"Oh nothing. Neither one sounds like a good choice to me."

You will be fine." She tells him, arriving at the screening line.

The agent tells Boner "Take your shoes off."

"But they're not shoes. They're sandals."

The agent insists "It does not matter what you call them. Please remove them Sir."

"Yes Sir. But they are not shoes." Boners again tells the agent.

"Sir, step to the side please. You have been selected for a full pat-down." The agent tells Boner.

"Sir would you like to do this in private or may we do it here?"

"Ok, let me understand. You are asking, if I want you to run your hand up into my crotch in private, where it is just you and me. Or I can let you feel me up out here where everyone gets to see you groping my crotch. Is that the deal?"

"Sir, you may have it here or in private and it will be done by an agent of your gender."

Now getting irate with the TSA Agent, Boner asks "An agent of my gender? So because I'm a man, you will have another man put his hands where I don't want them? Would it matter if I told you I'm gay and that is offensive to me?"

"William, please don't be this way. The agent is only doing his job. Please, let us just get this over with so we can leave."

Boner tells the agent "Ok ok, I'm sorry. I guess I'm just a little cranky this morning. Lets just do this."

With a silly devilish grin, the agent warms his hands "Thank you Sir. Please, spread your legs and raise your arms."

Chapter 49

Once they start boarding the plane, Boner starts to relax from the screening he just endured. Now they are standing in line to make their way down the planes aisle to their seats.

"Is it always like this?" Boner asks her.

"What do you mean?"

"I mean, is there always this many people? Seems a little crowded."

"Yes William. After all, it is Thanksgiving and most of these people are going home to be with family."

As Boner waits for one person to put their baggage in the overhead bin, another passenger is pushing their way past him.

Boner is feeling more cramped than trying to get to the Bar area at Pete's place. Once seated all Boner can think is "Why in the world do people put themselves through this?"

It will be about a four and a half hour flight. And Boner can not wait to land. Not because of flying. But because of the children that keep banging the rear of his seat.

Fortunately for him, Splender-sky gives him one of her little pills to relax him and allow him to go to sleep. Boner doesn't like medications, but this time he accepts.

Deplaning in San Francisco is almost as bad for Boner as boarding. Everyone is pushing. People standing in the aisles and no one getting anywhere.

Splender-sky, having made this trip many times before, already made arrangements for their bags to be transferred to their connecting flight to Napa Valley, with her mother's G-5 waiting.

Still trying to wake up from those little pills, Boner asks "Where's the line this time?"

"Oh there will not be a line this time. We will be boarding through the Privates area."

"Where did you say we are going?", Boner asks, as she is guiding him through a private screening area.

"Hey, isn't that…"

"Yes William. It is. You may see many celebrities using this area. Mother would have sent the plane to pick us up in Columbus but she used it to come back from Honolulu.

The Co-Pilot tells Splender-sky "Good evening Ms. Bonito, Mr. Morgan. Your bags are already on board and we are ready to takeoff on your say so."

Boner is confused. "You're not going to pat me up or take my sandals?"

Laughing, the Co-Pilot tells him "No Sir." Turning, she tells Splender-sky, "Please let us know when you are ready Ms. Bonito."

"Thank you Connie."

"You're kidding right? Where are all the other people?"

"William, there are no other people. This is Mother's plane. We are the only passengers."

Boner is beside himself. He lives in a small mansion and now flying on a private jet.

"Your mother's airplane?"

She giggles. "Yes, William. Are you surprised?"

"Well, its not what I expected after the flight to get here. This is..., I just..., wow."

"I am surprised your family does not have a private plane?"

Boner laughs "An airplane. No, that will mean we will be leaving the island. No, it will take more than an airplane to get my dad to leave the island."

"Mother uses it to travel from Napa and Sacramento to Washington and other business meetings around the country. It saves her a lot of time. And you know what they say William, time is money."

Pressing the intercom, Splender-sky tells the Pilot they may take off when they are ready.

Once the wheels of the plane have retracted and the plane levels out for the short flight to Napa, the Co-Pilot comes back and asks "Ms. Bonito, Mr. Morgan will you care for anything to drink?"

"Yes, thank you. I'll have a white wine, mother you know." She laughs. "And William will have a B&B on the rocks please."

"A what?. B&B on the rocks? I don't know, you know I'm not a drinker."

"Oh don't be silly William. You have had a long day and besides B&B is not a drink. You sip it slowly. Please, you can do this for me while we are here."

"I guess. Sure, ok one B&B on the rocks."

"I've never seen the land and the water from the sky before. This is really beautiful."

"I am glad you like it."

Upon landing in Napa, the Co-Pilot comes back to the cabin. "Ms. Bonito we will have your bags placed in the car once we stop."

"Thank you so much Connie. And I will be sure to tell Mother how wonderful the flight has been."

"Thank you Ms. Bonito, will you or Mr. Morgan be requiring anything else at this time?"

"No Connie, thank you."

"Shame we couldn't have flown like this out of Columbus." Boner says to her.

"Sometimes we will be able to, depending on Mother's schedule."

"Then I wouldn't be forced to have a TSA Agent..."

Splender-sky cuts him off "Now William."

Chapter 50

"Ms. Bonito, it is a pleasure to see you.", The chauffeur tells her.

"Thank you Jason. This is Mr. Morgan. He will be accompanying me."

"Yes Ma'am. Your bags are in the trunk and I know your Mother is excited about you coming."

"Thank you Jason." Splender-sky tells him, as she enters the limousine.

Whispering, she tells Boner "William, you need to use the door on the other side."

While driving out to Splender-sky's family home and Vineyard, Boner tells her "This does appear to be a beautiful part of the country."

"Yes. We take great pride in our heritage."

"How long till we arrive?"

"It is a shorter drive, than the flight. Why, are you nervous?"

"Nervous? No we conchs learn to be ourselves and if people can't accept us for who we are, its not our problem."

"Please William, don't take that attitude while we are here. Mother deserves respect."

Now questioning her "I understand that. But don't you think I also deserve respect?"

"William, of course I do. I am just asking that you be patient with my Mother."

Boner laughs. "I am always patient."

Finally arriving at the Vineyard, she tells Boner "It is good to be home."

"Home? I don't see a home."

Pointing to the Vineyard's Entrance sign. "There, that is the start of the Vineyard's property. I should have had the Pilot fly over it before we landed. Remind me and I will make sure they do when we leave."

"What type wines do you grow?"

"Silly. You do not grow wine. You grow grapes. The Vineyard produces Cabernet Sauvignon and Merlot from the grapes we grow."

Embarrassed for his question, Boner tells her "I know you don't grow wine. The vines couldn't hold the bottles." He laughs.

"Wow. Is that your house?"

"No William. That is the Tasting Room. It is used for the tourists who are looking to taste and purchase our wines and Mother uses it for her parties."

"I wonder if Seven-Eleven will ever let you taste a beer before you purchase a six pack?"

"William."

"What? I'm just saying."

"Ok there is the main house. Now please watch your manners."

Thinking to himself "Oh this is going to be fun, not."

As the limousine crawls up the long driveway, Boner still can not take it all in. The towering three story sprawling home from a Victorian time long gone.

As the driver opens her door, Splender-sky tells Boner "You may exit from my side."

With Splender-sky exiting the car, Boner is thinking "Well thank you Ma'am."

"Just place our bags to the side." She tells the driver.

"Come William, lets go in so I can introduce you to Mother."

The steps leading up to the porch remind him of Splender-sky's sorority house.

Entering the front door, open by a member of the house staff, Boner sees a woman descending the main stairs. As she walks the fifty or seventy steps to greet them, he notices this woman walks like she has gas and is trying to hold it in.

Getting closer, Boner can see she is expressionless and wonders if that's because of the gas she is holding in and starts to chuckle.

Splender-sky says under her breath "William please."

"Mother, I would like to introduce you to William Morgan. William, this is my Mother, Ms. Bonito."

"Is a pleasure to meet you Ms. Bonito." Boner says extending his hand.

"Yes William. And my daughter has told me a lot about you. Splender-sky, William will be staying in the Viewing Room suite."

Turning to a member of the house staff "Please take Mr. Morgan's luggage to his quarters."

"Let us receive our afternoon meal on the terrace, we can talk there." Nancy tells Splender-sky.

"You have a beautiful home Ms. Bonito."

With no expression, Nancy tells Boner "Thank you William. I expect you will enjoy your stay with us." As if she expects nothing less.

The terrace, connected to the rear of the spacious home, sits level upon a graded hillside over looking vast vineyards below. The warmth of the sun shines down feeding the vines as it seeks to find the evenings horizon.

"William, Splender-sky, I have taken the liberty of inviting several guests for a small party tomorrow evening. William, Splender-sky tells me you play with the universities Jazz Band, is that correct?"

"Yes Ma'am. Next year, I am to enter the full band. But yes, for now I play with their Jazz Band."

Nancy using her skills, sets out to involve him in tomorrow nights party. "That is wonderful. I take it you enjoy playing music?"

"Oh yes Ma'am. I also play at a local Jazz and Blues club in Columbus."

"Splender-sky, you did not tell me William plays at a Club?"

"It must have slipped my mind. I am sorry."

"Well William, I will love to hear you play. Later will you entertain me by playing something?" Nancy is not asking as much as instructing Boner he is going to play for her.

"Yes Ma'am, I'd be happy to."

"Oh that is wonderful William. You can play for us at tomorrow nights gathering as well. That will be just wonderful."

"Ms Bonito, Splender-sky, if you don't mind I'd like to go to my room and take a short nap, its been along day for me."

"Certainly William. One moment and I will have someone show you to your room."

Chapter 51

The next day Splender-sky gives Boner a tour of the Vineyard. They take a long morning walk through the groves. Arriving back at the main house in time for lunch with Nancy.

"Did you enjoy your walk this morning?" Nancy asks.

"Yes Ma'am. I did."

"Well after lunch Splender-sky will show you the Tasting Room and where the gathering will be tonight. Did you find your room acceptable?"

"Oh yes Ma'am. It is very nice. Of course I didn't really get to enjoy as much sleep as I'd like."

"Well I know, it may not be as nice as what you and your family are used to, but after all this is a working Vineyard." Nancy explains to Boner.

Boner laughs. "Not what I'm used to? It is very nice, thank you."

"Splender-sky, please take William to the Tasting house and show him around. William if there is anything you need for tonight, please let me or a member of the staff know."

"Yes Ma'am" Both Boner and Splender-sky say in unison.

During the long walk to the Tasting Room, Boner is feeling something but just can't place it. Something just seems a little odd to him. The way Nancy talks, the manner of her walk. He doesn't know.

"Splender-sky can I ask you a question without you getting upset with me?"

"Why certainly William. What is it?"

"Your mother. Why does she walk with her butt cheeks squeezed together, like she's holding in a fart?"

"William!" Exclaims Splender-sky "That's not anyway to talk."

Boner starts "I'm sorry, its just…"

"William, do not continue with that thought. Remember when I ask you to please show respect for my family while we are here. I meant it. Please, be respectful."

"I didn't mean anything. I was just wondering if maybe she has a back problem or something." Boner tells her, trying to save himself from more of a beating.

"That is ok William, I guess I get a little touchy when it comes to my family. I did not mean to jump on you like that." Splender-sky tells him, in an effort put him back at ease.

"This is the Tasting Room." Splender-sky tells him, while opening the door.

Inside Boner sees what to him is a huge warehouse with rows and rows of wines, glasses, trinkets, and souvenirs. The temperature inside feels like the fifties to Boner and he wishes he had brought a jacket.

"Wow, this is huge."

"This is only the front part. The gathering tonight will be held in the rear and on the Tasting Room's veranda."

Walking through the room Boner is amazed with all the wines. Laughing he tells her "This is like a Wal-Mart for wines"

Smiling Splender-sky tells him "You will not find our wines in a Wal-Mart William."

"This is where the gathering will be held." She says, showing Boner all the tables and chairs already in place.

Looking at all the tables, Boner asks "How many people will be here? I thought your mom said it was only several people. This looks more like a small crowd."

"My Mother wants to welcome you to our home. So she has invited a few friends."

Thinking to himself "A few friends. She should be charging admission."

"I only brought my guitar. Can you find me a small PA system and maybe a fifty watt amplifier?"

Pointing to the stage. "They already have been setup for you. Mother often invites musicians to perform for the guests and the tourists."

Tugging on Boner's arm, Splender-sky starts guiding him outside and back to the main house. "Come along, lets take a trip into town. I want you to see our historical area."

"Speaking of historical areas. Before we leave to go home, I'd like to go to Grant Street in North Beach., if that's ok?"

With a puzzled look on her face, she asks him "North Beach? You mean in San Francisco?"

"Yes, I'd like to see some of the places I've heard about from other musicians."

"Well I guess. That just means we will need to leave earlier than expected."

"Great! Thanks. I can't wait. This is good. We go where you want and we get to go where I want."

"Ok ok, settle down silly. We will take one of the house cars, if that is ok with you."

"A house car? Sure I guess, you know where you're going, I don't. But what's a house car?"

"Come on silly."

Splender-sky spends hours walking Boner around the City of Napa's Historical District and the nearby parks.

"This is fun William. I am so glad I am able to show you some of our history."

Much of the buildings he sees seem like the buildings you will see in the movies of the old west. The only standouts to Boner are the Holden Mansion and the Noyes Mansion. Other than those, all Boner sees is some old buildings from a time he knows nothing about.

"I have enjoyed your tour, but if I'm going to play for your guests tonight, we need to get back so I can get setup."

"Oh yes, William you are right. We should be getting back."

After they arrive back at Vineyard, Boner takes his guitar out to the Tasting House to check his setup and practice a little. While Boner is in the Tasting House Nancy takes Splender-sky out on the veranda of the main house for a woman to woman talk.

"Well Splender-sky, William seems like a nice young man." Nancy starts off the conversation.

"Yes Mother, I think he is."

Splender-sky knows Mother is always right whether it is at home, in Washington, or at the sorority house in Columbus.

"I know you want to make the right choice, so I took the liberty of looking into his background for you. I know you wouldn't mind."

"His background? You mean like he is some type of criminal?"

"No no settle down. We do want to make sure he is all he says he is. As you yourself know, after the last one, you can never be too careful."

"Yes Mother, but George never told me he was a polygamist with six other wives. I mean after all he was only twenty-two years old."

"I know darling. And you didn't know George had a fetish smelling women's shoes until you found him in my bedroom kneeling with his face in my Australia Ankle Boots either." Nancy reminds her.

"Yes well, anyway, I had him checked out. And it does appear his family does have money. His father owns a Seafood Business in the Keys. And William does not have any criminal record nor is he married. Not to six, three or even one other woman."

Excited, Splender-sky tells her mother "That is wonderful news."

"Yes dear it is. This one, may just be the one."

"I hope so mother. I have done everything you have told me to do to catch one."

"Well maybe this one is a keeper dear. Now shouldn't you be getting ready for our guests?"

Chapter 52

With all the guests seated and their glasses full, Boner is told by Splender-sky he may start anytime he wants.

"Good evening ladies and gentlemen. My name is Boner Morgan and I'm from the Florida Keys." He tells the guests. And in doing so, receives applause from them and an evil stare from Splender-sky, as he was not to use the name Boner while at the vineyard.

"A family friend told me this first song is about his family. And because he is as close to family as I know, I feel it must be about my family also."

And with that Boner starts playing the song, Dueling Banjos from the movie Deliverance.

Dada-dit-dit-dit-dit-dit-dit.

Dada-dit-dit-dit-dit-dit-dit.

You can see Splender-sky trying to bravely hold back her embarrassment. All the while watching, as the guests whisper to each other about the song, Boner and it being about his family.

Being deeply involved in playing the song, Boner doesn't notice the stirring of the guests. Upon completing the song there is only a few claps to be heard.

"Ok lets see if you like this one." Boner says into the microphone, as he starting playing the Simon & Garfunkel "Mrs. Robinson".

"I'm going to play this one for Ms. Bonito." Boner not realizing the song is a classic about an older woman having an affair with a recent college graduate.

He starts singing, replacing "Mrs. Robinson" with Ms. Bonito throughout the song. "Here's to you Ms. Bonito"

Now the heads are not just whispering, now they are turning and looking at Nancy and then back at Boner.

Hands cover their mouths. Some appear appalled while others are giggling. Still others appear nervous or uneasy. All of them are wondering.

Unlike the last song, Boner is now watching the guests . Towards the end of the song Boner can see the guests are uncomfortable with his choice of songs.

When he finishes, several more guests leave their tables. Politely thanking Nancy for the evening and leave.

Boner, does not know Nancys guest's taste of music. Nor did he know that the first two songs were going to be received badly.

Seeing the response from the guests, Boner decides to go back to what he knows.

"Folks, I'm from the Keys and I guess we do things a little different on the east coast than you do here on the west. So rather then try to find songs you may like, I'm just going to play what I like and I hope you come to like them too."

Boner takes a few seconds to re-tune his guitar and load the backing tracks for the songs he is going to play.

"Now I know one thing the east coast has in common with the west coast and that's the water. So I hope you will enjoy this set.", With that Boner starts to play "Southern Cross".

About halfway through he sees the guests are responding, moving with the music and some nodding their heads.

From Southern Cross, Boner enters into Buffett's "Son of a Son of a Sailor" then follows it with his favorite Red Stripe's rendition of Nat King Cole's "Calypso Blues"

"Wa oo oo. Wa oo oo. Sittin' by de ocean, Me heart, she feel so sad.

Sittin' by de ocean, Me heart, she feel so sad.

Don't got de money , To take me back to Trinidad

Fine calypso woman, She cook me shrimps and rice."

As Boner ends the song, all the guests are clapping. He wins them over after all.

"Being it is Thanksgiving, If you don't mind, I'd like to perform a song that has become a tradition in many parts of the country."

Boner tells them "It is Alice's Restaurant by Arlo Guthrie"

"Here we go…"

"This song is called Alice's Restaurant, and it's about Alice, and the restaurant, but Alice's Restaurant is not the name of the restaurant, that's just the name of the song, and that's why I called the song Alice's Restaurant.

You can get anything you want at Alice's Restaurant You can get anything you want at Alice's Restaurant Walk right in it's around the back Just a half a mile from the railroad track You can get anything you want at Alice's Restaurant… "

As the last note is struck and the last word uttered, the entire party stands up with applause for Boner. Nancy is so proud, as is Splender-sky.

Nancy has organized the receiving line so that all the guests may be introduced to William. And of course, for her to accept congratulations and honors from her guests.

"Well William, I think your performance was enjoyed by all the guests. Thank you so much for doing this for me on your vacation."

"My pleasure Ms. Bonito. I'm glad they enjoyed it."

Taking Boner in her arms for a hug of appreciation, she whispers in his ear "You know east coast people look and feel the same as west coast people, in the dark." She tells him while drawing him closer.

Not knowing how to respond, Boner lets his arm release Nancy.
"Thank you Ms. Bonito. I'm glad you're happy."

"Oh, more than happy. I like the song you sang for me." She tells
him with a wink in her eye.

Chapter 53

The next day after breakfast Splender-sky and Boner, using the chauffeur, take the house car into San Francisco rather than the G-5. Unlike the limousine, the house car is your standard Lincoln Town car.

Reaching the city, Boner tells the driver to take them to North Beach. North Beach is a traditionally historical Italian neighborhood in San Francisco or so Boner hears.

Driving in North Beach, Splender-sky is griping Boner's arm a little tighter than usual as the car passes strip club after strip club after strip club. They pass Blondie's, Lust, Centerfolds, Broadway Wonders, and the Hustle Club. A strip club is not quite the place Splender-sky believes she is going to be taken, she hopes.

Wondering if Boner is studying music or the female anatomy, she has to ask him "William are you sure we are going to the right place?"

"Splender-sky it'll be fine. We're going to a well known blues club. Besides I thought people in Frisco are ok with the nightlife."

Twisting on the car's seat, she tells him "William, we are."

"Didn't you ever come over here before?"

"No, Mother would never approve."

"But you just said…"

"Never mind what I just said." She tells him.

"Splender-sky, this is part of your history. This area is known as part of the Barbary Coast. I mean it has a hard past and the signs make you think its nothing but strip clubs, but its far more."

"So just where are we going William?"

"Driver, please take us to Grant Street."

"I can't believe you never came here. I'll bet your mom has been here."

Splender-sky scoffs. "No, Mother will never be in this area."

"Oh I think you'd be surprised about your mom."

Sounding indignant she asks "And just what does that mean?"

Thinking back to last night with what Nancy said to him, he decides it is best to let it go.

"Nothing. Its just that this area is rich in history and I'd think everyone from Napa would come here at one time or another."

Seeing the sign and not wanting to arrive at the door with a driver, Boner asks the driver to let them out and they will call him when they are ready to leave.

It is Boners first time here but he has heard about the place for years. First from Red Stripe and then at college from people around campus.

"Darling are you really sure this is where you want to come?"

Walking up to the corner entrance. "Yes, this is the place. It is where one of my Professors talks about quite often."

"But William look at those people. You don't expect us to go in there do you?"

"Splender-sky, it will be fine. This is one of the oldest blues bar around. It may look like a dive but the music is suppose to be out of this world."

Moving past a few biker types outside the doorway, Splender-sky again holds on to Boner's arm, as if holding on for her life. And to her she was.

It is Saturday night and Boner is in luck. Dave Workman will be on stage tonight. Workman plays one of Boner's favorite songs titled "Slip Away" and Boner has practiced it almost daily, since Red Stripe taught him how.

Looking around, Boner already starts to feel at home. The place reminds him of Tony's in Key West, as do the people and the décor of the bar.

Splender-sky is not comfortable in the dive's setting nor the people she is surrounded by. As her eyes adjust and she gets to look around, she sees what is to her, her worst nightmare.

There are so many strange people. People she has always steered clear of. People her mother told her to stay away from. She is walking past bikers, drunks, tourists and mutants from all walks of life.

Walking over the old wooden floor, Boner is able to get two seats across from the a long bar near the stage.

He prods her "Is this great or what?"

"I would have to say or what?"

"What? This is great. A real blues dive."

"William I am not in the habit of going to what you call dives. And yes this place qualifies as one."

Laughing, he points to the sign. "Ok, we won't stay long. Like the sign says no loitering."

"Good. Because I can not see us here. And what on earth is that smell?"

"Smell? Oh that. That's the smell of over one hundred years of spilled beer, booze and sweat. I wouldn't expect it to smell any different."

"Well it does not smell like any place I or mother have ever been."

"Lets get something to drink. What would you like?"

Looking around casting demeaning looks. "I will have a white wine. That is as long as it does not come out of a box."

"I think most wines come in a glass."

"Oh funny funny. " She said sarcastically. "When does the band start to play?"

"According to the sign, they should start about nine-thirty."

"Well I sure hope you do not want to stay long. I don't feel safe here."

"You don't feel safe. You really have led a very sheltered life haven't you?"

"William I have not been sheltered. I just have never been taken to such a place as this."

Boner laughs. "Ok sure you haven't. Let me go get those drinks."

"Bartender, let me have a draft and any white wine you have not in a box."

As Boner watches the man behind the bar draw his draft he starts reading all the signs behind the bar. Then he has to laugh as he watches the Bartender draw a cup of white wine from one of the beer taps.

Boner thinks to himself "Boy she is going to love this."

Sitting the drinks on the table, Boner tells her "Here you are and no he didn't pour the wine out of a box."

Sarcastically she tells him "Well I know good wine and crappy wine. So I hope it didn't come from a convenience store."

While looking around, a group of bikers walk through the door and Splender-sky does all she can do not to stare. The bikers don't affect Boner in the least as there are all types of people in the bars in Key West.

As the burley bikers move past her, she turns her head towards the wall so as not to make eye contact. And thus preserve her life.

Once the bikers have walked by to their seats, Splender-sky watches them out of the corner of her eye.

"William, I really do not like it here. How long must we stay?"

Almost in a pleading way He tells her "Please, just a couple of songs and we'll leave."

"William. William." She says trying to regain Boner's attention.

"Yes, I'm sorry, I was just taking everything in."

She tells him in an almost frighten voice "Well I too am taking things in and one of those bikers won't stop staring at me."

"Where. There are quite a few. Which one."

"Over there." She states while tossing her eyes in the direction of the biker.

"Looks harmless to me. Come on, just drink your wine."

"William, he is getting up."

"Splender-sky, please." Boner states, now getting a little irritated.

"William, he is walking towards us. William." She tells him turning her face to the wall. In an apparent effort to bury her head into the sand.

Boner watches carefully as this biker makes his way towards their table. He doesn't appear drunk. Just big.

"Excuse me Miss." The bike says as he approaches the table.

Boner now aware of the biker, his presence and the area between them, he places one foot on the old wooden planks of the bars floor.

"Miss." The biker again says wanting her attention.

"What can we do for you?", Boner asks him, now with one foot on the floor and a hand wrapped around his beer bottle.

"I wanted to come over and say hi."

"Splender-sky." Boner utters.

Looking at Boner for help, she does not know what she should do.

"I know you, don't I?" The biker questions.

She replies with a nervous voice "I do not believe so Sir."

"Sure I do."

"Sir, I'm sorry but she said she doesn't."

The biker will not take no for an answer. "Sure I do."

Then looking at Boner "In fact I know both of you."

"Sir", Boner says, now slowly without notice sliding his stool away and placing both feet on the floor.

Boner repeats "Sir, I'm sorry but you're mistaken, really."

Splender-sky now, being filled with fear, can only look into Boner's eyes for help and guidance.

Boner now states in a sterner voice "Sir really, She said she doesn't know you."

The biker laughs in an ever so mocking way. "No, I know her and you."

"You don't recognize me. Either of you?"

"No sir, I'm sorry we don't." Boner tells him, while starting to gain a better grip on his beer bottle.

With voices now starting to be elevated, the bikers who remained at the table are now turning to look towards Boner, Splender-sky and their friend. Even the Bartender and the bouncer are glancing towards them.

"Look Mr., we don't want any trouble. We're just here to listen to the music."

"Trouble!", the biker says with a slightly raised voice, turning towards Boner.

"Please, just let us listen to some of the music and we will be leaving."

The biker asks Boner "So, you don't know who I am?"

Noticing movement from the biker's table, Boner again tells him "No sir. We don't know you. I'm sorry."

During this showdown, Splender-sky is also slowly moving her stool back from the man and closer to the wall.

Boner can see one of the female bikers is now coming towards them. Hopefully to return this man to their seats.

"What is taking you so long Robert? Just do it.", the female biker tells the man.

Boner is now only seconds from an all out bar fight he doesn't want. Nor did he ask for. The bartender is giving a sign to the bouncer to start to move closer to Boner's table.

As the bouncer starts to move towards their table the female biker heads him off.

Boner can see the entire table of bikers are leaving their seats and heading towards him and Splender-sky.

Boner is thinking "This isn't going to be pretty."

Boner is running through his mind, the moves he may need to make to ensure he and Splender-sky get out without getting into a broken bottle bar fight.

He knows he is out numbered by these bikers and now even the bouncer is cutoff from helping them.

The biker turns his attention back to Splender-sky. "So you are sure you do not know who I am?" He again asks her, while reaching behind his back.

Almost in tears she again tells him "No I don't know you."

Boner watches the biker's hand and tries to keep track of those coming to their table. Bringing something around from his back, Boner raises his beer bottle off the table.

Something is in the biker's hand but it doesn't look like a weapon. Its some type of card.

Handing her the card, the biker tells her "Here is my card. I was at your mother's party at the vineyard last night. I am State Senator Robert Marshall."

In shock, Splender-sky says "Who? You are a biker. You can not have been at my mother's party."

Boner takes the card from his hand and reads the imprint.

Boner still leery asks "You're State Senator Marshall?"

"Yes. I am. I wanted to come over and tell you how much we enjoyed the party. And Boner, you sure play a great guitar."

Splender-sky still not understanding tells the biker "But, the way you are dressed?"

"Oh I know. Sometimes people take us for hard core one percenters. But look, he says turning around, no patches. We have a small group of us who like riding motorcycles and cutting loose once in a while. That's all."

"You really are a State Senator?"

He laughs. "Yes Ma'am I am. You didn't think we were real bikers did you?"

Splender-sky now showing slight embarrassment. "I..., I didn't know. I..., we have never been here before."

Again laughing while he talks. "I am sorry. I forgot how we are dressed. I guess we didn't look the same last night."

"Anyway, I just want to tell you how much we enjoyed the party and the music."

"Well thank you Senator."

"You two have a good time tonight."

"Thank you Senator. And..." Boner tells him, while gesturing to the crowd of bikers behind him.

"Oh them. They just want to meet Boner. I've been telling them about the party and his guitar playing."

After all the hand shaking, praise and thank you's, everyone returned to their tables. Where they wait for the music to come to the stage.

"William, I am sorry, but I was so afraid. Please do not take me some place like this again."

"I won't. I'm sorry I didn't know you would get upset." He tells her, while hiding the fact that he too had become afraid for their safety.

"Do we really have to stay for the band. I just do not feel comfortable William."

Thinking to himself "Darn. Geez." He tells her "Ok, go ahead and call the driver and we will leave."

Disappointed, Boner finds his eyes staring into the top of his half full beer bottle, wondering. Just wondering.

Chapter 54

With an uneventful ride to the airport and flight home, Boner drops Splender-sky off at the sorority house.

"William, thank you for going to Mothers."

"It was my pleasure. Just remember Christmas we are going to Key West so you can meet my dad."

Yes William, maybe we will be able to have mother join us. I am sure she will like to meet your father also." She tells Boner, while walking up the stairs to enter the sorority house.

Once settled back into Columbus, Boner calls his dad to catch up on the Keys life he misses so much.

"Hi son, how is it going?

"I'm sorry I couldn't get back for Thanksgiving."

"That's ok son. You are coming for Christmas aren't you?"

"Yes Sir. I hope you don't mind, I'd like to bring Splender-sky and maybe her mom down also. Is that ok?"

"Sure son. I'd love to meet them. Make sure you get them a nice place to stay. Like the Popular House, Avalon, or the Curry House."

"Yes Sir. I am thinking about that now. How is Red and Babs doing?"

"Looks like this will be the last Christmas at Moms. With all the local commercial fishermen slowly leaving, Babs is having a hard time even paying the property taxes."

"I'm sorry to hear that. What is she going to do?"

"I don't think she's decided yet. That Developer is still trying to squeeze her out. They already bought the property on one side and have blocked people from seeing Moms, from the road on the other side."

"Blocked drivers from seeing her?"

"Yeah, the developer has a truck with a large sign on it and Code Enforcement says they can't do anything about it."

"That's sad."

"I know son but what can you do. I'm still looking at some places just North of the Fort Myers and the Cape Coral area. Should know something by the time you come down."

"Ok dad, I'll let you know our plans."

"Great son. Be safe."

In the meantime, Splender-sky is telling her sorority sisters about her trip home. One thing she does not tell them is what took place in the Blues Bar in San Francisco.

Over the next several weeks Boner starts to get things ready for his trip back to the Keys. For Boner it has been too long that he has been off the rock and can not wait to get back and see everyone.

Splender-sky is talking with her mother almost everyday to also finalize their plans.. Both for the trip to Key West and the possible landing of William for Splender-sky's husband. Her and her mother have worked towards this event for most of their lives.

Classes end on December fourth and will not start back until January fourth so Boner will have a lot of time to enjoy the Florida sunshine.

Chapter 55

Rather than take a flight down to the Keys, Boner is going to drive down. This way he can also take all of his gear and maybe sit in with a few of the local bands while he is home.

Splender-sky's mother agrees to use her airplane. Nancy will fly to Columbus to pick her up. And then fly them to Key West.

Splender-sky likes it much better when she gets to fly in her mother's airplane than having to fly commercial.

With the normal high temperatures being only forty-one degrees in December, Boner sees no reason to stay in Columbus during any of the holidays.

Calling his dad, Boner lets him know his plans.

"Hi Boner, you're still coming for Christmas aren't you?" His dad asks in an almost worried tone.

"Yes dad. Why wouldn't I be coming? You haven't moved yet have you?"

"No son. Haven't moved yet. Just want to make sure you haven't changed your plans."

"No I haven't changed my plans. It fact that's why I'm calling."

"How's that son."

Dishearten, Boner tells his father "I've tried finding a place for Splender-sky and her mother to stay but seems like everyone is full up."

"Everyone?"

"Yes Sir. I tried everything from phone calls to the Internet and everyone is booked."

Laughing, his dad tells him "Well you know the best place to be is the Keys and during winter even more people want to be here."

"Yes Sir I know. I can't wait to get home. But I don't know what I am going to do with Splender-sky and her mother."

"Well, you can stay on the crab boat with me and let them stay on the houseboat and it wouldn't cost anyone anything."

"Have them stay on the houseboat?"

"Sure, why not? It was good enough for you all these years."

"Nothing wrong with it. I just didn't even think about that."

"Well there you go. I'll get Bait to come over and give it a good cleaning."

"Thanks dad. How's Macky doing?"

Surprised, his dad replies "Macky?"

Laughing Boner says "Yes dad, Macky. How's he been doing?"

"I thought you had forgotten about that bird. Red Stripe is looking out for him."

"Looking out for him?"

"Yeah, looking out for him."

Excited, Boner asks "You mean he got out again?"

"No son. He didn't get out. Red Stripe feeds him, talks to him and even cleans his cage once a week or so."

"Wow you scared me there for a minute."

His dad is now laughing. "Don't worry. Macky is being well cared for. Red Stripe even takes him out on walks. You should see him and that silly bird. They're a sight to see."

"I'll bet. Ok let me get with Splender-sky and see if she will stay in the houseboat." Boner says, thanking his dad for the idea.

Later that night Boner calls Splender-sky to ask her if she will mind staying at his home while in Key West.

She tells him in an stern voice "You were suppose to call me hours ago."

What have you been doing?" she asks him.

"Doing?"

"Yes William, doing. Why did you not call me when you were suppose to?"

Sheepishly Boner says "I didn't know there is a set time I'm suppose to call."

"Do you respect me William?"

"Sure, I respect you."

"Then you should know there is a proper time to call."

Now Boner is wondering why he even tries. Seems like there is little he can do right for her.

"William"

"Yes, I'm here."

"If you are there, then why do you not answer me?"

"I'm sorry. Yes I respect you. You know you can call me if you want to."

"William, A proper lady does not call men."

"Ok, ok. I'm sorry. Look I tried finding you and your mom a place to stay in Key West but they are all booked up."

"William you have known about this for months and you are just now finding out there are no rooms available?"

"Again, I'm sorry. I didn't think they would all be booked. I guess a lot more people are learning how great Key West is during the winter."

Starting to get more upset, she tells him "You guess!"

"But listen. There is good news."

"There had better be!"

"I just talked to my dad and he made a great suggestion."

"A great suggestion? Ok, what is his great suggestion?"

"He said why don't you and your mom stay at my house. I mean dad says its not much but…"

"But nothing." She states, thinking how wonderful Boner's summer home is.

"Yes. Yes. Tell your father we will love to stay at the house. That will be wonderful. Oh I can not wait to tell mother."

"So you won't mind?"

"Oh no William, that will be just perfect. I am sure mother will agree." She tells him, while thinking of how nice his real home must be compared to his families summer home.

Immediately after hanging up from the phone call with Boner, Splender-sky calls her mother at the Vineyard.

"Mother I have some great news."

"Slow down child. I do not even deserve a hello or how am I doing?"

"Yes Mother. I am sorry. I am just so excited!"

"Yes Splender-sky I hear the excitement in your voice."

"It is what William just asked me. About going to Key West."

"And what is that dear?"

"William asked if it is alright with us, that we stay at his house instead of a hotel!"

"He said for us to stay at his families home in Key West?"

"Yes mother. Isn't that just truly wonderful. At his home rather than a hotel."

"That is very nice dear. Have you seen his families home?"

"No mother I have not, but I have been in their summer home."

"And mother their summer home is breathtaking. I can only imagine what their real home must look like."

"Well as I said everything the Investigator showed me about his family makes me believe you may have found the one."

"I will take the G-5 from here to Columbus and then we can fly directly to the Key West airport. You will need to make sure there is someone there pick us and our bags up."

"Yes mother. I will make sure William has that taken care of for us. I will call you in a day or so to let you know all the plans."

Chapter 56

With finals done, it is time for Boner to start packing the Thing for the trip to the Keys. For Boner, he's been homesick for a while, missing the blue turquoise waters and the sweet salt smell of the islands.

Because he doesn't know when or if JR will return for a visit, Boner hires a cleaning crew to make the home look the same as he found it when he arrived.

But before he leaves Boner must make a trip to Wal-Mart. Over the past several months he's grown to really like this store. This time the trip it to make some type of top for the Thing.

It isn't bad going on the short trips around Columbus. But going sixty-five miles per hour on the Interstate, in winter, with no top or windows, is another story.

It is December third and Boner has already said goodbye to the crowds at Pete's place. He has the Thing packed and ready to go.

The blue tarp top is bungeed onto the Thing and plastic sheeting covers the doors. It may not look good but it gets the job done. Or so Boner hopes.

"Have you heard from Boner yet?" Red Stripe asks White Boots.

"Yep. He called yesterday. Looks like he'll be driving back instead of flying. Should be here in a couple of days."

"He's driving? Not in the Thing again?"

"Yeah, he said he's been working on it. Fixing some things and making some changes."

"Don't take this wrong boss, but the Thing is ok for the rock but another long drive? Is it safe?"

"I know. But Boner has a good head and if he says it will make it, well than I have to trust he knows what he's doing."

"Any idea of when he will arrive?"

"No, not yet. He's suppose to call me while he is on the road."

Boner wants to hear some new Trop Rock on the drive down. So he is going to use the laptop the school gave him. He is using an air card in the laptop. And with a twelve volt adapter he is able to keep the laptop turned on. He even setup the laptop's speakers to play thru the cars radio speakers.

Before leaving out of the driveway he fires up the laptop. Connecting to the Internet he opens his web browser to www.tropreock1290.com .

With Chris Rehm's "Key West Blues" playing on the station, Boner starts up the ramp to the interstate.

Excited, he cranks up the sound and starts beating the steering wheel keeping time to the Trop Rock music of the islands.

Boner is not wanting to pack and unpack the Thing after installing his new top. So instead of stopping at motels, he plans on driving straight through, only taking naps in the car.

Once Boner exits the Interstate in Florida City, he knows he's almost home. As he heads down the eighteen mile stretch his body starts to relax. It is nice to slow down, as the speed limit is now forty-five instead of sixty-five.

Passing through a few bare spots in the road known as Key Largo and Rock Harbor, his smile is growing even bigger on his face.

Getting hungry, Boner decides to stop at the Lorelei Restaurant & Cabana Bar in Islamorada located at mile marker eighty-two.

The view at the Lorelei tells him he is indeed on his way home. From the boats anchored out, to the dinghies and skiffs with their painters tied to the dock. He can feel the lifestyle of the Keys he's missed.

After a slow enjoyable lunch Boner pays his tab and heads back out onto the Overseas Highway. Only a mile or so later the traffic comes to a slow crawl. Seems like every tourist is heading to Key West. After all, who wants to spend their vacation in freezing cold when they can enjoy the Florida sunshine.

For Boner going slow is fine as he gets to think about his Keys and how he has missed them. He keeps thinking about the saying his dad always tells him. "Son, don't ever leave the rock."

Boner is only about sixty-five miles from home, but with the heavy traffic from the tourists, Christmas Breakers and the locals, he knows it will be late when he gets home. So instead of driving the last sixty or so miles in two to four hours of heavy traffic, Boner decides to stop by Boot Key Harbor in Marathon.

Boner has been there a few times to listen to a few of the local bands. But he never stayed more then a few hours and then returned home.

A lot of people think everyone drinks all day and night in the Keys due to all the Bars and music. What they don't know is these Tiki bars are not for heavy drinking. At least not for the locals. These bars are the local's living rooms and meeting places.

The Tiki bars are a place where the locals come after a hard days work and talk about their day. They catch up on the gossip and happenings of the Keys.

In the morning hours you will find the locals drinking their coffee, just as you will find people on the mainland sitting in a Perkins, Starbucks or Dunkin Donuts.

Although Boner plays for months at Pete's Place, he never understands why people only come in during the late afternoon and evening just to drink.

Turning off the Overseas Highway onto Sombrero Boulevard, Boner is heading to Boot Key Harbor and the Dockside Bar and Marina.

He checks into a room at the Sombrero Resort just a short walk from Dockside. And because he doesn't want to leave all of his things unattended, it takes him almost an hour just to unpack the Thing.

Chapter 57

It is Taco Tuesday and Dockside is packed with locals, tourists and snowbirds. The one man band has yet to start playing. But with fifty cent tacos and dollar beers, it seems like everyone in Marathon is there.

Lucky for Boner, the picnic table at the entrance next to the kitchen is empty. While most of the other tables closer to the stage are taken. The crowd ranges in age from the mid-twenties to over sixty. All the people are there to socialize and have fun.

Boner is sitting at the table for a minute or so when he notices some excitement out on the back dock and in the parking lot.

There in the parking lot is a rather small flat-bed truck with what appears to be a makeshift crane. It looks like they are getting ready to lift a wooden crate of some type.

He sees the workers struggling with their crowbars and mallets. They are trying to strip away the sides of the crate. Opening the crate, they reveal a large new diesel engine.

The small crane looks ready to lift the engine. The workers will be moving the engine from the parking lot across the wooden dock and onto the waiting boat.

He watches the men shouting at one another on how to lift the engine. Then, looking to where the makeshift crane is pointing, he sees another man standing on the deck of a large powerboat waiting for the engine.

There are many sights in the Tiki bars of the Florida Keys. This one might be interesting.

Looking around the restaurant, Boner sees several tables put together making one very large table. Where the locals appear to be sitting. They are far more involved with each other than what is taking place out on the dock.

Boner, wanting a closer look, leaves his table and food. He lets the waitress know he will be right back. He walks down past the long wooden bar and out past the dingy dock. He wants to watch this orchestrated operation.

While he is walking out to the docks, He sees the small crane starting to lift the engine over the wooden dock. With a loud snap, the cable holding the engine breaks.

The brand new engine slams onto the dock. The planking of the dock is unable to absorb the blow and breaks. Boner watches as the engine falls and splashes into the harbor's water below.

Once the large splash is over, there is silence. Everyone is in disbelief. They are looking at the hole in the dock and a brand new diesel engine sitting on the bay bottom.

Then as one starts, there is another, then another and within a minute or so everyone is laughing. Once the shock and laugher subsides the workers start scurrying around the boat, the dock and the hole like ants searching for food.

With the excitement over, Boner returns to the picnic table and his tacos.

Looking down at his tacos, Boner sees there is a big bite out of one of his Tacos. He starts looking around the tables and the people nearby. No one is looking his way and all of them have their own Tacos.

Then looking over at the grill shack, he sees the cook pointing to somewhere behind him. Turning around Boner sees a man getting on his bike. One look at the man's bike and you know he is either homeless or an eco-tourist, as the bike is piled high with packs.

Boner starts to get up from his table to say something but the man using the leg strength of Lance Armstrong is far down the road by the time Boner is able get his legs from under the table.

He looks at the Cook. Who only laughs and shrugs his shoulders. Making Boner join in his laughter.

Boner is beat from another long day. He wants badly to get a good nights sleep before he arrives home tomorrow morning. But this being his first time at Dockside, he also wants to listen to some of the music he has only heard about from others.

Chapter 58

As Boner leaves Marathon he crosses over the seven mile bridge. Just as he starts crossing the bridge the Trop Rock station plays Chris Rehm's "My Little Island Town" . A smile grows on Boner's face as he listens and looks out across Florida Bay.

Coming into Big Pine Key, Boner remembers to slow down to thirty-five miles per hour after coming off the Seven Mile bridge. As he is looking at his speedometer the Florida Highway Patrol Officer is checking his radar.

With a knowing smile exchanged between him and the Officer, Boner has his sights set on Stock Island.

Boner will be in the Keys long before Splender-sky and her mother arrive on their the jet.

As Boner is driving through Big Pine, White Boots is having breakfast with Red Stripe at Moms.

"I just heard from Boner and looks like he'll be in sometime around midday or so." White Boots tells Babs and Red Stripe while she is taking their orders.

"Today? You'll come in for breakfast in the morning, right?"

Laughing, White Boots tells her "Of course. You know Boner won't miss your breakfast."

"So boss, I'm guessing we won't be going out in the morning?"

White Boots chuckles. "No, not tomorrow. I want to give the day and of course the night to Boner."

"I can't wait to take him up to Charlotte Harbor and show him what we found."

"Figured out what you're going to do with the boats yet?"

"No, not unless you want to buy them and the traps."

Red Stripe laughs. "Me? No I'm too old for running things. I just like to make a little money and play my guitar."

"Well I better get going. I don't know what time he'll arrive and I want to be there."

Once back at the marina White Boots is pacing like a father in a delivery waiting room. He hasn't seen Boner in almost four months.

Chapter 59

Meanwhile on Nancy's G-5, flying over the Gulf of Mexico heading towards Key West, Splender-sky is also excited.

"Mother, I can not wait to see William's family home."

"The Pilot says we will be landing in another twenty minutes."

"I know Mother. Isn't it exciting. I have never been to the Keys, have you?

"No darling. I never have a need to come here. But I hear it is wonderful."

The Co-Pilot tells them "Ladies, please fasten your seat belts. We will be landing shortly."

"Oh Mother, look at the water and the islands. This is so beautiful."

"Yes. It does looks like paradise. Maybe I should buy a winter home here."

"Well if everything works out, William will ask me to marry him and we will have a winter home here, his." Splender-sky tells her mother.

Landing at the Key West Airport, the small jet taxies on the tarmac up to the terminal building.

Splender-sky's mother asks "Is William picking us up or sending a car?"

"No. For some reason he said it is best to call Key Lime Taxi and they will know where to go."

Outside the terminal they locate the Key Lime Taxi. Splender-sky walks over and asks the driver if he knows where they are going.

"This is the address. Do you know where this is?"

"Yes Ma'am. In fact I have been expecting you. Let me get your bags."

"You have expected us?"

"Yes. Boner told us you would be coming in and we should take good care of you and your mother."

"Mother, William did have someone waiting for us after all."

Smiling, Nancy tells her "Ok, show him where our bags are please."

"Miss, that is alot of luggage, I don't know if they will all fit. I may have to place some on the roof."

Nancy tells the driver "Well, we expected a much larger car. But if you must put them on the roof, please be careful."

"Yes Ma'am. It's a very short drive. It will only take about five minutes or so. Will you be staying long?"

"We will be staying for a few days. Christmas you know."

"Oh yes Ma'am. No better place to spend Christmas than in the islands. Here let me get that door for you and we'll be off."

As the driver leaves out of the airport and turns on to A1A, Nancy remarks "There appears to be a lot of quant little houses mixed in with new buildings."

"Yes Ma'am we try and keep the homes we grew up in."

"Mother look at the water."

"Oh I hope William's home has this type of view."

"View. Boner's place has a great view. Its on the water." The taxi driver tells them.

"Mother it is on the water!" Splender-sky exclaims.

"I take it, this is your first time in the island?"

"Yes. We are from the Napa Valley." Nancy tells the driver.

"Well I hope you enjoy your stay. We are a very laidback and relaxed people. We don't care for big city things. It is the water that drives our soul."

Nancy and Splender-sky just look at each other not understanding what the driver is talking about.

Pulling up to the front gate of the marina the driver tells them "Ok ladies here you are."

"Here we are where?" Nancy asks the driver.

Opening his door and getting out of the taxi tells them "This is the marina. I'll get your bags out for you."

Nancy looks at her daughter. Splender-sky looks at her mother.
Neither one able to say anything.

As Splender-sky opens her door she and her mother are greeted with
the sights, sounds and smells of a working commercial fishermen's
marina. The smells of the salt air mixed with the smell of fish and
sweat.

Standing in the road, Nancy holds her credit card in her hand. As the
taxi driver takes the card out of her hand she still does not utter a
word.

Splender-sky is also silent. Not a word being said between them.

After Nancy signs for the cab fare, the driver backs into a driveway
turns his cab around and heads back to the airport.

There they are. Two women standing in the center of the road with
ten to twelve pieces of luggage between them. In a strange town and
no one around except the seagulls cawing at them.

Looking at each other, Splender-sky asks Nancy "Now what do we
do Mother?"

"You do have William's phone number, don't you?"

"Well yes."

"Then why don't you call him dear?"

"Mother, I'm afraid."

"Splender-sky, just give William a call. Let us hear what he has to say."

While Splender-sky is calling Boner, Nancy is taking in their surroundings. It is nothing even close to what she is expecting. The sounds of the birds and a salt smell she is not accustomed to, not in Napa Valley.

"William, this is Splender-sky, please call me when you get this message. Where are you? Call me!" She tells the voice mail.

"I left him a voice mail. Mother what are we going to do?"

Chapter 60

Looking down the road from where they came, Nancy sees a raggy old man sitting on a crate. "Maybe you should ask that, that gentleman where William's house may be located." Nancy tells Splender-sky.

"Mother! No, I can not just walk up to that, that man."

Starting to get frustrated, Nancy takes matters into her own hands.

"Sir, excuse me. Sir." Nancy yells down to the man.

"I don't think he can hear you mother."

"Sir! Hello Sir!" Nancy yells louder.

"Maybe he is deaf mother." Splender-sky says.

"Well we will not just stand here. Lets walk towards him." Her mother tells her.

While walking towards the man, Nancy keeps yelling at him. But he doesn't look up. Nancy keeps trying to get his attention, yelling more, as they get closer to him.

Now no more than ten feet away from the man, Nancy angrily asks "Have you heard me yelling at you?"

The man slowly looking up, meets Nancy's eyes.

"I asked you a question, Did you hear me yelling at you?"

"Lady, do you see a chain on my neck?" The man asks Nancy.

"No, but what…"

Interrupting her "Do you see a plate of food at my feet?" He asks her.

"Well no, but as I…"

Again cutting her off, the man asks her "Then lady, why do you think you have a right to yell at me like some dog? Do you always treat people like that? Or is it just because you think I am below you, uneducated, broke and homeless?"

"Is that what you think?" He asks her.

Taken back, at the man's directness and soft tone, Nancy is speechless.

"Well lady? You did hear and understand the question didn't you?

Having time to regroup, Nancy starts in on him. "How dare you talk to…"

Cutting her off again, he too starts in on her. "How dare me? Lady you are the one who is yelling at me. Like I am some form of animal you are calling. That is not how we address people here in the Keys."

He continues "We expect you to bring your manners with you when you visit here. Now I must ask, did you leave your manners at home or do you not have any?"

Nancy is taken back again. She is a powerful person. No one talks to her in that way. With her anger now building Nancy looks at him and tells Splender-sky "Come darling. This man is of no help." And turns to walk back down the street to their luggage.

"Are you looking for Boner?" Red Stripe asks them as they are turning to leave.

Stopping in their tracks. Both women turn and look at each other. To Red Stripe seconds feel like minutes as he turns back to his work.

Seconds go by as Nancy tries to decide her response.

Splender-sky wanting to see Boner tells her mother "Please, talk to him. He knows William."

"Yes, dear, but how did he know we are looking for him?" She asks her daughter.

Slowly turning around, Nancy walks back towards Red Stripe. Except this time she has changed her attitude.

"Sir, I am so sorry for yelling at you. Even though we have come a long way and we are very tired, that is no excuse. And I am sorry."

Thinking for a minute Red Stripe again asks her "Are you looking for Boner?"

"Yes. Yes, we are looking for Boner, I mean William. Does he live near here?" Splender-sky asks him.

"Yes. Boner lives near here."

"Will you please tell us where or how we may find him?" Nancy asks him.

"Well, first things first. You may want to move your bags inside the marina, else someone may start tossing trash bags on the pile."

"Trash bags?"

"Yes Ma'am, Trash bags. You see when people see a pile like that, it usually means its put out to be given away or to be picked up by the trash truck."

"Surely you are kidding."

"Miss, I don't know you. Why would I kid you?" Red Stripe asks her.

"Fine, we will do that. Will you please tell us how to find William? Nancy inquires.

Red Stripe showing the patience of a Keys local, slowly puts down his project and stands up. "Lets first move your bags inside the marina." He tells them.

Still leery of this bearded man, but Nancy and Splender-sky agree and all three walk to their bags and follow Red Stripe inside the marina, placing their luggage in the location he shows them.

Turning back to Red Stripe Nancy asks "Ok, now will you please tell us how to locate Mr. Morgan?"

"Well Mr. Morgan is down on his boat. But Boner isn't here. He'll be back in a few minutes or so."

Nancy, looks between Splender-sky and Red Stripe "Ok, just so we understand. Mr. Morgan, Mr. Morgan is William's father. And William, Boner will be here shortly."

Red Stripe laughs "By golly, you got it."

"Well then, is there somewhere we can wait for William?

"Sure. Just a second." Red Stripe tell her.

Red Stripe walks over to an area beside the dock office and grabs a gray navy horse blanket.

Placing the blanket over some old crab traps Red Stripe tells them "There you go. You can sit there if you want."

"Nancy looks at Red Stripe then Splender-sky and back at Red Stripe.

An indigent Nancy asks "You expect us to sit on that?"

Smiling at her Red Stripe says "No Ma'am. You can just stand there, if you like."

Nancy is now beside herself. She left her Vineyard on her G-5 private jet and now is expected to sit on a nasty old blanket, that only God knows what has been on it. And to sit on it over a pair of wooden crates that smell like dead fish.

Nancy can only think, things can not get worse.

First two minutes, then five minutes and another five minutes go by. Then fifteen minutes.

"Please call William again!" Nancy now instructs her daughter.

"Yes mother. I have been texting him."

Nancy says "Well?"

Splender-sky with a sheepish reply, lowers her head and tells Nancy "William has not responded yet."

Finally, after almost an hour, Boner drives up in the Thing.

Chapter 61

Seeing Boner it is all Nancy can do to control her emotions.

She understands this is the man or boy her daughter may marry and she does not want to take that wealth away from her. Nor the happiness which will come with the money of course.

Splender-sky walks over to Boner as he gets out of the car greeting him with a hug and a few words.

"William, why didn't you return my phone calls or my texts to you?"

Hugging Boner, Splender-sky whispers into his ear "Mother is very upset. You do not want mother upset do you? You know if mother is upset I am upset. Now you need to apologize to her."

Sternly, Nancy tells Boner "William, we have been waiting for you."

Pointing down the road to Red Stripe, She tells Boner "You see where that man down there put our luggage."

"And he had the nerve to want us to sit there." She tells him, now pointing to the crab traps with the blanket laying over them.

"Miss Bonito, Splender-sky, I'm sorry. I wasn't expecting you until tomorrow. I didn't get your calls because my phone is turned off."

In disbelief Nancy states "Your phone is turned off."

Boner, starting to feel a little defensive tells her "Yes Ma'am. I use it to make calls, not to take calls. So it's turned off when I don't need it."

"William, mother and I have had a long flight. Will you please take us to your home so we may freshen up."

"Sure, lets take a walk and I'll come back for the bags."

"Take a walk? Come back for our luggage? William I don't understand." Splender-sky tells him.

"Miss Bonito, Splender-sky, please." Boner gestures with his hand. "Come with me."

As they start walking down the dock, Splender-sky asks "Do you know that homeless person out on the street?"

"Homeless person. What homeless person? We have a lot of people without homes in the Keys. But it's the way they like it. Living under the palm trees on the beach or in the Mangroves. They like being free."

"William, I mean the man who helped us bring our luggage inside the marina."

"Oh, you mean Red Stripe. He's not homeless. He works with my dad."

"Works with your father. You mean that man has a real job and at your father's company?" Nancy asks Boner.

"Yes Miss Bonito. Red Stripe has worked for my father for as long as I can remember."

"Well William it would be real nice if we could go to your home and freshen up." Nancy tells Boner.

"Splender-sky said the same thing so that's what we're doing." Boner tells her.

As Boner stops between his dad's crab boat and the houseboat, Splender-sky asks "Where are we going William? I don't want to be on this smelly dock anymore."

Looking up to the pilot house on his dad's crab boat, Boner yells out "Hey Dad, they're here early. Come on and meet Splender-sky and her mom."

"Your father?" Both Nancy and Splender-sky say at once.

Nancy says "Your father must be a real hands on owner."

"Hands on?" Boner questions.

"Yes, hands on. I mean for the owner of a company to come down to the docks to check on his boats and workers. Are all these boats your fathers?" Nancy asks Boner.

Boner gesturing to the houseboat and the crab boat, tells her "Oh no Ma'am. My dad only has these two."

Splender-sky hesitantly asks Boner "Where does he keep his other boats?"

"Other boats? What other boats. All we have are these two."

"But your father owns a seafood company." Nancy states.

"A seafood company?" now Boner doesn't understand.

"Yes, we were told your father owns a seafood company." Both the women blurt out.

"No this is it. My dad is a crabber. He works our crab traps with this boat and I used to live on the houseboat, but dads been living on it while I am at school."

Looking at Splender-sky, Nancy states "I think we have been mislead."

"No mother. Something is not right. This can not be. It can't!"

"Wait, let us ask his father."

"Hello ladies. Excuse me for not shaking your hands but as you can see." White Boots says showing them his hands covered with grease from the boats diesel engine.

Nancy asks "You are William's father?"

"Yes Ma'am. That's my boy. Boner hasn't told me much about you. Other than you all are from the Napa Valley."

"Mr. Morgan, I, we, don't mean to be rude, but our family was under the impression you owned a seafood company in Key West. And now William is telling us the only, company you own it this crab boat."

"A seafood company." He laughs. "Now who in the world is telling you that? I know Boner didn't."

"We had you investigated." Nancy blurts out without thinking.

While still wiping his greasy hand with his rag, he asks "You did what? Why?"

White Boots is confused. "Boner, you mind telling me what's going on."

Looking at his dad then back and forth between the ladies. "I don't know dad. What is your mom talking about?" He directs his question to Splender-sky.

"William…", she starts.

Being interrupted by her mother. "Mr. Morgan, William tells us this is your home." Nancy says pointing to the houseboat.

"Well yes Ma'am. That's our home."

Nancy asks White Boots "Mr. Morgan I think there has been a terrible mistake. Is this where we are expected to stay?"

"Well yes Ma'am." He tells her, not understanding what she is trying to say to him.

In a very pointed manner Nancy states "This is your home. This is your only home."

White Boots with a huge smile tells her "Yep that's it. Better than you expected hun?"

With Nancy now in shock, Boner tells them "I'll go get the dock cart and get your bags."

"NO!" Nancy exclaims.

"No?" Comes Boner's reply.

"William there is some type of mistake." Splender-sky says.

"Mistake?, I don't understand. What do you mean a mistake?"

"William, mother and I thought you, I mean your father had, had…" She says stumbling over her words.

"Had what? Splender-sky, Ms. Bonito?"

"William, Mr. Morgan, I am sorry but I need a moment with my daughter." She tells them, while taking Splender-sky's hand leading her towards the dock house.

"Boner, what's going on?" His dad asks.

"I don't know dad."

"This is your girlfriend, you should know something."

"No dad. She's not my girlfriend. We are just friends at school, nothing more."

"She's not your girlfriend?"

"No Sir. Bait is more of a girlfriend than Splender-sky."

"Well they don't seem too happy about something. Have they ever been to the Keys before?"

"No Sir, I don't think so."

Chapter 62

While Boner and his dad are trying to figure out what just happened, Nancy is on her cell phone with the Private Detective she hired to investigate Boner and his father.

"Listen to me, I pay you to do what I want, not what you think!" Nancy tells the detective. "You told me this boy's father owns his own seafood company and had property, a home, in Key West." She continues on.

"Now you tell me what is going on!" She demands to know.

"Miss Bonito, according to the report I gave you, Mr. Morgan owns and runs a crabbing business."

"A crabbing business! He owns a single boat. No correct that, he owns two boats. One crab boat and a small derelict houseboat he lives on! Now you explain how you missed that please." She asks the detective.

"Miss Bonito…"

"Don't you Miss Bonito me. I am not looking at a wealthy business owner! I am looking at some Florida Keys local! What did I pay you for? My daughter can not be seen with these people. And now they want us to sleep, sleep on these, these things."

Living a life of status and standing, Nancy is beside herself. She does not understand how people in the Keys do not care about a person's status and standing .

Nancy is expecting a rich catch for her and her daughter with a huge home on the ocean. What she is getting is a taste of the true local flavor of the Keys.

A local flavor where the people care about the hearts of people, not their money. To the locals, your heart tells your wealth, not your bank account.

While Nancy is on the phone, Boner sees Red Stripe coming into the marina with his guitar. So Boner goes and retrieves his guitar from the houseboat.

"What's going on with those two?" Red Stripe asks Boner and his dad.

"I honestly don't know Red." White Boots tell him, while Boner tunes his guitar.

"Well, looks like you're ready to play some." Red Stripe says to Boner.

"Oh you know me. I'm always ready to play."

So with Boner and Red Stripe sitting and playing, White Boots goes back to his work, telling Boner "Call me when they come back."

Again minutes turn from three to five, then fifteen minutes go by as Boner watches the women talking and making gestures with their hands and arms.

When Nancy and Splender-sky walk back, Nancy is speaking as though she has walked into a foreign country.

"I am so sorry. It appears there's been a terrible mistake. Seems as though we are suppose to be at an important meeting. Some how it did not make it on my calendar. I know you will understand." Nancy is telling Boner.

"I, I'm sorry? Did I miss something? Splender-sky, what is your mom talking about?"

"It is as mother said. We have an important meeting. It is something completely forgotten about and we must attend. But thankfully mother flew us in on her plane so we will not miss it."

Boner looks over to Red Stripe and sees Red shrug his shoulders, as if to tell him he didn't know what they are talking about either.

"Splender-sky, I still don't understand a word of what you're saying."

Nancy bluntly tells Boner. "William, what my daughter is saying, is that we can not stay and must leave to return to a meeting."

Perplexed, Boner asks "You're not staying?"

Nancy firmly states "Yes, William we are leaving. As I said, there was a mistake."

"A Mistake?"

"Yes, William a mistake." Nancy affirms, glancing around the dock.

Boner now asks, putting Nancy and Splender-sky on the spot. "Miss Bonito, why do I feel like you were expecting something different? There is no meeting is there?"

"William, my daughter..." Nancy starts to say..

Boner challenges her "Your daughter. This isn't about your daughter. You thought I was rich! Didn't you? You thought my dad had money."

Butting in, Red Stripe tells them "Ladies, the Keys isn't about money. It's about loving life and being happy with just being yourself."

"And what would you know?" Nancy says trying to belittle Red Stripe.

"I know it appears you two do not understand the Keys and who we are." Replies Red Stripe, watching a limo driver retrieve the ladies bags.

Seeing the driver as well, Nancy tells him "Well maybe you are correct. Splender-sky, say goodbye to your, your friends and meet me in the car."

With Nancy turning and walking way, Red Stripe calls out to her "Miss Bonito."

Stopping and turning around "Yes."

"We may not be what or who you expected, but there is one thing you should know."

Defiantly she asks "And what would that be?'

"This is the islands. People come here to leave the world behind. Here, we find our wealth with the ocean breeze, and from the warmth of sun to our starlit nights. In the Keys, we seek the freedom to relax without all the pretences of the mainland." Red Stripe tells her.

Without a reply Nancy turns and walks to the waiting limo.

"William, I don't know what to say."

"Its ok, I think I now understand."

With the corners of her mouth turned up, she simply says "Goodbye William."

As everyone watches, Splender-sky walks to her waiting mother And Red Stripe starts playing;

Dada-dit-dit-dit-dit-dit-dit-dit.

Dada-dit-dit-dit-dit-dit-dit-dit.

And once again the sounds of deliverance fills the air.

Laughing, Boner looks at Red Stripe and says "Well, at least the Houseboat got cleaned."

"Yes Sir, that it did." He replies with a smile.

White Boots crosses over to the finger pier from the crab boat also grinning.

"Well son, where did they go?

"Something about a meeting they forgot about." He tells his father.

White Boots laughs "Oh I'm sure it was or something."

"Dad what are you talking about?"

"Lets just say the Island drums are telling all about those two. Not to be concerned."

"You mean the telegraph?" Red Stripe says laughing.

"Yeah, seems those two have been looking for someone with a lot of money for a while."

"Son, they thought the place you were staying in Columbus was mine. They thought I own it. Did you tell them it was our summer home?"

Laughing, Boner tells his dad "I told them it was a summer home. I guess I forgot to tell them it was JR's summer home."

"Well I think its time for lunch. You two want to grab some lunch at Moms?" White Boots asks them.

"Works for me." Boner replies.

"Yep, me too." Replies Red Stripe.

Chapter 63

Over lunch White Boots tells Boner and Red Stripe about his plans for selling the crab boat and moving up to the Charlotte Harbor area just north of Fort Myers.

"So you don't mind leaving the Keys?", Red Stripe asks White Boots.

"I don't want to leave. But with the developers wanting everything what can you do."

Concerned, Red Stripes tells him "Well you know the county is trying to make changes to save the working waterfronts."

"Yeah but our marina isn't considered one. Look, we have had a great time and I don't have any regrets. Besides, I can always take the ferry down from Fort Myers once in a while."

"How about you Boner. What are you going to do?" Red Stripe asks.

"I still haven't decided yet."

"Morning Babs. How's life treating you this morning?" White Boots asks her, as she arrives at the table.

"Be doing better if I knew how I am going to keep the place open."

"We see the truck is still blocking you from the road"

"Yeah, that is really cutting down on people seeing me. I've still got the locals, but without the tourists coming in, its making it hard."

After Babs takes their orders and returns to the kitchen they are still talking about the restaurant, the developer's truck and the truck's huge sign on the adjacent property.

Seems the developer put the large sign on the truck and parked it on the adjacent lot to drive Babs out of business. Then the developer can buy the restaurant for pennies.

The restaurant sits on a parcel that has frontage on U.S.1, the Overseas Highway. And then she has another ten acres that run across the back of the lot where the restaurant sits. Making her property an L shape with the short side of the L facing the highway.

The developer has his truck on the lot next door to the restaurant. One side of the vacant lot sides with the restaurant and the back of the rear of vacant lot butts up to the restaurant's property in the rear. The developer wants it all.

"I'd like to help Babs but with me moving off the rock, it will be hard." White Boots comments.

"Decided where you going to move yet?" Red Stripe asks him.

"I tend to like it up there at the Desoto Marina. You know the place. Its part of the Nav-A-Gator Grill up on the Peace River." White boots replies.

"Why do you like it there?" Boner asks his dad.

"Well son, even though its old Florida, which I really like, its just a stones throw from the Gulf of Mexico. And if I want something more, Fishermen's Village is just a few miles down river."

"Hey Babs, what was all that shooting we were hearing last night?" White Boots yells back towards the kitchen.

"Shooting?"

"Yeah, all that gunfire we heard. Sounded like a war going on for an hour or so." Boner pipes in.

"Oh that. We were hunting those spiny-tails."

"What are you doing shooting lobster?" Red Stripe asks her.

"Not lobster Red, those spiny-tailed Iguanas. We got fifty-two of them last night. I was going to put them on the dinner menu tonight."

"Was?" White Boots questions.

Babs laughs "Yeah, they should have used pellet guns for the hunt."

"Pellet guns. What were they using?"

"Bobby had a Mossberg and his snot face son had an AK47. Darn meat is so mangled couldn't even make soup." Babs tells them.

"So what did you do with them?" Red Stripe asks her.

"Using them as bait in the crab traps. Those boys shot off so many rounds they even took out all my hibiscus and my vegetable garden.

Take a look out back, isn't nothing but darn shell casings" She tells them.

"Sorry Babs. But you should know better with those two. I don't think they have a full brain between them." White Boots replies.

"You think that's bad. They went crabbing last year and rather than tying the chicken on the string, they tied the chicken parts to their shorts. Lord you should have heard them scream when those crab pinchers took hold." Babs said, laughing all the way back to the kitchen.

White Boots is laughing so hard he almost chokes on his food.

Red Stripes laughs "Guess that explains why those boys are out there with shovels and rakes. They're getting all that lead out of the soil"

"I got a man coming to look at the crab boat today." White Boots tells them.

"That's a good thing. Specially during the season." Red Stripe replies.

"Yes it is. He says he wants to buy the boat and the traps as a package. And it shouldn't be to hard to find a buyer for the houseboat."

"Well Boner, why don't we sit out and play some while your dad shows the boat." Red Stripe suggests.

"Cool, I'll get my guitar when we get back."

"If he buys the boat, how long before you'll be moving to Charlotte Harbor?" Red Stripe asks.

"If... If he buys it, I'll be moving up slowly, starting right after Christmas. And he'll take possession just after New Years. That way I don't have to rush and it gives me time to find a live aboard boat up there." Replies White Boots.

"So you haven't decided where you going to call home, yet?" Red Stripe asks him.

"Like I said, I'm still looking. But I really do like it up at the Desoto Marina and the Nav-A-Gator Grill." White Boots tells him again.

"I do know I'll end up staying at either Burnt Store Marina, Fishermen's Village or there at the Desoto Marina for a while. They have everything a person can want.", White Boots says.

Thinking about what White Boots said, Red Stripe responds by telling him "Yes but you know Brunt Store Marina is the largest marina in the area."

"Yes I know. But its only a few miles to the Gulf. Like I said I'm still thinking. I'm not sure yet."

Heading back to the marina Red Stripe starts thinking of ways to help Babs save Moms. And he thinks he can talk Boner into helping him. But that means telling Boner a secret he's been keeping for years.

"Boner, you really want to help Babs save Moms?" Red Stripe asks him.

"Sure. Babs has been like a mom to be. I'll do anything to help her. Why?"

"Well I think I know how together, we can help her."

"We? Together? What do you have in mind?"

"Come this evening, lets take my skiff for a ride and I'll show you." Red Stripe tells him.

Chapter 64

Later that night as the sun sets over the Gulf of Mexico, Boner walks over to Red Stripe's skiff. Red Stripe already has his ninety horse engine warming up, the running lights are on and the fuel tank is full.

"Where we going Red?"

"I rather show you then tell you. Hop in." Red Stripe tells Boner.

"I can't get over how quiet your engine is since you made that cover for it."

Smiling, Red Stripe tells him "Yep. You can walk twenty feet away and not even know its running. Not even when revving it up."

Untying the painter, Boner pushes the bow of the Skiff away from the dock.

Through the darkness, Red Stripe watches the markers leading them out of the Stock Island Channel. With the skiff he doesn't have to worry too much about going aground as they only draw about eighteen inches. And even less once up on plane.

But its not the channel markers he is really watching for, it's the Patrol boats of the FWC, HLS, Customs and the Coast Guard.

This is a run Red Stripe makes three, sometimes four times a week.

After a given point, Red Stripe picks up a heading of one eighty-six and tells Boner to be quiet for while, as their voices will travel and be heard more than the engine.

After about twenty minutes Red Stripes starts to slow down and comes off plane. He allows the skiff to settle in the waters, lightly rolling with the swells.

"What's going on?" Boner asks him.

"Shh." Red Stripe says, raising his hand to stop Boner from talking.

"Red" Boner starts, but Red Stripe again raises his hand to quiet him.

Red Stripe is listening. He is listening to the sounds of the night, in between the swells lapping the skiff's hull. He is seeking any noise that does not belong to the water.

After about ten minutes of sitting in the open waters, Red Stripe tells Boner "Ok, now you can talk. I have to listen to hear if there is anyone around."

Boner laughs "Anyone around? Red, we're in the middle of the Atlantic Ocean. Who are you expecting to be around?"

"Son , its not funny. There are a lot of people who want what I'm going to show you. So, I have to make sure no one is following us and we have to keep a watch out for the Coasties."

"Ok then. How much further are we going to go?"

"Not long. Maybe another ten minutes or so. Lets get her back up on plane." And with that Red Stripe has the engine back at full throttle.

Then, just as fast as they cut through the swells, Red Stripe slows the skiff's engine and raises his hand, pointing to the outline of an island just yards ahead of them.

"Here we are." Red Stripe tells Boner.

"And just where is here?" Boner asks him.

Reaching the island, Red Stripe tells Boner "Here, take the painter and tie it around one of those Mangrove roots."

"Ok now what?" Boner asks him.

"Follow me."

Boner tripping, asks Red Stripe "Red, what are all these metal signs?"

"Those. Oh I put them in years ago to keep out snoopers. I bought them cheap at an Army Surplus store. See. Danger Unexploded Ordnance. Danger Live Fire Zone."

Laughing, Boner asks "Ok, so why are you keeping people off the island?"

"You'll see. Just follow me on this path through the mangroves. There is another way in, but it's on the other side of the island and this way is a little quicker."

Following Red Stripe through the Mangroves Boner starts to wonder what did he get himself into this time.

"Watch your step Boner." Red Stripe tells him, as they exit the root barriers of the Mangrove and come into a clearing.

"Wait a second. Just stand there while I get the lights."

"Get the what?" Boner asking in disbelief.

"The lights. Just wait a minute." Then a few second later, there is now a soft glow running the inside line of the Mangroves and outlining what appears to be an old potters barn.

In amazement, Boner now asks "What is this Red?"

"Its how we are going to save Moms. Come on I'll show you."

As Boner walks behind, following Red Stripe, he sees row after row of Key Lime trees lit by the soft glow from the twelve volt LED lights.

Unlocking the door to the shed, Red Stripe holds the door open. "Go on in nothing is going to bite you."

Entering the shed, Boner's eyes look upon shelf after shelf after shelf of bottles. Walking over to one of the shelves Boner takes a bottle and reads the label. It reads, "Red's Real Key Lime Juice"

"You make this?", Boner asks Red Stripe.

"Yes sir. Every bottle."

"But how? Why?"

"I've been bottling Key Lime juice for the past eight, no make that nine years now. I've got a web site and even sell it on Amazon and through EBay. It's been a great little business."

"Now I understand why you want to keep people away from here. But how is this going to save Moms?.

"Take a seat and I'll explain."

Chapter 65

So over the next few hours Red Stripe tells Boner of his plan and what he has done about it in the past few days.

"I was able to locate the owner of the property next to Moms. You know, where the developer has that truck sitting. They told me there is a tax lien on the property because they can't afford to pay the property tax. Then they tell me the developer offered to buy the land, but they didn't want the property developed. So they told them no."

"Red, I still don't understand. How does all this help Babs?"

"I told the owners of the property what the developer is doing and they are outraged. So I asked them, seeing as how they are going to lose the property anyway, would they be willing to give it to Babs if she promised not to develop it."

"And?"

"They said sure. Anything to keep it away from developers. Here, read this." Red Stripe says, handing Boner a piece of paper.

"They gave you the Deed to the property?"

"Sure did. And this paper assigns the property to Babs."

"What about the back taxes?"

"I took care of those this morning using some of the profits from selling the Key Lime juice."

"Ok, so that will get the truck off the property, but Babs is still having a hard time with all the tourists staying in Key West and the locals being pushed out."

Red Stripe started telling Boner more of the plan to save Moms and once Boner heard it he is all in.

Leaving the island, Boner still finds it hard to believe no one has found out what Red Stripe is doing. But now he understands why he made the skiff so quite and is watchful when going to and from this island in the middle of nowhere.

Chapter 66

The next day, Red Stripe using the newly recorded Deed calls Dave's Wrecker Service. Dave is hired to remove the developer's truck and take it to the storage yard. And to ensure there is no problem, Red Stripe calls the Monroe County Sheriff's Office to have a Deputy standing by.

At first the Deputy tells Red Stripe he can not remove the developer's truck. Then Red Stripe produces the Deed to the property and after a quick review the Deputy grins and allows Dave to remove the truck with it's large sign.

With the truck being removed from private property by the owner of the property, all Dave has to do is report he towed it. And that it is being stored in the tow yard.

For the developer, the days go by without them even knowing their truck is in storage. In storage, where the fees are adding up by the hour.

Babs never heard the truck being towed as she lives in the far backside of the restaurant. She does not notice the truck gone until the next morning when she opens the restaurant for breakfast.

At breakfast, Babs is asking everyone if they know what happened to the truck with the large sign. Even the Deputies are shaking their heads that they don't know either.

"Hey Babs, a man called me the other day about saving the old Keys. He is talking about preserving the keys way of life for future generations and such." Red Stripe tells Babs.

"That will be real good. Someone needs to help us. What's his name." She asks.

Red Stripe tells her "Johnson, they call him Outboard Johnson."

"I told him how Moms is hurting right now due to the locals leaving and the tourists not knowing how great the food is. He said he'd like to meet you."

"He did? He would? Did he say how he is going help?"

"No. He wants to talk to you though." Replies Red Stripe.

"So when is he going to be coming?"

"Well see, that's a problem. He is in Miami. He said he wants you to come up there for a day . To see how the two of you can work together."

"But I haven't been to Miami in over thirty-five years. And besides, I can't just close the restaurant."

"You won't have to close it up. Boner will be here to cook and Bait says we'll be happy to wait on the customers if it will help save the restaurant." Red Stripe tells her.

"Well how would I get up there? I don't drive."

"Babs, you know us locals stick together. Taxi Jim said he'll drive you up, wait as long as it takes and bring you back. All you have to do is listen to the man and see if there is something you two can do together." Red Stripe tells her with a huge smile.

"And besides, Taxi Jim has a cell phone. So if you are needed he can just turn around and bring you back." Boner adds.

Not wanting to lose the restaurant, Babs says "Ok I'll do it. When can I see him?"

In order to get Babs to go on the right day, Red Stripe makes it sound as if Mr. Johnson is very busy and had to clear his calendar just for the meeting with her.

"He is tied up most days. But he made special arrangements to see you on Christmas Eve. He cleared his whole calendar and moved everything around just for you."

"He must be an important person to be so busy." Babs replies.

"He is but he really wants to save a part of Keys history." Red Stripe tells her.

"Ok. Ok. I'll do it. I'll do just about anything to save Moms." She tells Red Stripe and Boner.

Red Stripe and Boner are putting the plan in motion. With Babs away from the restaurant they will be able to carry out the rest of it.

Just then one of the developers employees comes bursting in the door mad as hell.

"Where's our truck?", he demands to know.

"Simmer down there buddy." Babs tells him.

"Simmer down my foot! What did you do with our truck?", he again demands to know.

"Mister if you lost a truck, that's not my problem." She replies.

"It sure as hell is your problem lady. You took our truck and we want it back. Now!"

As the man is yelling at Babs, the two deputies start to get up from their table, but Babs motions them to stay seated.

She calmly asks him "Mister. do you see a truck in here? Did you see me take your truck?"

He yells at her "No lady! But I know it was you!"

Babs is now laughing. "Ok, so let me understand you. You lost your truck. You don't know where your truck is. You don't see a truck in here and you didn't see me take your truck. So I can only guess, you must have had one of the telephone psychics tell you they had a vision that I took your truck. Is that right?"

Still yelling at her, he says "Lady I know you have our truck. I'm going to call the Sheriff and have him arrest you!"

At that point, Babs looks over at the Deputies and nods for them to come over. "Maybe these two men can help you with that." She says gesturing to the two Monroe County Deputies walking towards him.

Looking first at the deputies then Babs, the man tells her "Look I don't want no trouble. We just want our truck back."

"Sir, lets talk about your problem outside." One Deputy says, while gesturing towards the door.

With one Deputy leading the way, the man exits the restaurant with the other following behind him.

Once outside the man continues to yell about Babs stealing his truck. As the Deputies try to explain that there is no proof Babs stole his truck, he starts turning red in the face as his anger builds.

One Deputy asks him "Sir did you know there are children in the restaurant?"

The man yells "Sure I saw the children. What does that have to do with my truck?"

Then out of the blue the man's rage overcomes him and he rushes towards the restaurant. He only makes it three feet when his feet slide out from under him due to the gravel parking lot. His body falling, into the little white picket fence that runs around the building.

Picking himself up, one Deputy grabs his left arm while the other one grabs his right. "Sir, you are now under arrest." One Deputy tells him.

"Under arrest! Under arrest for what?" The man yells "I haven't done anything."

"Mister, you're in the Keys and we take crime very seriously."

"You can't arrest me. I haven't done anything!" He keeps yelling.

"Sir you are under arrest for assault, a misdemeanor of the second degree, obscenity for exposing minors to harmful exhibitions through your foul language, disturbing religious and other assemblies in that you willfully interrupted and disturbed an assembly of people meeting for the lawful purpose for having breakfast."

"Further more, you are also being arrested for criminal anarchy in that your exhibit was an attempt to intimidate, breach of the peace in that your conduct is disorderly. and the destruction of private property with regards to you breaking the fence." One Deputy tells him while the other Deputy asks him "How much have had to drink today?"

"Drink? What? Arrested, you're kidding me! She stole my truck!"

"Calm down Sir, we are now adding resisting arrest to the list of charges. Would you like to keep it up and have more charges?"

The man continues to yell, while being placed in the back of the squad car. "I'll have your badges for this. Do you know who I work for?"

It only takes four minutes for the Crime Lab trucks to arrive. With everyone still watching, the Monroe County Crime Lab sets out to document everything that took place.

The Lab Technicians start unloading their equipment.

One Tech is unpacking their Laser Levels, Prism Poles, Electronic Tape Measures, their GPS equipment and their Tripods, and Bipods. Another is already taking pictures of the broken fence from every angle.

While back inside, everyone is watching and laughing as the developer's employee is being taken away. With the locals every small victory counts and is a cause for celebration.

As Boner and Red Stripe walk out the door past the yellow crime tape, Red Stripe turns and tells Babs "I'll let Bait know to be up and over here Christmas Eve morning to take over for you."

Once back at the marina, Red Stripe starts going over the plan again with Boner, Bait and White Boots. As each one will have a part to play.

Chapter 67

Red Stripe calls Taxi Jim to let him know he will be taking Babs to Miami on Christmas Eve and bringing her back to Stock Island on Christmas day.

It is going to be a fast paced three days. And everyone will need to do their part to pull it off. But in the Keys, when locals pull together anything is possible.

The next day at Moms, Taxi Jim appears. Seldom do you see him out of his cab. But today he needs to talk to Babs about picking her up in the morning.

By car, traveling up the Overseas Highway can be easy and done in three hours or less. However, there are many days when it is stop, go, stop, stay stopped and creep. On those days it can take five, seven, even eighteen hours due to the Overseas Highway, US 1 being closed.

Taxi Jim arrives and picks Babs up at seven A.M. The road is fairly clear as most people are already where they are going. It makes the drive up quick with no slow downs or stops.

Arriving in Miami, Taxi Jim is able to locate the man's office without much trouble.

The man in Miami turns out to be an Attorney with an office located on Biscayne Bay. As the Receptionist shows Babs to a conference room she is starting to get that uneasy feeling. The one that comes over most people when they are called into the bosses office and they don't know why.

The Receptionist asks her "May I bring you something to drink or eat Miss?"

"No thank you. Do you know how long it will be? Babs asks her.

"No Ma'am. But I will let Mr. Johnson know you are waiting."

"Good morning Miss. I am Clarence V Johnson the Fourth. But most of my friends call me Outboard."

"Am I your friend Mr. Johnson?" She asks still puzzled.

"I hope you are or will be after we are done."

"My friend said you want to help me save my restaurant."

"Your friend is correct. I need to go over a few documents with you and then you can decide if you want to go forward, is that ok?"

"Yes sir, I guess that's ok."

For the next several hours the Attorney goes through each document and every part of the plan to save Moms.

Although she is more excited with each piece of paper she is being shown, she is still nervous.

The Attorney explains to her, an anonymous businessman is giving her one hundred percent ownership in a well funded company.

A company which has been in business for over eight years. The company she is being given is profitable and owes no debts.

That evening, other parts of the plan are taking place. Bait, Boner and other locals are working at Moms on their part of the plan, while Red Stripe and White Boots are doing theirs.

Babs is never told who is giving her such a profitable company. Only that she now owns the company one hundred percent.

Before leaving his office, the Attorney tells her she can keep the company and it's profits or even sell it if she wants to, as it is now all hers.

All through the moon lit night, the locals are pulling everything together. Boner, Bait, crabbers and construction workers, they are all in the process of rebuilding Moms to the glory of old. With a few upgrades added in.

Chapter 68

While somewhere in the Atlantic Ocean off the coast of the Florida Keys, Red Stripe and White Boots are towing a barge to an abandon island.

It takes all night for them to remove solar panels, water barrels, and the Key Lime trees and put everything securely onto the barge for transport back to Stock Island.

In her hotel room Babs can not stop crying with joy. Joy that someone is so generous to her and the lifestyle of the islands.

It is Christmas Day. A bright sunny and warm South Florida Day as Babs pulls open the curtains of her room. Where she looks to the view of the sandy beaches and the ocean she loves. The tears of joy still have not left her eyes.

The drive back to Stock Island seems to be taking forever. Even though there are few cars on the road and barely a soul is on the Overseas Highway, it being Christmas morning. Red Stripe tells Taxi Jim to take his time.

As they are passing mile marker thirty-eight Babs feels her heart beating faster with the excitement of coming home. The excitement of knowing Moms will survive. What she doesn't know, is about the changes.

Taxi Jim pulls his cab onto the side of the road across the street from Moms, without saying a word. Putting the car into park, he just sits there. Sits there waiting for Babs reaction.

"Jim, why'd you stop. Is there something wrong with the car?"

"No Babs. Nothing wrong with the car."

"Then why are we stopping here?"

Smiling ear to ear, Jim tells her "Look around Babs, tell me what you see."

"Oh Jim, I'd much rather go home."

"Babs, just take a minute. Look around. Tell me what you see."

As Babs sits there in silence, she does as Taxi Jim asks and looks outside the cab.

Babs is sitting in the cab confused. But goes ahead and looks at the building where they are parked. Then she tells Jim "This looks just like the building across from the restaurant. Wait if this building is across from my restaurant then…"

Stopping in mid sentence she turns and can not believe or understand what it is she is seeing.

"What happened to my restaurant!" She exclaims.

"Jim, What is this? Is this a joke? On Christmas! Jim take me over there this minute." Babs demands.

Laughing, due to Babs confusion and knowing there is excitement to come, he simply tells her, "Sure Babs."

Chapter 69

Taxi Jim slowly pulls the cab out onto U.S. 1 and over to the restaurant's new parking lot.

Opening the door of the cab and stepping onto the newly laid asphalt parking lot, Babs is speechless. As Boner, White Boots, Bait, Red Stripe and the locals watch from inside the restaurant, Babs is putting her hands to her face. The tears start to flow as though a water main broke.

Where there used to be a weathered concrete block building with pealing faded paint, now sits a building twice the size of the one she left just the day before. The building still shows off the feel of old Florida yet presents a new update facade matching the resorts of the Caribbean.

Looking up at the new sign on the restaurant, Babs says, "What is this? I don't have any Key Limes."

Opening and holding the door for Babs, Taxi Jim tells her "You do now!"

Walking through the front door of the restaurant Babs is met by the locals from Stock Island and Key West. As well as a completely new décor.

Everyone inside yells at once "Merry Christmas!"

And there Babs stands, in the front of newly remodeled restaurant. No more rickety metal chairs or even wobbling tables. She is greeted back in time to old Florida Keys. A simpler time many forgot.

Where the metal chairs and tables once sat, are now glazed wooden tables made from old cable spools and chairs sanded, reinforced and painted from crab traps.

The walls now hold up paintings, photographs and art work from local Keys artists. Showcasing the life and history of the Keys for all to enjoy.

As Babs starts to cry even more, Bait takes her into her arms and laughingly tells her "Babs, you still have a lot more presents to open."

With the locals standing out of their way, Bait holds Babs's arm while guiding her out through a side door and into a processing building.

The Attorney never told Babs what the company produces. He only showed her the financials. And the companies name is changed to Moms, before she receives ownership.

With tears running down her face "What is this?" Babs asks.

"This. This is where Moms Key Lime Juice is made." Bait tells her.

"Key Lime Juice? But I don't have any Key Limes." Babs replies.

Walking out the back door of the Processing building, Bait says "You do now!"

There before her eyes, Babs sees row after row after row after row after row of Key Lime trees. A grove of trees surrounded by an eight foot tall wooden fence, hiding the trees from sight.

"But I don't understand? Where did all these trees come from" Babs asks Bait.

Bait tells her "Babs, it is all part of a Keys Christmas miracle."

During the night Red Stripe along with White Boots dug up all of Red Stripe's Key Lime trees. They dug up the trees, dismantled the solar panels and irrigation equipment. They loaded everything onto a borrowed barge and created Babs new Key Lime Grove and processing facility.

Turning to Bait, Babs wraps her into her body, hugging her with all her body will allow.

"Babs, its not over yet. Lets go back into the restaurant."

Upon re-entering the restaurant again everyone stands and claps their hands loudly as she passes through the door.

Bait guides Babs towards a table where Boner is sitting.

With Babs and Bait taking their seats at the table, Boner opens the menu in his hand and gives it to Babs.

Still in shock she asks "What's this Boner?"

Laughing, Boner tells her "Take a look at your new menu and order something."

Taking the menu in her hands, Babs starts reading off the list of items. "But I don't have a lot of these items." She says.

"You do now Babs." Boner replies, while handing her a three inch binder.

"While at college, I worked and re-worked every recipe in this book. And it is my present to you. Some of these recipes are now included on the restaurants new menu. Of course all of your great menu items are still on there also." Boner tells her.

Chapter 70

Over the following days, White Boots moves to Charlotte Harbor near Fishermen's Village. Babs is filled with excitement as the Key Lime Menu at Moms is an over the top hit with the tourists and the locals.

Boner moves back onto the houseboat while deciding where he wants his life to go. Bait keeps smiling while keeping the locals in line at the Hogfish. And Red Stripe, well some say Red Stripe went back to his families home. Others say he is on tour with Buffett.

Meanwhile shortly after New Years, sitting aboard his new boat, White Boots looks at the Newspaper opened across from him.

"Red, what were those coordinates of your island again?"

Red Stripe tells him. And after hearing the longitude and latitude of the island again, White Boots burst out laughing.

"Why? What's so funny?" Red Stripe asks.

Folding the paper back, Red Stripe reads the Headline from the Florida Keys.

Navy Bombers destroyed an island off the Florida Keys. Sending the uninhabited island which contained tons of unexploded ammunitions, to the bottom of the ocean.

Acknowledgements

I want to give many thanks to those who have helped in the creation of this book.

Bonnie Koon, Artist

www.koonberries.com and on facebook.
http://www.facebook.com/pages/KoonBerries/

http://www.facebook.com/pages/Bonnies-KoonKrabs-by-KoonBerries/

Chris Rehm, who provided photographs and Music of the Florida Keys.

http://keywestchris.com/

Nomadic State of Mind, The great sandals worn by Boner Morgan.

http://www.nomadicstateofmind.com

Trop Rock 1290, who's internet broadcasts brings the music of the Islands to those unable to be there.

http://www.troprock1290.com/

Matlacha http://www.pineislandchamber.org/

Burnt Store Marina http://www.burntstoremarina.com/index.htm

Fishermen's Village, a hidden Gem in Charlotte County Florida http://www.fishville.com

Sweet Treasures; The taste that you've been missing. And where you can find Key Lime Wine.

http://www.sweettreasureswine.com

Harpoon Harry's

http://www.harpoonharrys.com

Nav-A-Gator Grille, bringing you Trop Rock

http://nav-a-gator.com

Latitude: Tom and Michelle Becker

http://www.latitudemusic.net

J. Harold Lowry http://www.jharoldlowry.com

J. Harold Lowry has been called a Humorist, a Satirist. and A
Curmudgeon

As a Humorist and Satirist J. Harold Lowry can very well be the
Curmudgeon defined by Jon Winokur. As he steps back from the
drama. Seeking the lighter side of life. He believes there is laughter in
all things, be they good or bad. Knowing that life without laughter is
no life.

According to Jon Winokur, "A curmudgeon hates mankind's
absurdities. Curmudgeons are mockers and debunkers. Their
awareness is a curse. Perhaps curmudgeons have gotten a bad rap in
the same way that the messenger is blamed for the message: They
have the temerity to comment on the human condition without

apology. They not only refuse to applaud mediocrity, they howl it down with morose glee. Their versions of the truth unsettle us, and we hold it against them, even though they soften it with humor."

His careers include Banking and Finance where he rose to the level of S.R. Vice-President and wrote many articles about the Banking and Mortgage Industry. He goes on to help build one of the nations largest Telemarketing Companies and trained hundreds of successful sales people.

Again bored, he changes careers to become a Computer Systems Consultant for the likes of AT&T and Walt Disney World.

It is from these different careers and the breaks between them, that gives him, his cutting wit and humor.

J. Harold Lowry is able to bend and blend the realities of life into the illusion of fiction. For you never can tell the difference between what is Fiction and what is Reality.

You can find many articles written by J. Harold Lowry throughout Florida.

You can find his writings in regional publications as well as many Florida newspapers. His humor is often times cutting as he is seldom, if ever politically correct.

You can learn more about J. Harold Lowry on his Web Site at http://www.jharoldlowry.com and through the writings on his Blog at http://blog.jharoldlowry.com

12808489R00216

Made in the USA
Lexington, KY
28 December 2011